THE BAMBOO CANNON

THE
BAMBOO
CANNON

Donald McCaig

CROWN PUBLISHERS, INC., NEW YORK

Author's Note: This is a work of fiction. Although I've described real Caribbean islands, all the characters and political events are completely fictional; any resemblance to actual events or persons, living or dead, is entirely coincidental. Thanks to the will of its citizens, Dominica is a stable democracy today.

"Joshua Gone Barbados" originally appeared in *Sing Out* magazine, words and music by Eric von Schmidt. Copyright © 1965 by Minglewood Music. Lyrics from "More Fête" by Alphonsus Cassell (Arrow) used by permission. "Coming in from the Cold" lyrics and music by Bob Marley. Copyright © 1980 by Bob Marley Music Ltd. (ASCAP). All rights administered by Almo Music Corp. (ASCAP) for the world. All rights reserved. International copyright secured. Used by permission. "I Shot the Sheriff" words and music by Bob Marley. Copyright © 1974 by Cayman Music, Inc. (ASCAP). All rights reserved. Used by permission of Danny D. Sims. Excerpts from "The Schooner *Flight*" from *The Star-Apple Kingdom* by Derek Walcott. Copyright © 1977, 1978, 1979 by Derek Walcott. Reprinted by permission of Farrar, Straus and Giroux, Inc.

Published by Crown Publishers, Inc., 225 Park Avenue South, New York, New York 10003

CROWN is a trademark of Crown Publishers, Inc.

Manufactured in the United States of America

Library of Congress Cataloging-in-Publication Data

McCaig, Donald.
The bamboo cannon / Donald McCaig.
p. cm.
I. Title.
PS3563.A2555B3 1988
813'.54—dc19
88-14923

ISBN 0-517-56933-7

Designed by Leonard Henderson

10 9 8 7 6 5 4 3 2 1

First Edition

For Ivan and Dottie

PART ONE

CARNIVAL

When you break the law, you don't hurt the law, you don't change the law, you just make the law more the law; you stiffen the heart of the magistrate and set yourself to dodge and peep and every step you make, look over your shoulder for the police.
EARL LOVELACE

1

A Modest Little Airline

Every man says he wants to change the future but no he don't. It's yesterday he seeks to erase. Even a man like Winston Riviere who has most of his strong years ahead of him.

This morning—it wasn't seven o'clock—Winston rolled his front door shut, wishing he'd thought to dab grease on the rollers. He propped his motorcycle—a Honda 125—as he slipped the padlock through the door hasp and set it, muffling the click with his hands. He patted the wooden Obeah man who stood guard outside. Obeah man can do more than a steel lock to keep thief from thiefing.

A fine day in Charlotte Amalie, U.S.V.I. The sky was clean, pale blue. The trade winds were soft. Winston rolled his motorcycle down the cobblestoned alley toward Bjerge Gade; past Petty John's Disco & Snakbar (Open: 10 A.M.), past Ma Averill's house. Petty John's establishment was orange with parrot blue awnings. Ma Averill's house was one of the original Danish houses and it was a shame: her faded paint, her blistered veranda rails and shutters.

Even a small motorcycle is clumsy when you're pushing it. At the corner before the broad open street, was Mrs. Indarsingh's house; no fancy colors for her, by God, pure pink: pink from sills to rafter plate. Her garden fence was eight feet tall; salt-treated boards, each sharp pointed. Her coconut palm fronds shaded the alley and every May, her orangey Flamboyant blossomed. Winston had never been invited inside to admire the garden. He didn't know anyone who had.

He walked quietly, bumping his machine over the cobblestones one at a time. Freedom lay scant yards ahead.

A latch clicked and her garden gate swung heartily open. "Ah, Winston. Good-morning. How happy I am to intercept you."

For one mad moment, Winston thought to mount his motorcycle, kick it to life, roar straight ahead, and see who intercepted who; but the moment passed. He sighed. "Good-morning. Good-morning."

If St. Thomians are among the most polite people on earth, it stems from their conviction that St. Thomians, of all West Indians, are the most favored. Since Mrs. Indarsingh had been born in this neighborhood, she had marks up on Winston who had squalled his first infant squall twenty-five years ago, on the island of Dominica, far down island.

"And how are you, Winston? Montgomery, your brother, he is well? Your girl, lovely Rosemary, I have not been seeing so much of her lately."

"I have been working, Mrs. Indarsingh. DMS Airways. Day and night."

Mrs. Indarsingh's quilted robe was beige. Her steel gray hair was tightly pinned to the back of her skull. She stood uncomfortably—one bare foot resting on one that was shod.

Her stringy lips smiled but her black eyes bored into his brain. "Fifty-nine days you have had it, Mr. Riviere."

Winston toed his kickstand, rested his Honda, crossed his arms. "Mrs. Indarsingh, the parts for your mixer, they must come from Winter Rest, Florida, U.S.A. There are no such parts on St. Thomas."

"Mister Riviere, it is not a 'mixer' but a Cuisinart Supreme Automatic and for fifty-nine days you have it since first you accepted it, promising safe return in a fortnight."

"You blaming me they have no parts for this *mixer* in St. Thomas? St. Croix? San Juan? I wrote, myself, to Winter Rest, Florida, and then, it is a money order they demand, not accepting no personal check. Eighteen dollars and forty-seven cents, Mrs. Indarsingh. Perhaps you would like to pay for your parts now."

Brandishing her finger in his face. Made *that* noise with her mouth.

"Mrs. Indarsingh, it is rude to 'Tchups' your neighbor. Extremely rude."

"Not one penny until my Cuisinart is chopping and blending again, Mr. Riviere. No sir." Brandishing her finger she retreated through her gate as Winston jumped on his motorcycle and raced into the street, nearly striking a purple vanbus that had purple cowboys and cacti painted on its doors.

Winston zipped through the heart of town. The first week in August, there were no cruise ships in the harbor; the shops that sold duty-free watches, cameras, and perfumes were shuttered. A taxi wished to honk him out of the way but Winston held his ground until the taxi found a wide spot. The driver tapped his forefinger against his head as he passed.

"Because you are an elephant, you think you are big!" Winston cried.

Did Winston want Mrs. Indarsingh's mixer? No more than he wanted Jorge Delgado's air conditioner, Miss Averill's antique Motorola phonograph, his brother's two weedeaters—one with a scored cylinder—all the worn-out machines that cluttered the garage Winston called home. Winston was a wonderful fixer, everyone knew this for true. If Winston could fix an airplane, couldn't he fix anything?

He sped along Veteran's Drive toward the airport, just another neatly dressed black man on his way to work. Most cars passed him by. From habit, he slowed before Caribbean Rent-A-Car but no tourists today, trying to drive the wrong (right) lane, crossing traffic in improper turns, eyes frozen with fear, their arms locked to the steering wheel. Particularly dangerous to small motorcycles as Winston had told Rosemary many times. "In St. Thomas, only a car is safe from tourists. Also, picture my Honda during rainy season."

"You must do as you wish," she'd reply. "How much have you saved toward our house?"

The main terminal of the Cyril King Airport is a converted hangar. Departures and customs are located in a cinder-block building next door. Three taxi vans idled in front, their drivers gossiping. The early flight from St. Croix was due.

The cavernous building stays cool. Stout steel trusses crisscross far overhead. Tall photographic displays advertise the fancier resorts; Hertz and National promise competitive rates; local and charter air carriers are ready to serve.

The DMS Airways desk was tucked between LIAT and AIR CARIBE. Behind it, Mrs. Sanderson did accounts. Mrs. David Sanderson (Megan) was president of DMS Airways, bookkeeper, and reservations and shipping clerk. David Sanderson was chief pilot and director of flight operations. Winston, pilot and chief mechanic. They had it in writing in their FAA charter.

"Good-morning," Winston said. "David gone to San Juan?"

Though Mrs. Sanderson was somewhere in her mid-thirties, years of Caribbean sun had lightened and streaked her auburn hair. She was fretful, thin. "David said to tell you, the left throttle isn't locking."

"I tell him, set his friction."

Megan removed her tinted glasses and tapped them on the counter. "Winston, Sunday morning, yesterday, David was making his takeoff from Puerto Vallerta with three paying passengers, that throttle slipped right down to nothing, the wing sagged badly, and the passengers were, uh . . . painfully distressed."

"I bet they was hung over too."

She gave Winston the bad eye.

"I'll fix it," he said.

"Thank-you so very much." She attached a pleasant smile that didn't mean anything. Mrs. Sanderson was always nice to Winston when it didn't matter much. The Sandersons' new condo overlooked Hull Bay and they drove a Cherokee Chief station wagon, with four-wheel drive and air. When DMS freight customers were slow to pay, Winston's salary was late, sometimes two, three days —once a full week.

She said "Those DC-3 parts you were expecting. St. Croix radioed. They're coming in, this morning."

"The rudder cables."

DMS Airways' newest acquisition was a decertified DC-3 with low-time engines and instruments. The plane was 40 years old and slow (165 knots) but it'd carry 7,000 pounds, which was two-and-a-half times the twin Beech payload. Winston had been repairing it since May. The trim tabs, tail wheel, and port elevator were new, but Winston'd scavenged many parts from the junked DC-3s across Runway two-eight—tailless, motorless creatures, gradually dissolving into the bush.

David liked the zippy Beechcraft and Winston understood that he'd have the DC-3 to fly. Be fine. Winston had several hundred hours on a DC-3 from the year he flew Puerto Rico–Monserrat for Five-Star Charters.

"Once the DC-3's ready for the FAA, I'll start booking more freight and our cash flow will be regularized."

She meant Winston would get his salary on time but he had doubts.

"Richie can help you." She added the clincher.

Winston suppressed his snort.

She aimed her ballpoint at him. It was a gold Cross pen. "Winston, I want you to teach Richie what he needs to know. You're an easygoing man. Laid-back. That's all a teacher needs: patience, patience, patience." She restored a pleasant smile to her face. "If it isn't too much trouble, please pick up the landing fee receipt. David forgot yesterday."

"All right."

Jocko was perched on the lip of the luggage carousel and Winston managed a stiff "Good-morning" as he passed.

Jocko acknowledged the greeting with a flip of his hand. Jocko's black pegged trousers were inches longer than his legs and his heels frayed a circle in each cuff. Jocko's Hawaiian shirt was printed with fat flowers in brown, gold, pink. His hair was greased straight back on his skull and was, like his pants, dusty. He wore oversize, wraparound reflective sunglasses. He didn't weigh a hundred fifty pounds, wet. Probably his gold neck chain wasn't genuine, doubtless the rings weren't either.

Jocko waited for tourists. There'd be one or two looking for a man like him.

Jocko was Mal Esprit's dog.

The landing fee booth was at the end of Runway one-zero where the collectors wouldn't miss any small plane landing. A fee collector was chatting up Estelle, the customs lady. Estelle looked pretty foxy and Winston might have said so, except for their history.

Winston spoke to the collector. "Where David's receipt, man?

He need it, you know, for the tax man. You keeping he money for yourself?"

The collector snorted. "Six dollars, Winston, is not enough to tempt me." He riffled through a stack of receipts. "Here it is, made out already."

Estelle glowered at the runway like a severe violation of customs law might occur momentarily.

The collector said, "David very vex. Passengers, vex too. They was three swingers." He laughed. "Swingers, they all vomit all over themselves and the plane too. David take the hose to the cockpit after they gone." He turned to the customs lady. "Estelle, why you not out with the black plane?"

She muttered, "Plenty officials without me."

"They leave the junior officer behind?" His voice was cheerful.

Five years ago, before Winston met Rosemary, he and Estelle had had a thing. It hadn't been so serious, but when Winston took up with Rosemary, Estelle went raging mad and stayed so. Got so Winston hated to see Estelle on the customs desk when he landed. No smile, no good-morning, "Open the suitcase," and "You got a manifest for that?" Only time she didn't pick was when Winston brought in the fish. Even Estelle wasn't willing to search five hundred dead snappers, groupers, and tuna.

Now Estelle said, "Somebody has to do the customs work," and marched off, trim hips rolling slightly despite her intentions.

The collector shook his head. "Winston, you playing the ass, give that up."

Winston spread his hands apart. Life, love, who knows? "What black plane?"

"See? There by American Air Freight."

"Is the customs car."

"And, the immigration truck and that St. Thomas police and the dark green sedan from DEA. Can't see much black plane from here, just its wingtips and rudder. Police on that plane like worms on ripe guava."

Winston folded David's receipt. "Doper plane?"

"Oh yes, definitely yes. It came in four-forty-five this morning as they was taking the X off the runway. If pilot waited fifteen minutes he would have been lawful but he didn't wait. You know that old Rican who sets the X? He was just loading the barricade in his pickup when that plane come down and he nearly shit himself. Flopped on his face, plane so low. Oh, he wild. He jump in his truck in hot pursuit, going to bring them to law, you know. But they quit they plane, out of it and running. They was carrying a duffle bag he said. Old man never got too close. They jumped into a cab and sped away without hesitation. Old man honking he horn, but that didn't slow them. Winston, you know who own this black plane?"

Winston shook his head. "No, man, I seen plenty planes but never no plane like that."

"How long you been flyin' in these islands?"

Winston laughed. "Too long, man. Too long."

Winston took the receipt to Mrs. Sanderson who was explaining rates to some bone fishermen. She tucked the receipt under her account book without a word of thanks.

DMS Airways had the Monday-Wednesday bread run from San Juan, shuttled Eastern Airlines passengers to Virgin Gorda, ferried bone fishermen to Anegada, and had a Saturday afternoon run to Puerto Vallerta in the Dominican Republic. Since the only tourist feature in Puerto Vallerta is several whorehouses, Winston nicknamed that run "The Coxsman's Express" but never to the Sandersons' faces. Winston piloted the fish run. Every Friday, out to Anegada, where he'd purchase the fish right off the dock, and straight back to St. Thomas. Last month, Megan's cousin Richie arrived. Thus, Winston had a copilot he didn't need.

DMS Airways shared a Butler building beside Runway two-eight with U-Can-Fly Inc., Five-Star Charters, John's Small Engine Repair. Winston snapped on the fluorescents and rolled up the big doors facing the runway.

It was a comfortable shop; twenty by thirty feet. Winston's steel workbench and toolboxes along one plywood wall, metal lathe and electric welder against the other. Its #1 cylinder removed, a Lycoming engine dangled from an engine hoist. The rags stuffed into the block would prevent rusting.

Besides maintaining DMS Airways' Beech and working on the DC-3, Winston did custom work for private pilots and charter services who didn't have facilities or a mechanic of their own.

A man brought in a gas line, seeking a new female fitting, $\frac{3}{4}$ inch, did Winston have one?

"Give me a break, eh. I just now here. Let me get into my coveralls."

Winston's office was a plywood and wire cubicle. Gray metal desk, yellow two-drawer file cabinet, clipboards, manuals: *The Lycoming Engine, Lubrication Procedures for the Piper Aztec, Beechcraft Twins 140-160-180, Joy's Hydraulic Systems.* A bright poster—MODERN WARPLANES—decorated the back wall. Winston hung up his trousers and shirt, and unfolded light blue coveralls from the cleaner's bundle. Over his right breast he wore red and gold wings: DMS AIRWAYS.

When Winston flexed the fuel line several braids separated. "Man, you don't need no new fittin'. Line bad, that's why your fitting leak. I fix you a brand-new line and you don't go sprayin' your engine compartment with gasoline."

"The boss says, just a fitting. No new line."

Winston shrugged. "You want that kind of work, you go somewhere else than here. In town, maybe. Try the Datsun dealer."

So the man bought a complete new line and Winston noted that most manuals advised they should replace all lines and hoses every three years and the man said, "Yeah, sure. You betcha," and signed the purchase order.

Richie was from California. North Hollywood, California. His blond hair was chopped, rough but *right*. His teeth were even, slightly too big. Richie bopped into Winston's office, "Winnie, you got to check it out."

Winston made a note for inventory control. "You talkin' 'bout that doper," he said.

"Big twins. Speed fairings, radar, the works. The ident numbers"—Richie set his hands close apart—"you'd have to fly into that damn thing before you could read those numbers. . . . Winnie, you ever think . . . ?"

Winston said, "That's the third doper since February. We'll need an awning to work on the DC-3. Sun bounce off that runway, very hot."

Richie was Mrs. Sanderson's nephew and came from the same side of the family the money came from. Richie had his twin-engine commerical ticket and was building up hours.

"You ever think about that?" he persisted. "Extra fuel tanks in the back, and you could make it from Bolivia to Anegada easy.

Friday morning on the fish run, cover the stuff up with fish and bring it in here. One run, just one."

Winston carried the lightweight plastic awning and poles. "Bring nylon line. We lash the grommets to the fin."

"One run, Winston, and you could buy the house you're always talking about."

Winston said, "New rudder cables should be in customs, please get them. Don't tell Estelle they are for me."

AIR ROYALE had been the previous owners of the DC-3.

AIR ROYALE's colors were white with a red stripe set off by two lighter blue ones. The hole for the elevators yawed open, and on the metal edges you could count the layers of paint. Red, silver, white, silver again, over the original military dark green. Winston wondered how much that paint cut the payload. The green paint had been applied fourteen years before Winston was born, ten before Winston's father had joined the U.S. navy, convinced that his part of making the world safe for democracy was waiting officers' mess on the USS *Glebe*. When his turn came, Winston chose the army. His mother spoke so poorly of his long-gone father that Winston believed the American navy was, at best, frivolous. Besides, the U.S. army was willing to teach Winston to fly. On his first leave from helicopter school, Winston was greatly surprised to learn that Americans don't have any special respect for a pilot. On his home island of Dominica, pilots were held in high regard.

Carefully, Winston reamed old rivet holes and identified bad rivets with a crayoned X. After a bit, Richie returned and Winston had him unpack the cables.

"Go over them, inch by inch." After Richie passed them, Winston would repeat the inspection.

Nine-thirty, David Sanderson came in from San Juan with a cargo of rolls, bread, and pastries for Charlotte Amalie's fancy restaurants. Richie helped him unload into the wholesaler's truck. David took off for Anegada with the bone fishermen.

The sun bounced off the tarmac and flashed from the silver planes parked in rows beside the runway. On the dark green hill behind the airport, the water catchment basin glowed like a rusty badge. St. Thomas is a dry island and each summer people have to purchase water from Puerto Rican water barges. Winston couldn't understand why someone didn't get the tremendous water catchment system working again. It must be a thousand yards across.

At noon, Richie and Winston drove to Frenchtown for lunch. Winston had changed into street clothes. Richie wore his DMS Airways coveralls like a uniform of distinction.

The Barbary Coast Café was a bit fancy for Winston's tastes, but Richie liked it and it was his car. The café was a smallish place, just ten tables with unglassed windows facing the marina. Airline posters of Paris and Notre Dame adorned the white walls and fresh flowers in drinking glasses were on each table. Gift shops and boutique workers came here for lunch and a few cleverer tourists always found the place.

Winston slid the menu away. "Catch of the day, please, and ice tea."

"Winnie, why do you bother to look at the menu? Every day you have the same thing."

"I am Winston. I am not Winnie."

"That's what they called Winston Churchill, man. They called him Winnie to show how much they liked him."

"I do not wish to be so much liked."

"I don't know why you're so damn touchy."

"*Ja vou, ja vie,*" Winston said—which is to say: "a day comes, a day goes" or "one day, brother, you'll get yours."

Richie never asked Winston to translate his patois. He just shook his head. Richie turned around in his seat to inspect two women who'd come in and sat at a corner table. Like him, they had blond hair, good teeth. Unlike him, they had lines at the corners of their eyes. Winston had a vague feeling he knew one— the woman with the oversized jade ear cuff. Somewhere, he'd seen her before.

A banana quit zipped through the window and hovered over the shallow bowl of sweetened water, kept there just for him.

Richie said, "Excuse me," and beelined for the women's table. When he arrived, he leaned over and said something and a woman (not the one Winston remembered) smiled.

Winston was the only black man here. Whenever blacks came into the Barbary Coast Café, they dressed respectable. Some white tourists arrived in tattered painter's pants and runover boat shoes. Some were completely unshaved. When white people relax, they go all to hell. The waitress brought Winston red snapper with creole hot sauce. Not so hot as Dominican hot sauce.

Richie had pulled himself out a chair and was settling in at the women's table. They were all laughing at jokes.

The harbor was all pleasure boats. Used to be fishing boats too, but St. Thomas waters fished out, too polluted. St. Thomas all grown up today. Many exfishermen worked the pleasure boats. Winston had done that work himself, in between flying airplanes, when he first got out of the army. Return a 32-foot Morgan to Boca Raton, deliver a 78-foot steel-hulled schooner to its new owner in Buenos Aires. Carefree days.

Winston's brother, Montgomery, did some captaining too. Montgomery had an easy way about him and a soft grace Winston lacked and, at first, Montgomery found it easier to find boat work than his older brother did. But Montgomery was always dreaming about girls. When he put the 85-foot motor sailer, *Samson's Reward*, onto La Balien rock coming into St. Barts, he was thinking about the English girl he planned to meet that night. They managed to kedge *Samson's Reward* off La Balien but Montgomery wasn't so fortunate with the *Tanager*, a 40-foot charter he was bringing up island from Antigua. Montgomery went aground off Necker Island on the Invisibles and sharp coral heads tore the bottom out of the *Tanager* before they could do a thing to save her.

"You a great blue-water sailer," Winston said at the time, "but you play the ass coming into port."

Montgomery's companion had been a pretty brunette from Houston, Texas, and inquiry failed to determine if anyone had actually been on deck when the *Tanager* struck.

So Montgomery took a job at the Agricultural Station on St. Thomas. Winston kept on skippering. He was living on a boat when he first met Rosemary.

Winston was mopping up his creole sauce with french bread (probably flown in by DMS Airways) when Richie brought the women over. "This is Connie, Winston. Winston, Connie. Susan —she says she knows you."

Susan was tall, flat chested, and wore a peasant blouse. Her smile fluttered. She tugged at her ear cuff. Winston's age, maybe a couple years older.

"I don't think I forget a pretty lady like you."

"Carnival, Brewer's Beach. Oh, must be five years ago."

Winston made a sad gesture with his hands: maybe so, maybe no.

"You were pretty drunk." Ruefully she laughed.

Richie's mouth was surprised. "Winston? I don't think I ever saw you take a drink."

Winston said, "I was a bad john those days. Now, I sorry at what I missed."

She pursed her lips, looked away, drawled, "You didn't seem to be missing it at the time."

And Winston said, "Yes, well, thank-you," because he couldn't think of anything else.

On the way back to the airport, Richie quizzed him but Winston honestly couldn't remember her. There'd been so many quick white girls.

When they unlocked the shop, the Lycoming motor's owner was waiting. Winston told him the cylinder wasn't in.

The man said the motor would have been ready days ago in the States.

Winston felt like asking why he flew around the Caribbean if things were so much better in the States but instead he said maybe tomorrow, maybe day after that.

At 3:47, Eastern flight 506 came in from Miami. The 757 is the biggest plane to attempt the short St. Thomas runway and from habit, Winston glanced up as the big jet touched down and the captain reversed engines and stood on the brakes. Three years ago an American plane overran and crashed through the barrier, across the roadway into the gas station there.

"If I was to crash," Richie observed, "I'd rather go down taking off. Least you'd have some chance over water."

Winston said, "I know a lot of people gone down in this ocean. Don't know none of them swam back."

The tremendous airliner taxied toward the terminal. It turned its tail on the rusting DC-3s in the bush—primitive, tiny, ruined ancestors. Eastern's ground crew rolled out stairs.

Winston looked back to his work. What business had he with tourist passengers?

In the first-class section, Carly Hollander said, "I want more champagne." In a moment, she added, "Please."

Her mother said, "They don't serve on the ground, dear. We've landed."

Carly said, "It's hot in here." She pushed her champagne glass at the stewardess opening the overhead bins. The stewardess smiled and said, "Thank-you" and made Carly's plastic glass vanish. Carly licked her lips.

"It's hot because the air-conditioning is off," her mother said.

The stairs bumped against the fuselage.

The stewardess laid garment bags on the seat across the aisle. It hadn't been crowded in first class—never was in August. Just the mother and her mousy daughter. The daughter, thumbing through one fashion magazine after another, finished the better part of a bottle of champagne since Miami, and she'd been sloshed before she got on the plane. The stewardess smiled her professional smile, "Hope you have a nice time here in St. Thomas."

Carly's mother said, "Oh, we're just changing planes, here. We're going on to Sandpiper Cay."

The stewardess had never heard of the place. Since the passenger expected some response the stewardess widened her smile.

"It'll be a first for us. They say Linda Gray was there last month."

Again the stewardess showed appreciation though, for the life of her, she couldn't think who Linda Gray was.

"'Dallas,'" the mother said.

"Oh! My! Well, there's the door. Excuse me. It was our pleasure to have you aboard."

Carly said, "They expect us to climb down that thing?"

"That's how we all used to do it, dear. When your father and I first arrived at the Orange County airport, we . . ."

Carly tuned her out. It was something she was very good at. She could watch her mother's mouth moving and not hear a single word. Not just her mother, either. Anybody.

Carly wore her hair like Jackie Kennedy used to wear hers—in a lustrous helmet. Her small face was lost inside the hair like a small animal peering out of a cave. Her green eyes were bloodshot and puffy. Her too-thick mascara was smudged. She was a slender girl, not much on top and less on the bottom. Her legs were set wide on her pelvis. She wore jeans and a LUCAS PRODUCTIONS T-shirt.

"How'm I going to carry all this crap?" she asked. Besides her royal purple garment bag (Cardin) and carryon (Vuitton) she had a wicker purse (Giorgio's Rodeo Drive).

"It's just a few steps, dear," her mother said.

The stairwell was a rectangle of brilliant white light and the sun-heated air was very much hotter and more lively than the air inside the aircraft. It looked a great distance to the ground.

When one must, one must. Carly took a deep breath, slipped her wicker purse over her forearm, and floated down the steel steps to the tarmac and safety. At the very bottom, a flight attendant offered his hand, but Carly shrugged it off. She'd got this far under her own power.

On the ground, right away, her mother made her move and a rather astonished Eastern navigation officer found himself carrying a passenger's garment bags on the long hike to the terminal.

Burdened like a turtle, Carly hobbled along behind the officer, while her mother strode out front, seeking new worlds to conquer.

Inside the terminal building a heavy black woman in a voluminous skirt, vivid blouse, and beads was singsonging, "All welcome to St. Thomas. All welcome. Please sample St. Thomas free rum."

Another woman, similarly dressed but older, presided at a stand-up booth. Carly made a beeline.

"Carly, honey. Our luggage comes in here. Over here!"

Sullenly, Carly altered course for the carousel where her mother was dismissing the navigation officer, and with her free hand summoning a porter.

The porter said, "Taxi, miss?"

"We are booked for Sandpiper Cay. Take our luggage direct to the connecting flight."

"Miss, I do not know what airplane." He pointed at the bank of charters. "See, how many."

"Sandpiper Cay. Sand—Pi—Per Cay."

"Yes, miss. I am the porter for the taxis."

"But we do need your help." Carly's mother switched on her special smile. As always it worked. Though he muttered, the porter dragged their carryons into one pile and waited with Carly's mother for the rest.

"There. The blue. On, no, not that. There!"

Carly didn't have anything against black people but there were too many here and they walked around like they owned the place.

Of course, she'd slept with a black boy, once. He'd been no different. He had wanted to show Carly off to his friends—otherwise, no different.

In St. Thomas the whites wore shorts and black men wore long pants. Carly wondered why. Perhaps blacks' legs didn't get as hot? One black was eyeing Carly in an interested fashion. Horrible-looking man with greased-back hair and fake gold neck chain. He lifted one hand to his puckered lips and made a sucking sound. Ganja. Carly turned her back. She'd been found out too easily. "Mom, I need to use the facilities."

Mother pressed a hand to her brow. "Why couldn't you have gone on the plane?"

The porter plucked another bag from the carousel. Carly said, "Have to," in a little-girl voice that sometimes worked.

"Don't be long. Porter, that gray two-suiter. The Mark Cross."

Carly angled away from the ganja man. He wore reflective sunglasses so she couldn't see his eyes. He grinned at her in a presumptuous way.

Carly took a cubicle in the ladies room, sat, and opened her purse. Sandpiper Cay meant customs. Two years ago, she'd been detained at Heathrow for five hours because of customs. If she'd known she would have done up the half gram *before* she landed.

Carly had fifty Valiums (prescription). She gobbled thirty milligrams so she wouldn't be afraid. Then she flushed her toilet and washed her hands and marched close past the ganja man like he was nothing, nobody.

The Hollanders took the shuttle service to Beef Island, Tortola. The Connair plane was a ten-seater, and Carly and her mother were the only whites. Even the pilot was black. Carly closed her eyes tight when they took off, because she didn't know how black men could pilot a plane.

They flew over a mottled turquoise sea dotted with delicate islands and brilliant sand beaches but Carly had her eyes shut and didn't see any of it. Twenty minutes later, Carly and her mother were standing before the British Virgin Islands customs officer. The officer wore a starched khaki uniform and wondered if they wanted a driving permit.

"Yes," they said.

Carly's mother said, "There's no reason to spend money for two permits. One please." She added, "You drive on the wrong side here." A joke.

The customs officer showed his teeth but didn't laugh.

Beef Island is flat savanna, brush and sea oats. A bridge connects to mainland Tortola. The Connair plane rolled to the end of the runway and revved its engines for the return flight.

"Not many tourists this time of year," Carly's mother ventured.

"No, miss. Not so many."

"Of course this is the hurricane season."

"Oh no, miss. No danger. Hurricane track has shifted. Hurricanes go south of the Virgins now."

Carly's mother said, "July, stand by,/ August, you must,/ September, remember,/ October, all over."

Carly didn't know how her mother could smile and say such awful things. Carly's mother had always been able to smile and had always said awful things.

The Connair plane took off with a shattering roar, scattering birds at the end of the runway. It banked toward St. Thomas where a person could catch a flight to civilized cities all over the world.

The customs officer said, "Sandpiper Cay launch be here soon." And vanished through a door marked PRIVATE.

Carly plopped down in a red plastic chair. Her forehead was greasy with sweat but life is a dream, isn't it?

"Let's wait down on the quay," Carly's mother suggested.

"Screw it."

"Dear, why must you be so vulgar?"

Dragging her bags, Carly followed her mother to the concrete landing. Across the bay must be Tortola. It was brown too.

Her mother said, "Isn't this exciting?"

Carly sat on a suitcase.

A white launch rounded the point and purred steadily toward them—an old-fashioned Chris-Craft runabout: a 20-footer with varnished mahogany deck and cream-colored canvas canopy, cockpit to stern. A Sandpiper ensign whipped jauntily from the bowstaff. A black man in coveralls was steering and he held the boat to the dock, motor burbling while another black made the bow lines fast. The boat backed neatly so the stern lines could be fastened too.

A young white stepped up onto the dock, hand outstretched. He was theatrically handsome. Heavy dark hair, full Roman face, patrician nose. "Ringo Dragotti, ladies. You must be the Hollanders. Good trip, I hope."

"Oh fine, fine."

"Sometimes that Connair can be a little rough. My father is sure looking forward to meeting you." Such a wonderful smile.

"He doesn't know us from Adam," Carly said.

"Carly!"

"Dr. Dragotti gets to know all his clients," Ringo said smoothly. "Sometimes better than they know themselves."

Carly muttered, "Christ!" but not so loud her mother could hear.

The black men loaded their bags and everything was so effortless that the Hollanders relaxed, because they were again safe in the hands of professionals.

"It's an hour trip—give or take. We're a bit beyond Great Camanoe. Just take your seats with me in the stern. There's a light lunch and refreshments in our cooler."

Carly said champagne would be fine. The plastic champagne glasses, Ringo Dragotti explained, were used because the passage could be rough, but the champagne was real enough, ha ha. Before Ringo Dragotti had finished filling his own glass (he sat on a jumpseat facing them), Carly had her glass out for a refill. If Ringo was surprised he didn't show it.

"That's Marina Cay, over there," he said. "The harbor is full of yachts during the season. And, that faint smudge on the horizon there, that's Virgin Gorda. We often arrange day sails to The Baths there."

The channel was shallow and the water clear. Coral heads wavered beneath; mottled greens, yellows, and blacks and of all the Impressionists, only Renoir could have painted them.

Islets, cliffs, and rocky beaches slipped by while Ringo Dragotti made conversation. No, there weren't any notables at the clinic right now—"Present company excepted"—but a certain well-known English party was expected next week and he wasn't naming names but she was somebody dear to the hearts of Charles and

Lady Di. "She's really something. You'd never take her for royalty."

Carly tuned him out. She pushed her glass for more champagne
and got it too, despite her mother's warning glower. She watched
the green world slide by and tuned that out. She wished she had
some real drugs. Maybe this time next year she'd be dead.

The cylinder and gaskets for the Lycoming arrived on the late Pan
Am flight and Winston had Richie stow the tarp while he replaced
the cylinder. He'd replace the gaskets tomorrow.

As Winston was cleaning traces of grease from his fingers, Richie said, "How about it Win . . . ston. Sun's down. Connie—from
the restaurant—promised to meet me for drinks."

"No, man. Rosemary expecting me. Suppose you put these
tools away. Put the metric sockets in the top tray. If they scattered
all over the world you not find them tomorrow."

Richie made a face, but did what was told. There wasn't anything really wrong with Richie. He was just another spoiled white
boy. At five, promptly, he left and Winston sat at his desk to price
the gaskets on the Lycoming's bill. He heard the distinctive roar
of the Beechcraft, the prop's Chuck, Chuck, Chuck as David
Sanderson cut power.

David Sanderson had got hurt bad—gunships in Vietnam—
and limped whenever he was tired. He was a short man, and wore
khaki pants and overblouse, with epaulets and pilot's wings. Although he only had a fuzz of hair on the back of his head he
compensated with a fierce handlebar moustache. "Christ, what a
day."

Winston placed the bill in its job folder. "Bone fishermen fly
back with you?"

"Nope. They want to fish again at dawn. I'll pick them up at
0830." David stretched up on his tiptoes, yawned, rubbed his
back. "How's Richie coming along? How many hours he got in the
copilot seat?"

Winston looked away. "Ask Richie."

David Sanderson laughed. "Winston, don't get your ass in an
uproar. Pilots are a dime a dozen, but good mechanics are worth
their weight in . . ."

"Fish," Winston suggested.

And his boss smacked him between the shoulder blades and

said, "Hey, hey! Winston. You're all right. Megan tell you about the left throttle?"

"Uh-huh. If you just tighten the friction . . ."

The good nature drained out of David Sanderson's face. "Buddy, I do think you have told me about that."

"I got to pull the entire console get to that friction lever. Look here . . ." Winston plucked the fat Beechcraft shop manual off the shelf and opened it.

"If that's what it takes, Winston. Do it."

Stiffly, David walked away.

Winston could have asked him when he'd find time for one more repair with the DC-3 to certify and more private customers than he could handle. He might have reminded David that Winston was supposed to be doing more piloting as the airline grew, not less. Winston closed the Beechcraft manual and returned it to its place on the shelf, just so.

Winston heard David's Cherokee start. That four-wheel drive would be handy on St. Thomas's steep hills during the rainy season but what a price: as much as twenty thousand dollars!

At six o'clock, St. Thomas Airport officially closed and a pickup hurried to the runway's end where they'd erect the X barricade. The crew'd be watching the sky tonight, afraid some other crazy doper going to land on them.

Winston rolled down the big doors, swept the concrete floor, and dropped his soiled coveralls in the laundry box.

The summer sun was behind the mountain. A few lights at Five-Star but everything else was dark. The blue dusk crept out of the bush, through the ruined airplanes, eased across the tarmac. Winston walked through the rows of parked aircraft: Pipers, Beechcrafts, Jimmy Ohl's old Mustang. The black plane stood, on a slant, where they'd left it. Its cockpit door dangling open. It was all-over black; a glossy black that reflected all the black in the sky, took blackness into itself. This was the blackness that swallowed light.

The fuselage was slippery. Every inch of surface had been polished into sleekness.

Oversized Navaho engines—460 horsepower each—jutted from the wings. Someone had welded the luggage door shut and cut a clamshell hatch—like a bombdoor—in the floor.

Pirate black. Blacker than Winston's hands. Though he hadn't been inside a Catholic church in years, Winston crossed himself.

2

It's Never Too Late for a Dog to Go Mad

Winston's sweetheart, Rosemary, was a formidable woman. Second eldest of ten children (oldest girl), Rosemary had always been more mother than child. By age seven, she could put a meal on the table; by eleven, she was sewing most of her brothers' and sisters' clothing. Rosemary's mother, Urmilla, was, as her third husband put it, "Nothing to boast as a housekeeper, but how she love a fête."

Some of Rosemary's siblings lived in the Virgins, some down island, her eldest brother was in the States. Urmilla, herself, was in Florida. The two youngest children, Joshua and Leontine, lived with Rosemary.

Rosemary Parmassar was a nurse at the East End Clinic. She had wished to stay in school long enough to get her Registered Nurse license but had to go to work with just the Practical Nursing. Each morning, on the way to work, she dropped Leontine at the Tutu day care center.

Joshua, who was eight, played with older project boys after school and was learning plenty mischief. Rosemary wanted to send him north to his mother, who had a new husband now and a bit of extra money, but Urmilla didn't want Joshua and said to

Rosemary last Sunday on the telephone: "All my life I have children. Now, I want to have life for myself."

Lights blazed from the projects. Everybody's window was open and the night cried loud with radios: the calls of calypsonians; the wails of reggae and religion. In the gravel parking lot, a dozen cars clustered around the single lamppost. Each car was fresh-painted, cleaned, and waxed and the poorest among them had new Sears seatcovers but their working parts—transmissions and drivetrains—oh, my. Car hoods were raised in prayer while their owners lounged about, drank beer, and told falsehoods.

Winston dismounted quietly and wheeled his motorcycle through the darker end of the lot but Charlie had sharp eyes like a frigate bird. He jogged over, oily rag wrapped around the socket wrench in his hand. "Hey, Winston. Good-evening. Going to see Rosemary?"

"Charlie, good-evening. Yes. Cooking on the table." Winston grinned and made a great show of rubbing his stomach as he trundled forward.

"You know I got the disc brakes . . ."

Winston kept his eyes fixed on the light over the project's stairwell, like it was a mariner's beacon calling him home. He stepped up his pace.

"Winston, the little brushes, one come loose and the other gone and I don't know what to do."

Winston had spent too many Saturday afternoons under cars in this gravel parking lot. For no pay.

"You should junk that Peugeot, Charlie," Winston said, hoisting his Honda into the stairwell. Since Winston couldn't flee through the intertwined bikes and strollers he faced Charlie direct. "Man, I cannot help you."

Charlie's eyes glittered with desperation. "You should own a car yourself, man. Then, you know what a headache they be."

Winston squeezed past and jumped up the stairs. "I have headaches enough without you give me yours."

Three flights up, Winston paused outside Rosemary's door and breathed deep. He would not bring trouble to Rosemary's home. When Winston felt proper, he knocked.

On Rosemary's salary, she could afford a nicer place than this combination living room–kitchen–dining room, with one small bedroom for her, and another, no bigger than a closet, for two kids. But Rosemary was saving her money.

"Good-evening, Winston. You are very late. You must come to the table before the paté is cold."

Rosemary was light-skinned and sturdy. Winston loved how she smelled at the nape of her neck in the precise spot where the shoulder takes rise, the spot where arm might still become wing. When he bent to snuffle her there, she ducked.

"I could not get salt fish so the patés are beef. They were ready an hour ago."

Patés are meat pies in a pastry crust. Chicken, beef, pork but usually salt fish, which was Winston's favorite. "Where are the children, Darlin'?" he asked.

"I wished a dinner with you alone. Children play at Mrs. Childress's. She keep her sharp eye on them."

"Mrs. Childress, she too quick with blows," Winston complained.

"I tell Mrs. Childress, leave the blows to me." Rosemary sat down at the dinette, but set no place for herself. When Winston needed ice tea, she brought it.

A shout of laughter from the parking lot. A yell. A fragment of a calypso tune.

Rosemary's front windows faced the lot and beyond, the highway. Heavy trucks traveled from Sub Base to Tutu, all airhorns and smoking exhausts. Rosemary's curtains were yellow velour with blue butterflies. The butterflies were too plump but perfectly stitched. The Colonial American couch was upholstered in broad blue stripes that matched the overstuffed chair: Winston's. Rosemary's floor was glassy golden oak (sanded and shellacked one long weekend by Winston). Rosemary waxed it weekly. A fan in one window kept the air moving and doubled as exhaust for the stove.

Rosemary was a fine seamstress and an $800 Bernina sewing machine was tucked away in its cherrywood cabinet underneath the window. Rosemary made all her clothes and the children's too and they were practical designs in muted earth tones. Iridescent greens, brilliant pinks, startling lavenders were colors Rosemary strongly opposed. "Nigger colors" she called them.

Rosemary's dark hair was plaited into a single braid; thick as a mooring line it dangled to the base of her spine and Winston loved to play with it when they were naked.

Winston devoured three patés and a serving of pigeon peas. Rosemary poured herself ice tea, to keep him company. She said, "Joshua's hangin' around with the Rastas and bad johns down at the snack bar. He runnin' errands, fetchin' they rum. Winston, you got to straighten that boy."

"When I his age, Darlin', I was the same," Winston said.

"But you was doin' good in school. An' look where it got you. Finish the army as a warrant officer"—her voice underlined *officer*—"and then you get your pilot license and more licenses after."

Her praise made Winston gloomy. Pilot license, multi-engine, IFR, helicopter, Air Transport rating—all that work and study. For what? For what? He sighed. He said, "I talk to Joshua."

Rosemary stirred her tea. After a pause, she said, "I got two thousand four hundred dollars, fifty, saved up for our house. How about you?"

Winston pushed away his plate. "Same as last Friday when I get paid. No different."

"Winston, why you vex?"

He looked around the familiar room and cleared his throat. He said, "That Jocko, he hangin' around the airport again. I don't know why the authorities permit such outrage in public place. Jocko pimp and thief and drug pusher and they let him wander about free, like he the Lion of Judah."

Rosemary said, "Long as he don't bother you. Winston, how much money..."

"He Mal Esprit's—that's all he is. Jocko is Mal Esprit's eyes and ears, hands and legs."

"Mal Esprit's not in St. Thomas. Mal Esprit on Dominica," Rosemary said, impatient to put the matter to rest.

"Mal got men like Jocko everywhere. Mal taken up the political life, you know."

The manchineel tree is broad crowned, dark leaved, and its shade invites a picnic or children to play. It grows above some of Dominica's prettiest black-sand beaches. To touch the manchineel leaf is to burn, to pick a sliver of bark is to burn, to shelter under the manchineel in the rain is to be pelted with poison, to blister, suppurate, and die.

Like the manchineel, Mal Esprit had charms.

Winston and Mal (when he was younger, Mal had had a different name) had been boys together in the village of Soufriere. They'd been pals: the quick, dark, witty Mal and Winston, dogged, careful, more often the butt of the joke than the joke maker. They'd attended school under Mr. Soylo, the schoolmaster who, though dim-sighted, saw every mischief they did.

"Who would vote for Mal Esprit?" Rosemary asked scornfully.

Rosemary was a native St. Thomian, had never met Mal, and never once been on the island of Dominica—but plenty down islanders come to the East End Clinic and islanders like to talk. You can't keep a secret in the islands.

"I don't think Mal planning for voting," Winston said unhappily. He'd managed to shuffle from one topic he didn't wish to discuss into another. That was a habit of his. "I got the same saved as before: six thousand five hundred."

"More precisely, Winston." She laid an envelope on the counter, wrote down her balance and awaited his.

"Five hundred and thirty-two sixty."

She did the sum and nodded, pleased. "We get there pretty soon," she said. "Think, Winston, four years ago we hadn't a dollar in the bank."

"Near ain't home," Winston said. And, the truth was, they were far from satisfying Rosemary's dream.

Rosemary yearned for a real home. A modest three-room West Indian house, high on a hill where breezes would keep it free of mosquitoes, facing the ocean and the ocean's blue gleam but not too low where salt spray ate everything up. A good cistern, thirty thousand gallons, so they could take showers all year and flush the toilet every single time someone peed.

Cane sugar farming prospered in the Virgin Islands from 1700 to the 1850s. Danes and black slaves cleared the land, built stone terraces and sugar roads, erected great sugar mills beside the harbors. White sugar was the delight of European royalty. Sugar rum was the solace of the slaves who produced it.

On November 23, 1733, slaves on the Annanberg plantation rose up, hanged their masters, and burned the great mill. This uprising is still celebrated in the Virgins with considerable relish. It makes some white people very uncomfortable, creating a twitch just where the collar touches the neck.

Retribution was swift, imaginative, and horrible, but the uprising made its point. Slavery was outlawed in 1839 in the Danish Virgins; a few years later, on Tortola, the Brits followed suit. In 1917, the U.S. bought three of the Virgin Islands—St. Thomas, St. Johns, and St. Croix—from the Danes. They spent twenty-five million for them.

St. Thomas, a semiarid island, imports almost all its food. The stone terraces of the sugar estates have returned to bush. When they are cleared, it is for private houses.

While Rosemary was washing up, Mrs. Childress brought the children home. Mrs. Childress had tiny eyes and a Cupid's mouth. The skin on her hands and plump cheeks was exquisite.

"Joshua is a very good boy when he with me," she said, implying that in poorer care, he might go wild.

Mrs. Childress accepted several glasses of ice tea, and what with the chatting and the children finding release from good manners by wrestling with Winston, it was eleven o'clock before Mrs. Childress was gone and the children abed. Winston eased their bedroom door closed. Rosemary's hand evaded his. She gave him a fierce look.

"Winston. The children."

"Children sleep now."

"They might wake up, Winston, at any time. And if they should come out for a pee or a glass of water? Winston, you know how I feel about this."

Winston looked at his watch. "It is late for this fella. I go to my home, now."

Softening, she took his hand, "Winston, I'm sorry. There'll be another time. We go out one night for dancing. I'll leave the children at Mrs. Childress's home all night."

"Can we afford this fête, darlin'?"

For answer she touched his cheek with her fingertips.

At the door, her kiss was so soft, her lips so yielding, his manhood erected. Dazed, he watched the green enameled door swing shut in his face.

"Good-night, Winston," she murmured behind it.

Promises. Sometimes, Winston thought that was all they had between them: promises.

During the Danes' tenure in the Virgins, a French Creole mercantile class rose up and soon controlled most of the fishing, restaurants, and small markets and bought the old estates cheap when the sugar market collapsed. Fifty years after, the grandsons of the original purchasers sold off these steep, waterless acres, bordered by slave walls and terraces, for twenty-five thousand dollars an acre—if a purchaser was lucky enough to find a Frenchman willing to make Essau's bargain.

St. Thomas banks will not lend money on unimproved land. If you wish to buy property to build a house you must demonstrate your ability to put a cistern on the land. St. Thomas gets plenty rain in the spring and if your roof is broad enough and your cistern deep you can store adequate household water all year. Pools are definitely a luxury, and St. Thomians still talk about the wealthy American writer who bought a WWII naval gun battery, used one gun implacement for his cistern and the other as a circular swimming pool, 50-foot diameter, dark blue, overlooking the paler Caribbean.

The cistern Winston wanted cost $15,925. Add the price of pump and filters, and the backhoe work to set it in place. After four years of saving (Winston thought of them as the "Honda years"), they'd saved not quite half the money.

Turpentine Run is too steep for a Honda 125 so Winston took the Bovoni Road and didn't pull into his own alleyway until after midnight. The Obeah man glowered in his headlight.

The Obeah man was man-sized, carved from oiled mahogany. The carver had taken pains. You knew the book in the Obeah man's left hand was the Bible, because LIV SACRE was carved in the spine. His walking stick curled into a serpent, just above the grasp of his right hand. He had a heavy wooden beard and round spectacles mended with a piece of black electrician's tape at the bridge where they'd broken. His wooden nose was dented, like he'd lost a fight.

Winston bought the Obeah man from a fellow pilot, a Haitian, who needed quick cash when he and his wife split up. Two weeks later, in dead calm, not a cloud in the sky, the Haitian's plane went down off St. Croix and sank like a stone.

Winston often spoke with the Obeah man. Sometimes he asked him for advice. Winston would never sell the Obeah man. Obeah man hated slavery like poison.

* * *

Next morning, when Winston puttered off, Mrs. Indarsingh didn't come out but he saw a curtain flutter in her upstairs window.

Once he got to the DMS shop, Winston set to work on the Lycoming.

Richie was an hour late and wore the same clothes (more rumpled) he'd worn last night.

"Connie," he said. "Uh-uh."

"Those white women tear you up," Winston noted.

Richie ran his hands through his shaggy blond hair and grinned. He was restless this morning and less use than usual so Winston didn't object when he clambered into the DC-3 cockpit, trying controls. Winston torqued down the Lycoming bolts, each one, just so.

"Hey, Winston, how do you tell when the landing gear's down on this thing?"

"Stick your head out the window and look."

Richie laughed. "Jesus Christ, what a clunk."

Winston swung the Lycoming onto the test stand and rolled it out onto the apron. He brought out a fire extinguisher and set it where it'd be handy. He fueled the motor, attached oil pressure and temperature gauges and a battery. She cranked right away.

Winston yelled up at the DC-3, but Richie was gone—wandered off somewhere. Winston set up the DC-3 tarp himself.

The thrum of the engine on the stand soothed Winston as he cut rivets. This is how he liked it—alone, cut off from the rest of the world by the motor's roar. As he worked, he hummed last year's Carnival anthem. "Oh Lord, pee-pee gonna fall on me . . ."

The second-story windows of the St. Thomas jail overlook a pleasant oceanside promenade. Nice to walk beside the water, you and your girl. Last February, it was a great scandal (and became a song) when prisoners were observed, sneaking up to the open windows and, "Oh Lord, pee-pee gonna fall . . ."

When Richie returned, he brought two black coffees. Winston always drank his coffee with milk and sugar.

Richie said, "They towed the doper over to the bush with the junk planes. They didn't put no customs sticker on it either."

"They didn't find no dope?"

"No, man. Customs and DEA went over that plane with vacuum cleaners and everything but whoever was flying had his dope sealed. There was some marijuana ash under the pilot's seat but nothing they can confiscate the plane for. There were bloodstains on the prop."

"From where?"

Richie shrugged. "If you're not gonna drink your coffee, give it here. That woman was insatiable."

"Where blood?"

"On the tip of the prop. Must have hit a bird. Winston, they got a color radar in that thing."

"I look at it last night but I didn't see the instruments."

"Goddamned beautiful. Man, how long you figure it'd take us to get that radar out of there?"

"Thief it?"

Richie snorted. "How long you think that plane gonna last without a police seal? Week or so, the landing lights are gone and a week after that, the radios. Hell, those other dopers—you seen 'em lately, Winnie? They used to be twin engines but they zip engines now. And they were sealed—they had the DEA seal. And they wasn't registered in goddamned Nicaragua."

"Where?"

"For truth—some bullshit company registered the black plane in Nicaragua. Winston, if we don't get that radar, somebody will. Think how this old bird'd love to have radar in her." He patted the DC-3. "Honey, you'd really be something then, wouldn't you?"

Winston said, "You're sitting on the rivet punch."

At eleven, David came in from Anegada and taxied right over beside the DC-3, where the twin Beech would be perfectly accessible, if anybody wanted to work on it, repair the throttle friction, for instance. He gave Richie a pleasant wave before he walked off but ignored Winston.

Warmed up, the Lycoming wouldn't hold oil pressure and a smear of dark liquid appeared beside the number-four spark plug.

Winston said, "Goddamned son of a bitch" and shut down.

About then, the Lycoming owner arrived, delighted to see his motor on the test stand.

"No, sir, it is not fixed," Winston explained. "Either a bad valve or the new cylinder is no good. I will wait until she is cooled and take her down again."

The man set his lips in a thin, thin line. "If I had known this was going to be so much trouble I would have taken it to Five-Star."

Winston said, "Five-Star right down at the end of the building here. Richie will help you push it."

The owner looked at Winston for a long, long time. He had a magistrate's eyes. He said, "I'll speak to your boss about this."

He was just the sort who would.

Richie put the extinguisher away.

Winston rolled the Lycoming inside, pulled the big doors down, and washed his hands.

Richie said, "It's only eleven-thirty."

Winston shrugged off his coveralls and drew on street clothes. He inspected his face in the mirror above the washbasin. Winston said, "A hungry belly has no ears." He added, "Maybe you'll see your girlfriend."

But neither girl was at the Barbary Coast today and Winston's silence defeated Richie's chatter. Although the mellow sun streamed in the café's windows and the banana quit zipped to and fro, it was not a pleasant lunch.

When they returned and opened the shop again, Richie said, "Maybe I could start on that left throttle. Last night, David said he wasn't taking the Beech out until the bread run tomorrow."

Winston turned from the Lycoming. "When you talk to David?"

Richie was flustered. He wriggled around in his skin. "Well, it was last night. Me and Connie were invited up for cocktails. I mean Connie wasn't, I was, but I didn't think they'd mind. Megan liked Connie. Megan said Connie is 'real people.' It's pretty up there above Hull Bay."

"I never been to the Sandersons' house," Winston said. "You ever pull a console?"

Richie laughed at his own ineptitude. "Everything I know about airplanes is what you taught me, man. Hell, give me another year or two and I'll be a first-rate mechanic."

Winston thought his estimate conservative but didn't say so. "I think the Beech wait until I can get to it."

Richie wanted to work on the DC-3 and Winston said to cut rivets. A child can cut rivets. Winston pulled the Lycoming head and could see that the gasket was bad. When he miked the cylinder, it was three-thousandths fatter at one end than the other. It'd have to go back to the Florida machine shop and, of course, it'd need a new gasket too. Winston might have got away with the old one but: the Caribbean looks like a smooth place for a deadstick landing but it's not.

Winston had a rule of three: one thing wrong (bad weather), he fly; two things wrong (dubious fuel, an untrustworthy altimeter), he fly; three things, he no longer fly. Over the Caribbean, an oil leak counted as three things wrong.

He cleaned the mismilled cylinder with kerosene before re-packing it in the crate it had arrived in.

Richie asked, "What's the maximum overload for these DC-3s?"

Winston said, "Bob, that old pilot comes into Five-Star some-times? During the war, he flew seventy-two people off a dirt strip in Burma. Most of 'em was kids."

Richie did the weight calculation in his head. He whistled, "You believe him?"

Winston shrugged. "Japs was comin'. Take this to Mrs. Sander-son. Tell her to send it back."

"Sure." The young man dropped a broken rivet on the apron where it'd be sure to puncture a nosewheel one day. "What's she like to fly?"

"DC-3s good aircraft. Very forgiving."

Richie looked at Winston for too long before saying. "Yeah, sure, Winston. I'll get this off. Toot sweet."

Winston stooped and pocketed the rivet.

Winston changed from dirty overalls into clean ones. He sat at his desk with the Beech shop manual and read through the proce-dures.

Richie brought two black coffees. Winston said he never drank coffee in the afternoon. Richie sat both cups on Winston's desk, leaving wet rings. He was embarrassed but sincere, "Megan said the Lycoming owner stopped to bitch."

Winston grunted.

Richie scratched his head and examined the poster: FIGHTER AIRCRAFT OF THE WORLD.

"Said he was going to sue. Winnie, you ever fly one of these F-16s?"

Winston said, "I learn to fly on helicopters. Army teach me."

Richie said, "I'd give my left arm to fly an F-16." He banked with his hand. "ERROOOW," he said.

Winston said, "You thinkin' of flyin' that DC-3, maybe?"

"Well, yeah, I thought...You know, Winston, I mean, as a ground chief, there isn't anybody can touch you. I mean, shit, man, anybody can drive a plane."

"David in the Beech and you in the DC-3."

"And you keep us both flying." He ventured a laugh. "DMS is gonna grow, Winston. David says so. He thinks a lot of you, the world."

Winston said, "Don't leave rivets on the apron no more."

"Oh sure. Hell, yes. See what I mean?" And he beamed at Winston like "okay, no problem." Like they were pals again.

As Winston stared into his confident, witless grin, a tingle started in his body, low, in the webbing between his toes, and that tingle brushed every nerve all the way up, like an electric paintbrush.

A tremor shook his biceps and he crossed his arms to clutch them. He grinned. Couldn't have been a reassuring grin because Richie backed up and, at the door, waved a floppy wave that was silly even for him. Winston's laughter burst out of him like tears from his eyes and Richie disappeared.

That's how they do it to you. Innocently. And wanting so terribly to be liked. My, oh my. Weakened, laughing, Winston leaned against his workbench.

His mind so clear. Cold as a sharp knife.

They treat him so, he be a bad john again. Fine. He snorted. His laugh rattled off the tin walls of the shop. He would steal the black plane.

He would steal it and fly it to Puerto Rico where he knew a man who would buy it. While Richie slipped around, plotting to steal the plane's instruments, Winston would steal the whole plane, not leaving its shadow behind.

When he sobered, he wiped his eyes and said, "Man, man." He traced throttle linkages in the Beechcraft manual, identified the tools he'd need, and picked them from his toolbox.

An amateur mechanic came by, wanting to borrow Winston's impact wrench and Winston started laughing again so the man went away.

Richie returned to the DC-3, looking up from time to time to watch Winston. Richie whistled nervously.

Winston pulled the Beechcraft console and was squatting over the bare cables and solenoids when Tom Bledsoe came by to ask Winston about an irregular fuel injector. Winston said to check his ports, "Mike them, man."

At five o'clock Richie cleaned up his rivets. He swept the apron clean, which was a first. He climbed onto the Beech's wingstep.

"David's gonna want this for the bread run in the morning."

Winston said, "Where is David now?"

"How the hell should I know? Home, I suppose."

"And you be goin' now?"

"Uh-huh. Connie and me got a hot date." With his fingers, Richie made an obscene gesture. Bunny lust.

"Black man can't trust white man do anything right," Winston said.

Richie made a face. "Jesus, Winston, I'd hoped we were a little beyond that!" He glared at Winston but Winston was picking at the linkage with his needle-nose pliers. In a bit, Richie went away. Winston's watch said half past five.

"White men don't pay no overtime either," he muttered. He spread a plastic garbage bag across the open console. Wouldn't want dirt dropping in there. He locked the Beech, put tools away, manual back on its shelf. For the fourth time today he changed clothes.

Winston used the pay phone. "Rosemary, I got to work on the Beech tonight and so, can't come over."

"I hope they payin' you," she said. "I hope they ain't workin' you like nigger."

Winston said, "I'd hoped we were a little beyond that."

Rosemary snorted.

After the last stragglers left the airport and the X was across the runway, Winston crossed the taxiway. Even without a flashlight he could see fine: DC-3, DC-3, C-54, Piper Cherokee, a doper, DC-3, Lockheed Electra, another doper. Plenty of planes in the bush. Black plane.

A strong half moon climbed over Red Point. The black plane didn't seem Jumbie tonight. Just another quiet machine, waiting for a man's touch. Winston slipped aboard quietly and sat in the copilot's seat. The plane had color radar, with the double sweep. The radios were Collins Microlines, and it had Loran navigation. Winston held the wheel, wondering how it'd feel to fly those tremendous Navaho engines. A homemade red lever clamped the cable to the rear hatch release. They could drop their dope without scrambling around the rear compartment—one pass over the pickup boat and away.

Winston sat there, imagining, for a long time before he went home.

A note on his door said a package from Winter Rest, Florida, had arrived and was at Petty John's Disco and Snakbar. Winston could hear a radio playing in the Snakbar, jokes and laughter. He'd get the package later.

He showered and put on new undershorts. He gave his dress shoes a good polish and washed his hands again, digging every bit of polish from his fingernails. Just another black man getting dressed to go out. He pulled on pale blue pants and a guayaberra shirt. He exchanged his workaday Timex for the gold Seiko with matching gold bracelet.

Outside, he paused beside the Obeah man for some moments, two old friends enjoying the evening calm, the dusky air. Winston waited until he felt natural.

He found a taxi on Bjerge Gade and the trip to the yacht harbor cost $3.20, which Rosemary damn sure would have questioned.

In his pre-Rosemary days, the Beachcomber was one of Winston's hangouts. Pretty girls from the sailboats and tourist girls from the resorts and the food wasn't terrible and the drinks were generous. Of course he'd had too many of those generous drinks. He knew that now.

He caught the bartender's eye. "Robert Maroni, still working here?"

The bartender wore black pants, pleated white shirt, a red sash. He seemed very young.

"Jimmy Red? Tall fella, hooked nose?"

"Nope."

"Ma Dorothea, she still back in the kitchen?"

The bartender said, "Pal, this place was bought by Caribbean Restaurant Management two years ago. Nobody here from before."

"Okay. Rum and tonic." Winston put his elbows on the bar and remembered the room: bistro tables, wire chairs, windows overlooking the sailboats in the mooring. It hadn't changed but didn't mean anything to him. The room was smaller than he remembered.

The customers—were they old enough to drink?—they called out to each other and walked from one table to another, like bees after honey. The jukebox played white music. Video games had been installed and they hummed and clicked and blinked though nobody was playing them—like they were playing themselves.

Winston didn't send back his fried fish although he'd ordered broiled because getting it right wouldn't matter. He picked at his fish, drank half his stingy drink, and got out of there.

The sailboats hadn't changed though there were fewer wooden boats and more plastic ones. Anchored farther out, a 12-meter boat rocked in the swell. It was very beautiful and made Winston sad because he'd never be young again. He'd crewed one Bermuda race and navigated another. What a time.

When Winston first met Rosemary, he'd been living on a 21-foot catboat moored in Benner Bay. That catboat provided the first three thousand dollars of their savings.

Winston leaned against a piling, city lights at his back and black water gently chuckling at his feet. The taut whine of rigging, a loose halyard rattling, the squeak as a boat rubbed the bumper.

When Winston got out of the army, he was twenty-two years old and angry at life. He crewed and captained all around the Caribbean, Central America too. He flew airplanes—some of the worst clunkers still able to fly. He never flew dope—never had to. On most Caribbean islands, customs duties are a major part of government income. On Dominica, after customs, an ordinary household sink costs $2,000, a rebuilt carburetor, $300. A pilot able to land a small plane on a beach can make plenty without running dope.

When Winston wasn't flying, he was sailing or sailboarding or drinking or making love. He never gave thought to the future since he assumed he had none.

It was Carnival on St. Thomas and he'd been drinking nonstop for two weeks until, one morning about 10 A.M., he fell over in the street. When he came around he was in the East End Clinic and the doctor was telling him something alarming about his pancreas. Later Rosemary came in. She seemed so decent.

Winston and Rosemary never talked about his life before they met. It was a nontopic.

When Winston checked his dress watch, it had stopped. Dead

battery. When was the last time Winston dressed up to go out for a fête? One of Rosemary's sisters' marrying—Sudy? Doreen?

He took a cab to Mutt & Jeff's in Dorotea Estate and didn't count his change.

Mutt & Jeff's had been in business for thirty years, which is unusual in St. Thomas, where restaurants open one day and close the day after.

He came in through the downstairs bar; the bartender—happily—he knew her.

"Winston! I'll be damned. Do the dead walk?"

"Good evening, Katrina. Last time I saw you, you a waitress, at the Rainbow."

She shook her head. "Long time ago, Winston. The Rainbow's closed." Katrina was a pretty girl, cornshock hair, nice green eyes. Winston and she had never made it but he'd always thought they might one day. "Gosh, it's good to see you. Come over here and give me a kiss." And he did kiss her scented cheek and she was so welcoming. What had he done with all his friends?

"Winston"—she kept his hands clasped in hers—"you don't look much different. More sober, maybe."

He laughed, "Oh yes. That."

"You still flyin'?"

Winston made a gesture: so-so. "DMS Airways."

She brought him a Mountgay and tonic and took care of other customers. It was a nice bar, shutters thrown open to the fragrant night. The upstairs restaurant was open too, and you could dine amidst royal palms and banyan trees.

When she was caught up she rested her elbows on the bar and said, "Winston, where have you been?"

Winston felt funny. She was a fine woman and her face too close to his. "I marry soon," he said. "Rosemary, she a nurse."

Briefly, Katrina's smile froze before it deepened, "Hey, hey, Winston. Great! That is really terrific! How long you known her?"

"Oh long time. Long time. We been planning and saving, you know."

She bobbed her head like maybe she did know. She brought him a second Mountgay and tonic, unasked for, and took a glass of wine herself and raised a toast. "Good luck, Winston. Really, I mean it."

Winston hadn't finished his first drink and didn't really want another but he clicked glasses. "Thank-you," he said. They smiled at each other until it got awkward and Winston said, "Fitz still hang out here?"

Her smile vanished like she'd wiped it.

"You know him, white guy, thirty-five maybe. His legs..."

"Shit yes I know Fitz. Winston, I never knew you to be mixed up in *that*."

"Katrina, I am not mixed up in anything. I am wishing to talk to Fitz only."

Her eyes were sorrowful with doubt. "Uh-huh. He's here. Upstairs, in the corner." And she left and soon had a conversation going with a white guy at the far end of the bar.

Winston took one of his drinks with him.

The upstairs room was couples, finishing late candlelight suppers, talking soft and low. Waitresses glided between tables, pouring coffee, delivering desserts and sweet liquors. Most of the couples were white but a few were black.

Once upon a time, FitzRoy McDermett had been the apple of somebody's eye. Perhaps someone—a mother?—still had photographs lovingly preserved in a shoebox labeled: "At the Beach" or "Schooldays."

Today, Fitz was a bad man. He hadn't been so very bad when Winston first met him, but even then he'd had hard ways, and honest men found pressing business or other places to be when Fitz came around.

Fitz's face was fluid. It never stayed still long enough to pin anything on it: not a hope or a complaint, nothing. The top of his head was bald and he wore a sports car cap everywhere, indoors and out.

He sat alone, stirring a drink in a tall frosted glass.

Fitz wore tan shorts and a faded blue pullover with the insignia of the Boca Raton Hotel & Club. His awful leg was bare.

Fitz looked up when Winston pulled out a chair. Fitz clinked his ice cubes around his drink. He said, "These stupid assholes pour warm Scotch over warm diet cola and wonder why the drink's watery before it's cold."

"Been a long time," Winston said.

Fitz stirred his drink.

"I think it was the wooden boat race, four years ago."

"Some people think that shit's fun."

"Oh, it's nice, man," Winston said nervously. "Quiet, the wind, the waves . . ."

"Your pal, Mal Esprit, is into some heavy shit."

Fitz always zoomed in tight on his interests. Most of the world wasn't his business.

"Mal . . . I don't care what that boy do."

"You Dominican, right? You and Mal are tight."

"My mother was Dominican. My father a sailor: U.S. navy."

"Mal's growin' some righteous product is what I hear."

"That's what they do, Dreads and Rastas. They grow ganja."

Fitz grinned. He lacked two teeth top and bottom and Winston wondered if he'd lost them in the same accident that disfigured his leg. The leg had been broken below the knee and set by — field hands?—You could still see the bumps of sharp bone ends just underneath the slick scar flesh. It looked like it had hurt terribly and maybe still hurt in wet weather.

"I hear Mal is trading ganja for guns," Fitz said. He let the sentence hover in the air like a balloon.

"So?"

"Yeah. 'So.'" Fitz ran his eyes over the other diners. He said, "Everybody loves a lover. Ain't that a song or something?"

"Got something to ask," Winston said.

But Fitz shook his head and grinned, like a man remembering a good joke. "Remember those cult people down in Guyana? The ones killed themselves?"

"Jonestown?"

"Yeah. Jim Jones had him a white man for chief of security. U.S. ex-cop, ex-Special Forces, one of them. Everything goes along fine until one day, the Reverend Jim decides to close up shop and put out the lights. Mixes up a big vat of Kool-Aid, I mean *big* vat. Adds a bunch of poison to it, says drink up. Well, all the kids drink and the parents, they feel so bad account of their kids dead they drink it too. After while, ain't nobody left 'cept Jim Jones and his Security Chief. 'Have one on me,' says Jim."

Winston wished he hadn't had so many rum and tonics. He wasn't used to them.

Fitz chuckled. "When the soldiers fly into Jonestown, there wasn't nobody alive. Reverend Jim Jones was sittin' on his throne, dead as hell. Somebody had planted a pill between his eyes and they never did catch that Security Chief. Oh, he was a sweet-heart, he was. Know what they called him?"

Winston looked away. At a few tables, lovers whispered and smiled.

"Called him 'Mr. Bones.' Man, life is just a dream in the tropics."

"Why you saying this?"

When the waitress came, Winston decided he'd have another rum and tonic after all.

Fitz crossed his third finger over his second, "Mal and Mr. Bones, they're in the government. Get a few obstacles squared away and Dominica's gonna be a businessman's paradise. Can you dig it?"

Winston looked at his hands.

"I can get the items Mal wants. You tell him that next time you see him."

Angrily, "Him and me went to school together when we wore short pants like you. That's all. Long years since I seen him. Since he went away to University of West Indies and got to be a Dread."

Fitz lifted his glass and drank it in a single draught and rapped the glass on the table to signal the waitress, who brought him another, which he began to stir into coldness, same as the last.

Few dreamy couples remained. Below the balcony, car lights switched on, laughter, a door slammed.

Fitz said, "What are you doin' in my face? Why you taking my time?"

Winston said, "I come to ask about that doper landed at St. Thomas airport two mornings past."

Fitz's stirrer didn't pause or skip a beat, his vague smile stayed fixed and it might have been Winston's illusion that his eyes narrowed. Swish, swish, swish.

Winston said, "It was a black plane, twin Navaho—"

"I know what the fuck it was, Winston. I just don't know who the fuck you are. Four, five years since I seen you and you come on to me with questions. Who you workin' for?"

"DMS Airways!" Maybe Winston wished he hadn't blurted it out like that.

"Dandy."

"How long ago was it, Fitz, I flew you off St. Barts? Stupid white boy sellin' dreamy drugs to kids, turned out they was the magistrate's kids, and they wreck the car and lucky they still livin'. Not so many white fellas on St. Barts, that you hard to find. 'Please, Winston, fly me off island.' Me, I got a single-engine Cessna, and it got oil pressure like shit. 'Fly me off, Winston. I don't got no money, but I'll make it up to you.' Fitz, I still can't land on St. Barts. After that time, they never gave me no landing rights again."

Fitz swallowed his drink and rapped. Winston told the waitress, no thanks. The waitress showed irritation. Most tables were empty while waitresses removed tablecloths, flowers, refilled the salt, pepper, and sugar. One black waitress sat at an uncovered table counting tips.

Fitz aimed his finger at Winston. "You can't present this bill twice."

Winston didn't like Fitz. Probably, the reason he'd helped him was his horribly broken leg. Winston said, "Sure."

Dope is the middle-class dream of great wealth—California Gold Rush, oil boomtown, marque de privateer. Where else can an ordinary man with no special talent double, triple, quintuple his investment? Where else can a middle-aged dentist, in a Pennsylvania steel town overcrowded with dentists, and the mills closing and slow pay and goddamn fluoride taking the guts right out of the business because kids don't have tooth decay today unless their parents are too poor and ignorant to own a goddamned TV, how can such an ordinary man keep up the payments?

Fitz didn't know their names. One was a pudgy man, middle-aged, stylish hair, aviator glasses. The other man—the pilot—was short and swarthy and wore a dark handlebar moustache. He was bowlegged.

The dentist had put the deal together. Took investment money from other dentists, insurance men, realtors—other men terrified of not making the mortgage, of hitting the skids. The pilot had connections and found the plane. For two trips, it worked perfect. With extra tanks in the back, the black plane could fly all the way from the Bolivian highlands over the lighted marker in North Georgia, where they'd pull the lever and the packed duffel bag was dropped and they could land anywhere, clean. It was the pilot's idea to register the plane in Nicaragua. The Sandinista official who filled out the papers thought it was funny.

If they had ever had trouble, they'd just pull the lever and the evidence was gone.

"They'd been lucky," Fitz whispered. "They were buying from the Guiterez family and they'll kill you, quick as a wink, but they won't rip you off. They give good weight." Fitz turned his palm upright. "Good people."

For the dentist and the doper pilot, it had started out as a nice morning. A morning of sun showers, green forest below, the Andes winking through the haze. As always, the doper pilot buzzed the tiny dirt strip three times before he landed, and as always, the dentist had the Swedish Ingram machine pistol in his lap.

Business as usual. There was the dealer, his brother, and an armed bodyguard. The brother drove. It was such a routine piece of business, the brother brought his four-year-old son along for the outing.

The doper pilot kept his engines running as the Toyota Land Cruiser edged onto the strip. For a moment the two groups stopped and watched, but that was just perfunctory caution and soon the dentist was on the ground and the Bolivians were counting his cash: $200,000 in tens and twenties and fifties and he was sampling random bags of coke, $3 million back in Altoona if they didn't cut it, if they moved it all in one deal.

The pilot shut down and did his walk-around check. He paused to pat the child on the head. The boy had never seen an airplane so close before and was fascinated with its surfaces, its rare blackness. The dentist tucked the Ingram under his arm where it would be inoffensive. Arturo, the dealer, didn't carry a weapon, of course. His bodyguard had an AK-47 in the Toyota but he knew these Americanos, everybody did.

The dope pilot gassed up his wing tanks. The dentist smiled and shook everybody's hand and the bodyguard helped him lift the bag of dreams into the airplane. The pilot wanted to check something: oil pressure, carburetor, ignition spark advance—something—and kicked over the right engine. It was an accident. The boy had no reason to be there in the first place. But when the propeller flashed around and killed his son, scooped him from under the wing and hurled him to his father's feet, Arturo screamed and ran for the AK and the dentist found himself firing the machine pistol he'd never fired before. The Ingram jittered and spat and three men died. When the echoes died, the only sound was the pilot weeping and the dentist retching onto the dirt.

Well, there was nothing for it. They grabbed the money and took off but forgot they hadn't refilled the auxiliary tanks and they had $200,000 cold cash and a big sack of nose candy but only forty-two gallons of aviation gas and even feathered for maximum economy, that'd not take them back to the U.S. mainland.

The doper pilot remembered St. Thomas.

Other Guiterez men arrived at the dirt airstrip in time to see the black plane turning onto its heading.

"You know how those people are," Fitz said. "If the Guiterezes can't spend it or eat it or fuck it they shoot it. They don't have the same number of categories you and me do. Hell," Fitz said, "every thief on St. Thomas is looking for those two. Whoever gives them up to the Guiterez family will hit the jackpot."

Their waitress waited nearby. She took off one shoe and massaged her weary instep.

Laughter from the bar below.

Fitz said, "You find them and I'll get word to Guiterez. They paying fifty thousand. Split two ways."

"Ambition killed the rat," Winston said.

3

No Connections

"But I *know* her. She's an old and dear friend," Dr. Dragotti murmured, bending over his charcoal sketch.

"Then you won't mind if I get an imprint of her card." Arms folded, Ringo leaned in the doorway of his father's room. Ringo wore pale green designer jeans, loafers, and a square-necked striped Mexican overblouse.

His father waved his delicate hand. "Those zygomatic arches," he enthused. His charcoal dashed at the sketch. "There, and there."

Dr. Dick Dragotti's office occupied the top block at Sandpiper Cay clinic overlooking the terraces and roofs of the operating room, recovery room, and guest apartments. The terrace below with floral tubs and brilliant white tables was Café Schweitzer. The doctor's west windows faced green-brown Great Cameneo, rising like a humpback whale, circled by soaring gulls. From the south, he could see Guana Island (owned entirely, it is said, by a family of wealthy Chileans). Nobody had ever been seen to land at the rotting boat dock and nobody cleaned rubbish off the beach after the last hurricane. Rarely, patients at the clinic made a picnic there. Beyond Guana Island lay the featureless gray, serious Atlantic.

There was no desk in Dr. Dragotti's room; he did his sketching at the thick glass coffee table, working from a lightboard that bore four X rays of Carly's mother's skull and jaw. Dr. Dragotti perched on the edge of a Barcelona chair and shaded highlights into his portrait.

On the black-and-white Norwegian rug beneath the table were magazines: *Der Stern, Paris Match, Country Gentleman, Connoisseur.*

Dragotti turned his sketch—a dramatic, high-fashion rendition of a woman who did look a bit like Carly's mother, only more rarefied somehow. Her hair was longer too, and in the sketch it flowed free. "Isn't she a fucking stunner?"

Ringo glanced at the sketch that wasn't anybody yet and said, "Uh-huh. You knew her in the Silicon Valley days?"

The doctor sighed, "Those were the days, my friend. Those were the days."

"Stephen Jobs?"

"My yes. I was one of Stephen's first investors. And there was Max Frisch and John Carradine, and Magdellana's husband, Willy. The pioneers. They didn't know how to dress properly and they'd abandon the most amusing gathering to tinker with their crazy machines. Computer hackers. Well, they were right and the rest of the world wrong and that's how it goes."

Dr. Dragotti wore pleated linen trousers and a white silk shirt. The platinum watch fob that dangled discretely from his breast pocket was connected to a Gerard Pirregaux doctor's watch with two second hands. At one time this watch had belonged to Dr. George Harvey who revolutionized heart surgery in the twenties.

Dr. Dragotti's hair was soft, mousy brown. Behind the granny glasses, his eyes were soft too.

"The wives of those hackers were among the first to realize the benefits of my work," he said. "They were wonderful patients. Won-der-ful!"

"It's too bad about the daughter."

Dr. Dragotti drew on concern easily, like a comfortable shirt.

"She was so whacked at dinner last night, I was afraid she was going to flop into her mango sorbet."

"A little too much champers, no doubt. . . ."

"Uh-huh. She's got a great ass. One day you'll have a good time restructuring that one."

"Not my cup of tea, I'm afraid." Dr. Dragotti's eyes sparkled over his glasses. "I leave the gluteus maximus to the Big Stitchers. Human eyes—now there's a great challenge."

"I think Mama Hollander hopes to fuck her way to a new face. She pull that, back in Silicon Valley?"

His father set down his charcoal stub and took a sip of iced Perrier. Except for the glowing X rays, the gray office walls were bare. There was room for only one artist at Sandpiper Cay. He said, "Her husband always paid without complaint." He paused. "I suppose he still must."

"You been gettin' into that. You old bastard."

With a smile flickering at the corner of his mouth, the Doctor said, "She's a very special patient, Ringo."

"She's got a death grip on that platinum card. She's been here two days and I haven't got a glimpse of it."

Dr. Dragotti's stern expression was the one he put on while advising patients to stay out of the sun for ninety-six hours after the dressings came off. "Do you know what it costs to run this clinic?"

Ringo Dragotti, Sandpiper Cay's business manager, could have told him to the penny, but artists need special delicacy. He didn't say, "Our nut is 42 K, off season, higher in December and January" because that would have disconcerted the Doctor. "It costs a lot," Ringo said.

Ringo might have added they charged a lot too which was equally true. The simplest face-lift (rytidoplasty) combined with a removal of neck wattles (platysma-lift) was $22,000. It was a package plan: operation and three-week recovery on the island. A bank president's wife, or movie starlet, could spend a month in the British West Indies and return with a fine tan and new face underneath it.

Despite his preening, Dr. Dragotti was a first-rate surgeon. He'd studied under Boivin in France and done his internship with Hale Tolleth at Stanford Medical Center. Like Jean Boivin, Dr. Dragotti had initially studied to be an artist. Like Pitanguy in Rio, his patients were the rich, the famous, the would-be-famous.

"Make sure you get her card," Dr. Dragotti said. He closed his sketch pad, faced it down. He hummed a few bars of Bach's *Orchestral Suite*, the trumpet part. Music played everywhere at Sandpiper Cay. Bach before noon, Vivaldi until dusk, then Chopin. In the Café Schweitzer, at night, Frank Sinatra and Duke Ellington.

"What about Nurse Elwain's raise?" Ringo asked.

Miss Elwain was British, and had come with fine credentials as a surgical nurse. She was, Dr. Dragotti had said, "too stuffy, too darned polite." Although she didn't make mistakes, she never enthused "Yes, Doctor, no, Doctor," and Dr. Dragotti began to think her formality was stony disapproval. There was only room for one PROFESSIONAL at Sandpiper too. The doctor's lip curled, "Tell her to look around Roadtown and see if she can do better. If she's unhappy here, she can always apply with someone else."

Ringo raised his eyebrows. "I think we could be more diplomatic. She's only worked here six months."

Dr. Dragotti said, "You should see the looks she gives me. 'Ice Princess.'"

"I'll put her off. Tell her we don't have the cash flow in the off season. We'll advertise in the journals. When we get a new nurse, off she goes. Good-bye Sandpiper, hello Roadtown Emergency."

Dr. Dragotti changed X rays and placed a sketch of another face (the sketch resembled Candice Bergen in her modeling days) next to them.

Dr. Dragotti said, "I'll be doing a collagen implant on Mrs. Alvarez after lunch." He shuddered delicately. "I loathe yellow subcutaneous fat."

On the landing outside, Ringo paused to light a thin cigar. Sandpiper Cay had been built twenty years ago as a luxury resort on the model of Peter Island and Biras Creek. The architect had helped design Montreal's Habitat and his influence was unmistakable.

The building was a staggered V of concrete prefabs stacked up the leeward side of the island, like overlapping dominoes. Between the arms of the V was a rock garden, recirculating waterfall, gilded Japanese bridge. The physical plant was attractive but they never did manage to silence the hotel's generator and after dinner the café terrace was plagued by mosquitoes—the beach was too small, and the irregular tides of sea urchins that washed into the cove made it unusable.

In a hurry to recoup their investment the new owners took in guests before the staff was properly trained and, in consequence, food and service were legendarily bad. Several famous (and vocal) guests stayed less than a full day before leaving for other more congenial resorts.

Five years later, Dr. Dick Dragotti bought the failing resort and Sandpiper Cay Clinic was, he liked to say, "Transformed from my mind to concrete reality."

Broad wooden stairs wandered up the hill skirting the apartments, past the recovery room and surgery, past Café Schweitzer, past Dr. Dragotti's own room to the very brim of the island where a wooden gazebo overlooked the Atlantic, the Caribbean, all the dusty islands. Each hurricane destroyed the gazebo, but fastened to the leeward slope, the clinic itself was windproof.

At the bottom was the beach and boat jetty where the natives came to work every morning. (After 10 P.M. there were very few staff on duty. A kitchen worker to prepare late-night sandwiches, a bartender, nurses in the recovery unit.)

Ringo smoked his cigar. A white-tailed tropic bird circled overhead, dolphins sounded off Guana Island, a long red schooner heeled over in the Atlantic surge but Ringo was thinking about Carly. It was a long time since he'd had a girl so young.

The stairs were wide and gentle with benches for elderly patients fatigued by the climb. One patient had called the stairs "the stairway to heaven" and Dr. Dragotti relished and repeated this description.

Ringo Dragotti's office, in the recovery block, had no window overlooking anything. By computer he fired off a credit inquiry to a Florida agency. He checked reservations, ensured that boatmen would be ready to meet the Beef Island plane. He fired a cook's helper for petty theft, decided to keep another who was selling pot on the side.

At 10:59, the computer stuttered a reply to his credit inquiry and he tucked the printout and credit card imprinter in his leather case.

The patients' apartments were named after Caribbean fruits. Rose Apple bungalow wasn't Sandpiper Cay's best—Mr. and Mrs. Harrington, of the BBC, had that. But Rose Apple was in the second rank. Two bedrooms, two baths, and a tremendous living room with eastern and southern exposure.

"Good-morning, Mrs. Hollander. I hope you're enjoying your stay."

"Call me Magdellana! I hope I'm not so ancient young men call me by my last name." She touched his arm. There was something clinging in her touch.

"Magdellana, then. Lovely." He gave her arm a squeeze and his smile was as bright as her own.

"The Doctor asked me to invite you to lunch. I believe he'll have sketches ready." He looked her over rather severely. "I hope you know you're challenging."

"Oh dear. I'd rather hoped to be fascinating."

"Would you like to hear his exact words?"

"I'm breathless. . . ."

While they chatted, the daughter curled up on the couch reading yesterday's *Miami Herald*. Her hair was uncombed and she wore a thick flannel nightgown—the sort of gown only a young child or old woman usually wears. The drink in her glass might have been pure orange juice but probably wasn't. As she finished each section of her paper she let it drift onto the floor.

Magdellana wore a print jacket and wraparound skirt. The jacket was white, the skirt dull red. Around her neck she wore a triple necklace of the African trading beads so popular five seasons ago. Her bare feet were stub toed. Sturdy. Ringo would have expected more aristocratic feet.

Carly glanced up. "Hullo," she said.

"And how about you this morning?" Ringo asked.

"Fucking terrific." She looked at her newspaper. She sipped at her drink.

Ringo turned his ready smile to her mother. "My father posted your X rays in his office yesterday and he spent the morning conceptualizing." He chuckled. "I can't pretend I understand the Doctor's gift but I've rarely seen him so excited about a face."

Magdellana said, "Oh, pooh."

He accepted this invitation to proceed. "The drama in your cheekbones . . . Would you be offended by a comparison?"

"I don't, hah . . ."

"Meryl Streep?" he murmured.

"Oh, really now. Really . . ."

Carly licked her lips and drawled, "You do look like a Pollack, Mother."

Magdellana puffed up three sizes and flew to the couch, arms high over her head, jacket opened like a beetle's wings. Carly flinched and shrank. "Don't you use your tongue on me, little one, or I'll tear it out. I will spread mustard and horseradish on your tongue and lay it between thin slices of rye bread. I will chomp down." She wheeled, her jacket swirling like a highwayman's cape. She smiled a red smile. "My daughter is a runaway, Mr. Dragotti. She does not enjoy the real world." She gestured with elegant fingertips. "She always returns to Mother, don't you, dear?"

Ringo coughed politely.

Her voice dripped honey as she said, "Carly, don't you think it's time to get dressed? It is noonish, dear, and I'm sure Mr. Dragotti doesn't wish to see you dishabille." Carly's mother clamped her hands together so her rings interlocked into a single bright line.

It's too bad the doctor doesn't do hands, Ringo thought.

Sullenly, the girl dropped her paper on the floor and got to her feet and stretched so her breasts pressed the buttery flannel. Behind her mother's back, she looked at Ringo Dragotti and, deliberately, winked. It was a remarkable wink, a window into her soul.

The bedroom door hissed softly shut behind her. A moment later, hot rock-and-roll overwhelmed the Bach coming through the ceiling speakers. Dr. Dick hated it when patients brought their own tape players.

Throughout, Mrs. Hollander's face remained fixed, glittering, and her rings interlocked like a mace. She said, "But I'm sure, Ringo—you don't object to my using your first name...?"

"Uh, no..."

"That you haven't come down here this morning to enjoy the spectacle of me disciplining my daughter. Unless"—she put a thoughtful finger to her chin—"you're one of *those*...."

Ringo had taken too many punches below the belt. "No, Magdellana," he said. "I'm from the fuck 'em and forget 'em school. I never was much for whips and chains."

"Maybe you're not so, so special as you think, Ringo...." she said. "Luncheon with your father? Half past?"

"He usually shows up at one," Ringo reported.

"Late. How fashionable."

And Ringo found himself backing out of the Rose Apple bungalow with his briefcase unopened. In the briefcase he had a card imprinter and the printout of her credit check, which was terrible, just awful, of course.

Carly always felt stupid after reading the newspaper, which was why she read it. She felt stupid when she read a fashion magazine and subscribed to *Vogue, Glamour, Mademoiselle, and Twenty-one*. When she was fetched back from her attempts to start a new life, that was the first thing she did: catch up on the fashion mags. Drinking three mimosas in the morning stupified her and the Valium she took distributed her stupor so it was thinner and had a careless quality to it.

She drew on painter's pants. They were spacious in the legs, gathered at the waist, and gave her a sense of freedom. Carly loathed shoes. She considered another Valium but decided no, her supply was too low. If it hadn't been for that damn customs agent at Heathrow last year, she wouldn't be in this fix. She would have been confident enough to bring in the drugs she needed here. That was what the British government did—make people lose confidence.

A light knock on the door, "Maid, ma'am."

"Come in."

When the maid entered her eyes flicked to Carly's bare breasts and said, "Excuse me, miss, I didn't . . ."

"Don't worry about it."

"I just like to make up the room, miss. The housekeeper like us to be finished now."

Carly's suitcases were heaped on the dresser and she pawed through them, seeking the proper blouse. Sailor blouse, no; middy, no; T-shirts? Maybe. Most of the farts at Sandpiper Cay couldn't wear T-shirts without looking ridiculous. Definitely a T-shirt. No to: BANANA REPUBLIC, no to CARTIER'S EMPLOYEES PICNIC, no to RUSH, no to BOB DYLAN AUSTRALIAN TOUR. "Don't worry about my clothes," Carly said. "I'll pick up. Just make the bed."

"Yes, miss."

Penny, the maid, was Carly's age, with milk chocolate skin like Tobler's bon bons and her hair in a blue kerchief that matched her shift. She wore oversized white gym shoes.

Carly had an inspiration. "I hate shoes," she said.

The maid looked up from stripping the bed, "Oh, yes, miss, but it is the job." She stepped out from behind the bed, and spread her feet. She rocked back on her heels and bumped her fat shoes together. "I walk like the duck," she said. She giggled.

Carly was suddenly embarrassed because she was in bare feet and this black woman wasn't, because this woman was making her bed, because of her giggle. She said, "When you're done with the bed, I'll need more towels."

The woman's feet slapped back together and her giggle fell to the unvacuumed floor. "Yes, miss," she said, blank.

Carly selected a CANNES FILM FESTIVAL T-shirt. It had a hole at the right armpit and the slope of her breast peeked but that was how it should be with a Cannes T-shirt.

"Where can I get a newspaper in this dump?"

"The magazines and the newspapers come in with the afternoon speedboat."

Carly made a face, patted her hair, left.

Carly's mother was still in her bedroom making up for the CHEEKBONE SUMMIT. Beautifying the face she planned to trade in, oh my.

Outside, Carly squinted against the sunlight and eased the door shut. Mama would want Carly along at the SUMMIT—moral support—but there was no place she'd less rather be. Damn that sun. She didn't want to go back for sunglasses. Crested humming-birds dipped into the orchid blossoms beside the stair and a pair of palm swifts chortled to each other. In the rock garden, lemon trees were in bloom. The soft beauty angered Carly because it made her feel sad and she had enough to feel sad about, thank-you.

She thought about the Café Schweitzer. She needed a connec-tion—nothing formal, of course. "Could you let me have a couple Valiums? My shrink went on vacation and then we came down here, and I'm kind of in a crunch, you know. . . . " Half the dress-ing kits in this place would be full of drugs. Valiums, poppers, phenobarb, with luck a little oral Demerol. Carly had to make new friends.

She dreaded it. Vain men talking about their operations. Elabo-rately coiffed women with their faces swathed in bandages. Carly hated to be nice. But some of those ugly people were bound to have drugs, just a question of putting up with the bullshit long enough to score. Carly had to be realistic: grown up.

Maybe tomorrow.

The bridge over the waterfall was painted bright red. Carly watched the waterfall and idly picked the paint on the rail.

She didn't like the Caribbean. The islands were too close together, like tract houses. Too many people too. When her mother and father had still been living together, they'd had the big house on Pacific Palisades and you couldn't see another house from the terrace, just the limitless Pacific. She'd sit there and get stoned and watch the sun set past Catalina Island.

She descended the long wooden stairs, to the jetty where workmen unloaded supplies for the restaurant. Because the island was so steep, they had to carry everything in baskets balanced on their heads. Hams and frozen turkeys marched up the stairs borne by unsmiling black men in work shirts and gray work trousers. They looked funny. Carly wished she had her camera.

She wondered if her maid was married. She hadn't worn a ring but Carly didn't know if married women wore rings down here. Carly watched the men shifting the cargo from the boat to the dock, rhythmically, talking in a language she couldn't understand. She wondered if her maid was happy. If she ever had fun.

4

Every Fish in the Ocean Eats People, but the Shark Has the Bad Name

"Winston," Richie said, "why'd you have to aggravate David? Sure, David's a prick, but he isn't so bad."

Winston folded his hands in his lap as Richie forced a woman to jump off the road for safety. "I don't have the proper part to fix the throttle. I tell David that. Until it proper fix, he have to fly Beech as is."

"It was the way you said it." Richie blared his horn at a green jitney trying to take advantage. "I told you we'd be late getting back to the airport if we came all the way down here. Food stunk."

"And you disappear into the pay phone for thirty minutes. Don't you think Megan Sanderson won't notice we're late?"

"*Jou va, jou vie,*" Winston said.

"Don't go native on me, Winston. Christ! David comes in this morning for the bread run and his plane can't fly. I told you he expected it first thing."

"Maybe he start payin' overtime for workin' at night."

"And when you put it all back together the damn throttle *still* don't work."

Winston closed his eyes as Richie nosed out a jitney on a narrow turn. The jitney honked angrily.

"When I get the part, I repair it."

"David just wanted you to nigger-rig something. Christ, Winston, he's the one has to fly it."

The car jumped through the air by Drake's Lookout where the jitneys parked and tourists photographed the panorama while souvenir hawkers tugged at their sleeves. Winston looked at the view, the tremendous blue bay, the fragrant island, the soft sky. "Virgin Islands—American Paradise," he quoted off a license plate.

"What took you so long on the phone?"

Winston lied easily, "I was talkin' to Rosemary."

"Twenty dollars change to call across the island?"

"We planning our holiday," Winston lied again. Lies came so smoothly to him today. He'd never thought he had the talent.

"Winston, we've got the DC-3 down and the Beech needs work and that Lycoming is dangling in the motor mounts and David's talking about buying Jimmy Ohl's old P-51 and having you restore it. There's a market for those old army planes in Florida."

Winston hadn't heard a word about this and you'd think he'd be first to know since it was him supposed to fix the old warplane. David talked to Richie first. Winston was relieved he didn't have to get mad. With luck, he wouldn't have to get mad at David Sanderson ever again.

On the phone, Sr. Enrique Gonzalez, dealer in funny airplanes, had offered Winston $25,000 for the black plane. F.O.B. Puerto Rico. Winston said, "Me and Rosemary take a week off. Go over to St. John, maybe go Tortola for Carnival. You take the fish run," Winston said generously. "Build up you hours."

Richie didn't speak again en route to the airport. He didn't speak as Winston changed. He kept quiet when the Five-Star mechanic said Megan Sanderson had been looking for them, "Oh, about thirty minutes ago."

Winston turned to Richie then, "You think I get my pay early if I ask?"

The American flight from Miami had just come in and hundreds of tourists jammed the terminal, clotted the luggage carousel, sought information from the self-important taxi starter or free rum from the mother-daughter team dispensing it. Winston waited politely while Megan booked a honeymoon couple for a flight down island (St. Lucien) and two white males for Saturday's Coxman's Express.

When the customers were gone, Megan dawdled, filing papers, filling out forms. Winston leaned against the counter and watched the bright, childlike tourists. "Something you wanted, Winston?"

"They say you lookin' down at the shop."

"I expected you to be open for business."

Winston scratched his head. "Oh, me and Richie ran into bad traffic coming back from lunch. Very bad, traffic."

Megan's light blue eyes were hard as bottle caps. She said, "Beechcraft parts doesn't stock the throttle friction part anymore."

Winston said, "Call that Florida fellow, Johnson, the plane wrecker. He have one."

Megan said, not sweetly, "You're the mechanic."

Winston told her he planned to take a vacation, one week, starting tomorrow.

Megan Sanderson said, "Christ! You've got to be kidding." David was overnighting in Puerto Vallerta but Winston could talk to him first thing in the morning.

Winston said reasonably, "I can't talk to David tomorrow morning. I already be on holiday."

She said, "I hope there's a job for you when you get back."

"If you think you find a top mechanic so easy," Winston said, "I think you mad."

Her eyes glittered like the fer-de-lance. White slave owners imported the fer-de-lance to Martinique so the slaves would be afraid to run to the bush.

She did pay him. Angrily, she counted out bills. She said, "I just don't understand you people."

"Tell David not to buy that P-51 until I look it over. I hear it motor bad," Winston said.

At 4:30, Richie tossed his tools on the workbench and left without a word, without changing. Winston shook his head. "That boy know a thousand ways to show he careless."

Like tonight was just like every other night, Winston rolled down the door, swept up, put all the tools away. He sat in the side doorway of the darkened shop, hands on knees, as shadows slid across the field. The X truck hurried to the end of the runway and Five-Star workers called good-nights and went to their cars. Winston sat until it grew quiet and a bit longer.

He got up, stretched, and fetched the gas dolly, which he trundled across both runways. He lifted the dolly hose into the black plane's wing tank and pumped until the dolly was empty. Twenty-five gallons was plenty to reach Puerto Rico, but Winston never liked to fly without full tanks. He trudged back to the shop for a second dolly and used that to fill the other wing tank. He climbed into the black plane's cockpit and flicked the instrument lights on. The batteries showed plenty of charge. Check. Nothing to do now but fly her away.

He put the gas dollys in their usual place and locked up the shop, same as always. En route to Rosemary's, he made his Honda whine. Upstairs, he hugged the kids and bundled them off to Mrs. Childress for the night.

"What are you doing, Winston? We cannot afford baby-sitting every time you feeling gay."

"Darlin', you sit down, while I open this bottle of Mateus wine I bought special for this occasion."

Rosemary asked, "What occasion?" but she did sit, folded her dish towel, and laid it before her.

"You remember this sweet wine from Josephine's wedding? See this bottle here? When the wine is gone, you can make a vase out of it."

"Winston, what are you talking? Dinner is . . ."

"Rosemary, wait!" Winston held up a hand. He poured and handed her a glass of wine. He took a breath. "Rosemary, I invite you to become my wife!"

She unfolded her towel, refolded it.

"I wish to marry also, Winston. But, as we have agreed, not while I am living here in these projects and you sleep in a converted garage. We will marry when we start our house."

Winston clapped his hands. His grin occupied most of his face. "Set the date then, darlin'. Set the date."

"Winston!"

"October, September, you name. Try your wine. Very nice wine." He took a sip to prove it.

Rosemary's face went pale. A tear started down her cheek.

Winston kept pumping the conversation, "Woman, telephone your mama. Make the wedding announcement. September be nice. Next week, I will have the money we need to start. Twenty-five thousand dollars. We see what the bank say to that. They will change their opinion of Winston Riviere!"

Although the tear reached the corner of her cheek, she didn't brush it away. She just look at him. "Winston, how many times I say. I will have nothing to do with any man who flys drugs."

"Thank-you, darlin', for trusting me so much. Thank-you for making this happy fête a disgrace. Since when I fly drugs? How many years you know me? Have I ever fool with drugs? I am so happy you think I am a doper man."

Wanting to believe, her eyes softened. "Winston . . ."

"This is where I get money," he lied. "This morning I stand up to David and say I quit unless he loan me the money and David, he has so much money, is nothing to him! He say there is no better mechanic in the Virgins than me, and I pilot too. He wants to buy this old Mustang. A P-51—oh, it's junk, Rosemary, but I know I can fix it and he can get plenty for it in the States. That's how I pay him—extra jobs like that."

Her headshake was helpless, and she let him see her tears, every one. "Winston, I know you been so unhappy. I feared . . ." She wiped her eyes on her sleeve and snuffed and tried on a tremulous smile. "David say those things?"

"Rosemary, you going to call your mother?"

She lowered her eyes demurely.

"And drink the damn wine."

She did that too and while Winston picked at his dinner of chicken, rice, and tomatoes, she connected with her mother in Florida and with Winston correcting details ("What that you trying to say, Winston? Mama, I try' to listen to two people at once."), Rosemary gave her news.

September 23, which would be a Saturday so everybody could come, the whole family. "Winston, where we have the reception?"

Airily, Winston waved his hand. "We have it on our house lot— picnic style."

Winston called brother Montgomery and, for a surprise, Montgomery was home. First thing Montgomery asked, "Winston, is Rosemary pregnant?"

"Oh, man . . ."

"Why you marry so quick? I thought you waiting to have a house before you marry."

"We buildin' a house."

"How you buildin' it? You a rich man today?"

"I tellin' you later, man. Now I am asking you to come to our fête, tonight with me and Rosemary, our celebration."

Sure thing.

While Winston showered, Rosemary phoned her sister Doreen on St. Johns and her brother Samuel on St. Barthélemy. She phoned all her family and was heroine of the hour. West Indians will travel vast distances for a wedding and everybody promised to come.

Bluebeard's Castle is located on the steep hill over St. Thomas harbor and it was packed. Montgomery had saved a table by stretching his legs across the chairs.

"Winston, Winston! Congratulations! Oh, Rosemary, give me a kiss!"

"There there. Enough of kissing. Is not you marrying this girl!"

The steel band played. Two dreadlocked men and one handsome black woman sang:

> *"In this life, in this life,*
> *in this sweet life, oh,*
> *we're coming in from the cold . . ."*

Montgomery chatted up Rosemary. In any gathering, automatically, Montgomery turned to the women, turning the brightness of his eyes upon their dreams and skin.

Winston ordered a round of rum and tonics and Rosemary didn't protest and he knew he could have anything he wanted tonight and it made him feel humble and sad.

Montgomery was three years younger than Winston and (as he was quick to point out) "much prettier, man." His skin was the color of the sweet blue dusk and his black eyes gleamed with fun. He was built slight—like the boys who hung around on Back Street—and he wore a billowing-sleeved white shirt and gold neck chain same as them, but Montgomery lived for women, white women, especially.

"Them snowbirds, man, they all-sweet not some-sweet." And he grinned his sharp smile. Montgomery's hands were longish and he never wore rings.

Rosemary was saying, "I never guessed Winston had it in his mind to marry me. So many years he delay."

Like schoolchildren they laughed and Winston felt older than he was, and stuffier too. It was often like this when Rosemary and Montgomery got together.

After a bit, their drinks came and Winston remembered how

much he loved Montgomery and Rosemary and he put away his stern face and said, "Why you children not dance? They playin' your song." The band kicked into "Zion Train" and Rosemary covered her face with her hand to hide her giggle. When Montgomery was near, Rosemary was always laughing and gay. In Winston's company, Rosemary was sober as a magistrate.

While they whirled across the dance floor, Winston looked out at the harbor lights gleaming and thought it is very, very difficult to know what is on another person's mind.

When Rosemary went to the powder room, Montgomery slid into the seat beside Winston.

"Wins-ton," Montgomery said.

"Don't you worry," Winston said.

"Rosemary say David loan you this house money. Since when David doin' you favors?"

"Where he going to find another mechanic like me?"

Montgomery poked his elegant finger at Winston. "I know that and you know that. David not know that. David think mechanics fall out of the trees like breadfruits."

Winston changed the subject. "I hear things gettin' rough in Dominica."

"Where you hear?"

Winston shrugged, "Radio Neg."

Montgomery kept close ties to their home island. Not Winston. Last time Winston was in Dominica was six, no, seven years ago, for his mother's funeral. Soon as she was buried, Winston was gone, not even staying for the condolences. When Mr. Soylo, Winston's old schoolmaster, had written him his need for a Seeing Eye dog, it was Winston who arranged to obtain the dog (a big black Labrador named Mrs. Polly) but Montgomery had to make the flight down island with the dog.

"Dominica government in ruins," Montgomery said. Sir Rollo-Long Pre acting more like king than president, many government ministers resign. Rollo-Long Pre appoint some Dreads, I hear, to the government. . . ."

"Mal Esprit?"

"I hear he is minister of information and he Dreads patrol the streets of Roseau like they official constables and the people, they won't stand for this disorder no more and go on strike. Dominica an island shut down. New government confiscate the private planes so striking people block the airstrip at Melville Hall. Cane-field Airport not blocked but no airlines landing there for fear once they land, government not let them take off again. Mal Es-prit, he riding high."

"Who cares who rules Dominica?" Winston said. "Poor agricul-tural island. Whoever rules got to export bananas, the grapefruits and limes."

Returning, Rosemary overheard the last of this and made a dis-agreeable face. "This my engagement fête or is it not? Winston, how long since you and me danced?"

She was so light in Winston's arms. His spirit, which had been trapped in his memories, was lifted by her.

Later, they took Montgomery's immaculately clean 1982 Dodge Aspen downtown. Montgomery had a pine tree deodorizer dan-gling from his mirror. "Lady don't like to sit in car smells like the agricultural station," he solemnly advised.

Usually, on weekends, the Cosmopolitan Hotel had a zouk band, sometimes Trinidadian soca-calypso. Before Rosemary, Winston often came here to dance and in the morning, sometimes breakfasted with the girl he'd danced with, night before.

Wrought-iron balconies faced the enclosed courtyard where the band played and people danced life's cares away.

Everybody wearing his best. Man or woman in between lovers, this was the spot to be seen.

The band was playing "Hot! Hot! Hot!" when they came in, but the horns wavered and were not so hot. Three couples dancing, the crowd restrained, and most tables empty. Waitresses stood unhappily at the end of the bar drinking soda water.

Under his breath, Montgomery said a curse.

Four men lolled at a double table like they were waiting for the entertainment to start.

Dozens of green bottles on the table in front of them. Several smoldering ashtrays. The gigantic black man beside Jocko laid his head on the table. The white man was neat as a Kewpie doll. The fourth man wore his hair in natty dreadlocks, an aviator's jacket and scarf and an unblinking whacked-out smile.

Rosemary clutched Winston's arm pretty hard. "Winston?"

"You don't mind about them and they not bother us."

Montgomery said, "You want to leave? Go down to French-man's Reef?"

"Who the white man?"

"I not see him anyplace before. Look, he dressed like Sydney Greenstreet."

"Who?"

"*The Maltese Falcon*. I seen it on the Cable. *Maltese Falcon's* in color now. They never shot it in color but it's color today. Modern times."

Jocko was whispering in the white man's ear. The white man summoned Winston with the flick of his finger. That flick traveled across a forty-foot dance floor, but no doubt about it.

Winston said, "Why don't you and Rosemary take a table? Order me rum."

The unconscious black man snorted and rolled off his cheek onto his forehead. His head was big as a casaba melon.

The white man's cheeks were pudgy-smooth. His mouth red like lipstick. His linen suit was perfect, unsullied. He wore gold bands on every finger like he'd been married eight times. "You are Winston Riviere?"

Jocko said, "From Soufriere, him."

"Lovely village. Such a picturesque beach—if the citizens could refrain from using its tides to remove their garbage."

"I am Mr. Riviere," Winston said.

The white man laid one of his hands atop the other, like toads mating. "You have some reputation as a mechanic."

Jocko said, "He fix for that one-plane airline, DMS . . ."

"DMS got a Twin Beech and DC-3, buying a third plane next month. DMS going to grow. . ."

"Quite so," the white man said. His eyes were pale blue, almost colorless. His pupils were scratchy black. "You grew up with Mal Esprit?"

Winston nodded very briefly.

"Tell me, Mr. Riviere, what was Mal like as a boy? Was he an honest boy, kind to his elders?"

"He Leon then. Leon Balla."

"Le-on." The white man tasted the word and found it sweet, "Le-on."

The Dread with the white scarf smiled his stoned face. "Hello, Winston," he said. "What you doin' in this place?"

"Rupert."

"You know each other?"

Rupert said, "Oh my yes. Yes, we, uh, Nevis, St. Kitts, uh, not so much as used to be." Since explanation was beyond him, he smiled seraphically and used his hands to show how an aircraft climbs and banks. "My yes."

"You are a pilot too, Mr. Riviere?"

"I have my Air Transport rating," Winston said.

The white man beamed but his faded eyes were completely disinterested. "A man of accomplishments. My. We have need for able men down island. There's a crying need for able men down island."

"Plenty good fixers on Dominica. I know fellows can nigger-rig a 747 from three Piper Cubs and a spare parts box."

"We'll pay," the white man said.

The gigantic man lifted his head from the table. His left nostril ran and a fleck of drool hung from the corner of his mouth. His hair was done in tight cornrows. He put a hand around his glass of rum like he feared it would get away from him. His eyes swam in their sockets.

"As the U.S. Marines put it, Mr. Riviere, 'We are looking for a few good men' to help us turn a backward agricultural island into the showcase of the Caribbean. A thousand dollars a week?"

"Where Dominica get that kind of money?" Winston burst out, genuinely shocked.

The white man smiled a prissy little smile. "Suppose you let your employers worry about that."

"Suppose I tell you 'Go to hell.'" Winston developed a severe back itch but he wouldn't scratch it, not now.

The white man said, "Maboya."

Standing the giant black was even bigger. He had his height in his legs. He breathed through his mouth like a fighter, "Uh, uh, uh."

The white man said, "I despise rudeness. Note him, Maboya."

And Maboya's red-and-yellow eyes fixed on Winston, like a barracuda eyes a swimmer.

Maboya said,

> "Black man time is come.
> White man has had his fun.
> Black man stronger than white man.
> Black man sweeter than white man."

The white man said, "A thousand a week. U.S. dollars, not E.C."

Winston said, "I got a good job here. St. Thomas my home."

The white man said, "Change your mind, you know where to find me."

Winston said, "I know where but not who."

Jocko uncoiled across the table like a snake. "Mr. Bones," he hissed.

Though Mr. Bones's fish eyes searched Winston's face for opinions, he didn't find any, no.

Winston thought, I see plenty flesh, not so many bones, but didn't say a word.

And Mr. Bones's red lips formed a Cupid smile and, once, twice, thrice, he patted his paunch.

Winston felt blood draining from his face. Maboya went on breathing, Rupert dreamed. With a flick of his fingers, Mr. Bones dismissed Winston.

There were three drinks on Rosemary's table, all untouched. "Let's go," Winston said.

Rosemary asked, "Winston, who are those men?"

"Rupert, he's a pilot I know from smuggling days. The white man . . . I don't know. . . . Come along."

"Winston, what they want with you?"

"A job. They offer me a job. Let's go."

But the life had gone out of their fête. Although they went on to Frenchman's Reef and The Foolish Virgins, it was no fun anymore. Winston quit drinking while Montgomery drank too much. Rosemary picked a fight: "Who will be master in our marriage?" She said she wanted her house in Nordside or perhaps Nazareth Estates.

A true West Indian house, with open windows and hurricane shutters. They'd have three bedrooms and a big living area, with a kitchenette. They could put the laundry room downstairs, next to the cistern and they could get Montgomery to help them landscape the property, couldn't they, Montgomery, couldn't they?

"What say?"

"Won't you help us with the landscaping?"

"Sure, Rosemary."

Winston thought it was getting late and said so. Winston took the wheel and Montgomery got in the backseat, curled up with his hands between his legs.

Rosemary sat very close to Winston. Her body felt very warm and soft and it made him sad, like he was cheating her, like all love was faithless love, like life could never be just one thing but always had to be a thing and its opposite.

At Montgomery's house, Winston offered Montgomery a hand, which he shrugged off. Montgomery mumbled so Rosemary couldn't hear. "It's not them, is it? Not those shits? They're not the ones you gettin' money from?"

Winston got angry. "What you think?"

Montgomery's begging eyes skidded all over Winston's face.

When Winston got back in the driver's seat, Rosemary snuggled up. Winston said, "Montgomery can get his car in the morning."

Late Friday night at the projects, radios playing, laughter from open windows, teenagers dancing on the concrete apron outside the front door.

Rosemary unlocked her apartment and invited him in.

Rosemary said, "Winston . . ." She stood in her bedroom doorway, silhouetted by pale light. A burst of laughter outside. Someone dropped a glass bottle. A horn honked. A radio blared.

But Winston could hear every faint pop as she unbuttoned her blouse, the whiffle as it slithered to the floor. Behind her dusky silhouette the bedroom yearned. The zipper of her skirt. The heavier rustle as she stepped out of it.

Winston said, "Rosemary, I hope this thing gonna work."

She said, "Winston—is you."

He was so excited and his heart beat so fast and he stubbed right out of his shoes without unlacing them and his fingers sought buttons, snaps, and zippers of his own.

Took her in his arms. She whispered, "I glad, Winston," and her breath in his ear concentrated him. He nuzzled into the hollow of her throat and his tongue darted against her sweet skin and she chuckled like a cat.

Oh they were laughing outside and hooting and having a grand fête and calypsonians were dancing by the headlights of their cars.

Even as he lied, it was her that made him a man. Most of what was good about him was lost in her as they became one flesh on the white muslin coverlet she'd sewed herself.

He had a mental picture of the black plane, as he'd last seen it, tonight, him crouched on the wing, with the black cockpit beside him and the black bush looming behind.

She said, "Winston, do not go from me," and cupped his balls. She said his name and said it again, and her belly muscles clenched and bucked under his own wet slab.

After a bit he rolled off her and she nestled against his back. She kissed him between the shoulder blades. Moments later he heard her snore.

Winston set his wristwatch alarm and slept until it buzzed.

At four o'clock in the morning, the projects were quiet as Winston dressed, splashed water on his face, and washed his hands. He puttered across the sleeping island of St. Thomas, only a few cars on the roads, one or two trucks. Nighthawks fluttered in his headlight beam.

Nobody in downtown Charlotte Amalie except two police cars parked front to back on Main Street, the police leaning about, gossiping, and didn't look up as Winston went by.

An envelope was tacked to his door. He laid it on the table, and searched under his mattress for his passport. He folded two clean shirts, socks, and one pair of fresh pants into his canvas duffle bag. He shaved, put on a clean blue shirt.

The letter was in a plain buff envelope.

Mister Riviere,
From Mister Petty John I learn of a package for you from Winter Rest Florida USA. This blue package is the proper size and weight to be parts for my Cuisinart which you have now two months, three days. I am expecting my Cuisinart summarily!

(signed) Mrs. J.T.D. Indarsingh

Winston crumped the letter and dropped it into a cardboard wastebarrel into the rat's nest of appliance wire and snapped piston rings.

Outside, in the soft tropical night, he stood for a quiet moment next to the Obeah man. The night smelled like honey; it smelled like the sea. He laid his hand on the Obeah man's wooden shoulder and thought a wordless prayer.

The police were gone from Main Street. Probably gone to

snooze in the turnout above Sub Base. Through the sleeping heart of Charlotte Amalie, along Veteran's Drive, past Caribbean Rent-A-Car onto the airport road, Winston didn't see a living soul.

He rolled his motorcycle into the DMS Airways shop but kept the shop lights off.

The moon washed the wings of the parked aircraft. Plexiglas and chrome glittered. They seemed alive and hypercritical as Winston passed down their neat rows onto the taxiway.

The smell of jet fuel was strong on the tarmac. You'd think the night would wash it away but it didn't. Duffle over his shoulder, Winston hurried across the open space, a shadow man on black asphalt in the moonlight.

On the grassy median, he paused beside the 200-meter marker. Froze. Something. Heard something. Winston dropped to one knee beside the marker: black letters on white steel. Winston could see fine behind him, but the bush on the far side darkened the night.

A ground dove cooed. Pause. Cooed again. She'd have a nest somewhere near, in the median grass.

The night panted softly, or perhaps that was Winston's breath.

Cha-wuffa, wuf, wuffa, wuffa, the motor caught and the chill rolled right down Winston's spine to his tailbone. And as the first motor caught the second was firing, cha-wuffa, wuffa, until it caught too. Winston flopped on his belly.

It showed no running lights, just a black shape blurring the bush blackness, as it taxied onto the runway a hundred feet ahead. The pilot ran his engines up and the noise was so shattering. Winston had done it himself a thousand times and hadn't known how this noise tore the night. Poor dove!

The instruments glowed green as the pilot checked his pressures.

The pilot wore a white scarf. With fringe.

The mighty Navaho engines thundered and surged against the brakes and the black plane shuddered like a thoroughbred in the starting gate.

The pilot held the plane down until he had 80 knots of airspeed before he hauled back the stick and, for the second time, the black plane just skimmed the wooden barricades.

Too stunned to weep, Winston watched as the wing dipped slightly and his airplane banked, south by southeast, out to sea.

5

The Runaway

It was the Cincy Mummy's fault. Two solid days of flattery, a thousand minutes of fawning attention at "her" table at the Café Schweitzer; court to her queen, jester to her caprice, gofer— "Dear, would you please fetch me another Perrier, two slices of lime"—all because the Mummy had "oh oodles" of pills although she didn't call them that—"restoratives," for Christ's sake—and she wouldn't come through.

The Cincy Mummy was June ("Call me Juney, dear, everybody does") Mellenbarger and she was a talking head for the morning show, somewhere in the Midwest. "Did I ever tell you the time I interviewed Alexander Haig—charming! Let me tell you! And did a remote with Ted Kennedy that afternoon! It was at the airport, of course; Teddy was just flying through."

As Juney's bandaged white face droned on, Carly's supply of downs dwindled, every time she excused herself to go to the ladies room.

The mouth and lips were unbandaged and the Cincy Mummy had managed to apply pale orange lipstick without smudging the blinding white dressings. Disapproval. "If you weren't so quick with your white wine, you wouldn't need the ladies room so often." A touch on Carly's arm. "Just joking, dear."

Though other patients came to sit at the bright white tables on the open terrace overlooking the pale sea, none sat so long as the Cincy Mummy or her accolyte. Oh, Carly learned all her habits. How she had to take a little "nappy," after Le Dejunieer, how she thought Ronald Reagan was just "too masculine," and George Will—"Well, my dear, you know what a wimp he is." No other patient sat at their table though the Mummy greeted all of them gaily.

And Carly nodded and smiled until her jaw ached. When her head was sore from too much white wine and too much sun, she'd put on her perkiest expression and ask, "Did you ever meet, uh, George Lucas?"

"Dear," sternly, "you must know, he never gives interviews."

"Oh, sorry. You want some more Perrier?"

"You know, dear," the orange lips confided, "it's time a girl like you took up her career. You know what they say, 'Idle hands are the devil's workshop.'"

"Excuse me, I'll be back in a jiff."

And in the ladies room, Carly'd count the pills remaining to her and there had been twenty once and she'd worried then. Think of that—worried about twenty pills. Twenty would seem like a major score right now.

Yesterday, when the Mummy took her nappy, she'd turned over two standard-issue, ten-milligram tabs to Carly, like she was extruding a part of herself. Said, "Here, dear. I know how it is to be restless, unable to sleep."

And those two little greenish pills had given Carly hope. So she sat through the long afternoon and the evening too. The Mummy was indefatigable. She breathed in praise like it was air.

Carly's mother, Magdellana, was with the Doctor. Magdellana hung out in his suite while he drew his sketches, went sailboarding with him yesterday, and today took an excursion into Roadtown to see the Carnival preparations. Magdellana was making certain the hands that touched her skin, scalp, and skull would touch them lovingly. Carly thought Magdellana always overdid things.

By three, the luncheon crowd dwindled and left. In the afternoon sun the terrace was blazing hot and Carly had to keep her eyes shaded. The Mummy was going to get her bandages removed tomorrow. She'd been trilling about it.

She patted her regularized face. "My dear, you just won't believe the real me."

Carly's patience was very thin. "I'll just bet," she said.

"What?"

"I'm sure you'll be lovely," Carly hastened.

"I thought I detected an unbecoming hostility, dear."

Carly yawned elaborately. "I think I'll go take my 'nappy.' Could I have a couple 'restoratives'? Why not let me have a couple doz? It'll keep me from pestering you all the time." Carly smiled until the corners of her mouth hurt.

The Mummy picked at the bandage where her cheek must be. "I'm afraid I couldn't, dear. I've been watching you these last days and you've had far too many glasses of wine and, I believe, some medications of your own. At times, you are quite inattentive."

A red flash ripped through Carly's brain. Her hands ached to grip the Mummy by the wattles and rush her to the terrace edge and see if Dr. Dragotti could put Humpty back together again.

She bit down. "You certainly have a fine sense of humor," she said.

"Oh yes. My ratings are partly due to that. Of course, people don't tune in to watch little old me. My guests—"

"I really need some Valiums, Juney. I told you about not being able to get my prescription filled."

The Mummy reached across the table and patted Carly's hand. "Just talk to Dr. Dragotti, dear. I'm sure he can help you."

Carly went white. She wanted to throw her glass of wine in the Mummy's face, but why? What was the point? Carly was ruined. Four pills left—enough to last until nightfall if she stretched them. She stumbled to her feet and the chair crashed over behind her.

Juney's mummy face waggled in a concerned fashion. "Dear, dear . . . ?" Blindly Carly stumbled to the stairs and, gripping the stair rail heavily, she got down however many flights of stairs to Rose Apple. It was cool inside and the hidden speakers played Vivaldi's *Concert de Camera*. Carly's lips were dry. The carpet was grayish green and very deep under her feet.

"Miss? You all right, miss?" It was the maid. Her name was what? Cindy? Prissy? Cynthia? Penelope? Who the fuck cared? Carly's voice cracked when she spoke. "Who sells drugs on Sandpiper? You know: coke, grass, ganja, ups, downs, dope?"

"Missy, I not know."

Carly ran into her bedroom for her purse. She found a fifty dollar bill. She returned with the crisp bill hanging from her fingertips like bait. "Ganja? Who?"

With a pillowcase full of soiled linen in front of her, the maid was backing toward the door. "Missy?"

"Please!"

And the maid sighed and a look of great dignity crossed her face, like she was so much older than Carly, knew so very much more of life, though, for God's sake, she probably hadn't traveled off these rinky-dink islands ever in her life. "There is Gerry the kitchen boy. You talk to him."

And she turned and walked out the door and didn't take the money, absolutely ignored it, like it wasn't real currency that could buy.

Carly took time to splash cold water on her face. She changed her blouse. She took a couple of aspirins and one of her remaining pills.

In Café Schweitzer's kitchen they were preparing the evening meal. Carly went right to the cook at the big stove. She ran her hand through her hair. She said, "I want to talk to Gerry."

The man turned to her so slowly he seemed retarded.

"Gerry. You know. The kitchen boy, Gerry."

And the big black man smiled slowly and said, "Oh, that Gerry," like it was some kind of goddamned joke.

"My maid—uh, Penny—she said he worked here."

And the cook slapped his leg. "Oh, that Penny," he said. He rolled his eyes. The cook wore a starched chef's hat and immaculate apron. His pants were oversized black-and-white checks and his formal, lace-up shoes were burst through. Now the cook turned to another black man, who was cutting vegetables. He said, *"Fam sepul, kali we gren main li kouri."* The vegetable man stretched his mouth in a grin. He was younger than Carly but his grin was gaps and broken teeth.

To Carly, the chef repeated, "Ah, Penny."

Carly ran a nervous hand through her hair. "Gerry is the..." She pointed at the stack of dirty dishes. "There..." How could these people be so stupid!

"You wish another sandwich, miss? We fix you right up."

"No. No. I want to talk to Gerry. He works here."

—— 71 ——

"Lots work here, miss. Plenty workers in my kitchen." He inspected the vegetable chef's cutting board and said, "Make them peppers more fine, man. People bite down on stuffed quail don't want no pepper big as a house."

The vegetable chef's knife flashed up and down. If Carly stuck her hand under that blade she'd get some attention then.

The kitchen was quite clean and the chefs looked like real chefs except for their shoes. Nobody'd bothered to tell Carly about West Indian manners and she'd burst out with her question about the kitchen boy's whereabouts without so much as a "How are you?" or "Good-morning, I hope your family's well." "I want to talk to Gerry," and the smile stayed on the chef's black face but the light went right out of his eyes like he'd willed brain death.

After a few minutes—it made her feel like she was absolutely nobody, like she was nothing—they tired of the sport. With his knife blade, the vegetable chef nudged his vegetables into a stock kettle. "Gerry with the garbage," he muttered.

And the garbage was down at the dock. Carly figured that out herself.

Gerry was a gangly bespectacled youth. His hair was crisp and short and he looked studious. He wore scruffy corduroys and a T-shirt that advertised the Pepsi Generation. He hefted an empty garbage can from the well in the back of the launch, his stiff canvas gloves molded to his palms.

They were alone on the dock. Two small moored speedboats bobbed in the swell.

"Hi," Carly said, lifting one hand and letting it drop.

"Good-afternoon," the boy said. His accent was precise and British and this gave Carly hope because it meant he'd be smart.

"I'm Carly." She pointed up the hill. "My mom is a patient here."

Gerry plucked off his gloves delicately and slipped them through a can handle. "You like it on Sandpiper?"

"Far out," Carly drawled.

"Is not so far," he said. "Hour to Beef Island."

"We're in Rose Apple," she said. "You know."

He nodded too vigorously. "Oh yes, miss."

"The girl, uh, the woman, who comes in to clean—Penny—told me about you."

"Oh, Penny, one fine woman. Mad to dance."

"She said . . . I might talk to you."

"Me?" Pointed to his chest. "Oh yes, miss. I talk with you. Talk all day." He giggled.

"Maybe we can do business."

He closed his smile then and his eyes shrank and a false calm descended. "Business?"

"Yah. You know. I mean, half the people in the world take Valiums. I don't know why they make such a damn fuss. It's a free country, isn't it?"

"I don't know, miss."

Carly attached her biggest and, she hoped, most fetching grin. "D-r-u-g-s," she said. "Your uppers, your downers, your ganja, your hash, speed, coke, or acid. That kind of business."

His smile was a weak one. "Yes, miss," he said.

"Well, what you got? I got money. Got lots of money."

Gerry scratched his head foolishly. He looked away. He pulled his gloves back on and said, "Excuse me, miss." He humped a full can onto the work boat.

The voice came from behind, so clear it was like his lips were right at her ear. "I'm afraid Gerry can't help you."

She turned.

His smile was big and deep and zero. He had both hands stuffed in his pockets as he soft-footed toward her. "Gerry might be able to sell you a couple joints, but niggers don't do anything very interesting. It takes a white man to get well and truly stoned."

She shivered and wrapped her arms around her body. "Maybe . . . maybe you can help me?"

And Ringo swept his arms wide, like Sir Walter Raleigh casting his cape. "Why not?" he said.

6

Go Brave!

"Rosemary gonna go mad," Montgomery said.

The two brothers sat on bags of sphagnum moss in the potting shed at the Agricultural Station. Montgomery's eyes were hidden behind dark sunglasses and his slender hands shook. Winston had his face in his hands. He moaned.

"Where you get idea like that one, man? Steal a doper plane and fly it to Puerto Rico—that is playing the ass!"

"I know Enrique long time," Winston mumbled. "If he say he give me twenty-five thousand, he give it."

Montgomery wore the pale green coveralls they issued to all the Ag Station workers. Winston wore the same dark clothes he'd worn seven hours ago when he tried to steal the airplane.

"You doin' such rogueness, brother," Montgomery cocked his head in a particularly irritating manner.

"Oh, man. I see that plane takin' off, I glad I don't have no gun in my hand. I vow I glad."

Montgomery poured himself coffee from his Thermos, sipped, made a face, tossed drags at the jacaranda. "Rosemary not gonna want call her momma, say wedding is off. Oh, Rosemary. . ."

"You stop talkin' 'bout Rosemary! My fiancée, not yours!"

"Okay, Winston, sure thing." Montgomery burped. "Some fête," he said. He eyed the main greenhouse. "Overseer gonna be seekin' me, Winston. Couple hours we get lunch break. We go to Mountaintop Restaurant for West Indian chicken."

Winston lay on the cool plastic bags like they were his own bed. This made twice Mal Esprit had stolen from him. Through his closed eyes, Winston saw Mal as he'd been, a boy, at the cricket field in Soufriere, barefoot, short pants, bright yellow man's shirt, torn off sleeves, and no buttons at all. Saw Leon Balla clear as day, as he'd been before he took on the name (and some said the Jumbie) Mal Esprit. Leon was grinning at Winston, urging Winston to lovely mischief. How Winston wished he and Leon were still friends. How he wished Leon hadn't hurt him so.

Because Winston couldn't think, he slept. When he woke, his cheek stuck to the plastic and was sore and dry. The light was hot, clear, and hard. The island's floral perfumes lay flat under the brightness. His feet were asleep and he stamped and wiggled them. Smells of moss and a hot tin roof. Outside, the leaves of the great banyans hung, elephant ears, still in the sun.

A young white woman was inspecting the row of pepper plants, a child in a Snugli on her back. Pretty soon a West Indian worker came to help her.

Tropical things grow good on St. Thomas. Northern plants like tomatoes and onions don't grow so good and the Ag Station starts them because most gardeners can't.

Another worker trundled a wheelbarrow full of bagged saplings down the path. He turned to toss a joke to someone Winston couldn't see.

When Montgomery came, Winston was staring into the distance.

"Winston, you okay? We go to Mountaintop Café?"

"No, brother. I got no hunger now."

"You gonna tell . . ."

"Rosemary? No." Winston spoke out of the great calm that descends once a man has decided. "Twice now, Mal Esprit thief from me. He thief my examination and now he thief my house and my marriage-to-be. *Neg pape neg*—one man is not afraid of another man. Me, Winston Roosevelt Riviere, I had enough of this. I gonna go brave."

Montgomery took off his sunglasses. "What you schemin', brother?"

"I gonna get my plane back." Winston's voice had a lilt, like he was trembling on the lip of laughter.

Montgomery snorted. He coughed. Clumsily, he jammed his sunglasses on his face and smeared one lens with a thumbprint. "Mal Esprit? You gonna thief from Mal Esprit? Oh brother, I hope your insurance paid up. Rosemary be able to buy nice house with that insurance. Up on Nordside, maybe."

"The lines cast off, brother. The sail is set."

"You mad? Thief from him, Mal Esprit gonna kill you. His pilot took that doper plane and flew it away to Dominica and Mal gonna use it to fly ganja. It Mal's plane now."

Winston's foolish smile spiced Montgomery's wrath. "Mal never rest until he find out who thief from him. Can't hide nothing on Dominica, Winston. Mal gonna ask around. 'Oh, Winston Riviere was on the island, eh? I wonder why he didn't stop by. Oh, he disappear same day as my airplane?'

"Then he kill you. His man slash you with cutlass outside the Disco one night. He cut your fuel lines so you flyin' to Anegada and you explode. He put bamboo fuzz into your coffee and it take you weeks to die, bamboo workin' its way out your belly and no doctor can pick it all out, that fuzz so sharp and small. Winston, you thief from Mal and you dead man."

"Nobody gonna know."

Montgomery's head was pounding. His brother, Winston, the eminently practical pilot, sailor, mechanic, wearing the goofy grin Montgomery used to see on stoned-out hippy boys on Hull Bay.

"I go to Dominica by boat and land at night. Nobody see me. I fly the plane to Puerto Rico the same day. Three days down to Dominica and three hours to fly north. I get on Eastern flight in San Juan and home. Rosemary don't have to know nothing." More soberly Winston added, "I let Mal Esprit do this to me again, Montgomery, then Mal Esprit own Winston Riviere, just like I his slave. Rest of my life, I his."

Montgomery's heart sank to his shoes. He wished he felt better, his body stronger, than he did or was. "He gonna kill you," Montgomery said. "Maybe not this month, this year, but one day you take a nice cup of coffee and drink it and after while, bellyache. 'Oh my,' you say, 'I got me upset stomach,' because by then you forget all about Mal Esprit and how you thief from him. But Mal not forget. Winston Riviere the ass who stole his airplane."

"You gonna help me?"

Montgomery went to the foreman and asked for the rest of the day off. The foreman said, go ahead, but he'd have to work Saturday.

They drove downtown in Montgomery's car. A cruise ship had docked that morning and towered over downtown, stolid as a bourgeois wedding cake. All the little shops were open and hundreds of pale tourists promenaded Main Street.

Many of the tourists were elderly, all were clean scrubbed. The women had tinted coiffures and the men trailed a step or two behind their wives. They smiled at everyone.

Winston went into the bank to withdraw his savings. It frightened him to take all that money and fold it in his wallet and he was grateful Rosemary was not there to see.

Montgomery was drumming his fingers on the steering wheel. Winston said, "Let us go find a boat. Not too expensive boat."

Montgomery looked at him for the longest minute before a sweet grin came. "Brother, you mad as me. I think I know where a boat is."

"Okay." Winston settled back into the seat.

"On Tortola."

At the ferry dock Winston found his appetite and ate three salt-fish patés he bought from a vendor.

The ocean ferry had decks for cars and trucks, an enclosed lounge with rows of plastic-covered benches. A solemn, dusty-skinned black man sold beer and soda pop and Winston bought two orange juices.

Saturday night—tonight—would be the wrap-up of Tortola's Carnival, the parade and the grand fête. As the ferry rounded the point and got up on its hydroplanes, rum bottles and straw hats appeared and a man laid a vibraphone across his knees and began picking out Carnival tunes.

White tourists took his photo as he played Lord Invader rhythms, snap snap flash, until one got too near, took too much time, and the musician angrily set his vibraphone aside and stuck out his hand. "Give me dollar, man, you take my picture. You think I play for free?"

The tourist—a portly, freckled male—didn't know what:

should he or shouldn't he, and, anyway, what did it mean? He went into his pocket and found a dollar bill. "Okay, okay. But you got to pose with your instrument."

"Don't feel like that no more, man. I tired of playing."

"I didn't quite get . . ."

"The hell with you, man. You think you buy me for a dollar?"

It's an hour from St. Thomas, U.S.V.I., to Roadtown, B.V.I., and the passengers grew louder, more festive as the ferry neared British waters.

"This hurricane season," Montgomery noted.

Winston said, "Three days down. One day back."

"You know how much you have lived. You don't know how much life you got left," Montgomery said. Then he laughed.

The ferry reversed its engines and greenish billows rumbled under the hull as it slid toward the Roadtown quay. Roadtown has the biggest charter fleet in the Caribbean, and the harbor was rows and rows of anchored sailboats. During the season, the anchorages would be empty—buoys bobbing in the swell—and hundreds of fine triangular sails dancing over Drake Channel.

The immigration official hesitated over Montgomery's St. Thomas driver's license. Montgomery said, "Man, I U.S." He added, "It's Carnival!"

"Right you are," the official said, and let him pass.

Festively dressed drunks lounged on the wharves. A steel band banged away on the pier, another was playing on Main Street and a song flew by pursued by a burst of laughter.

The cab was dark blue. COURTESY SERVICE. The driver wore a rumpled seersucker and a string tie, knotted hard. He braked sharply when a couple wobbled from a rum shop into his path.

The driver made a sound with his mouth. "Tchups."

One drunk slid his face against the window glass. He said, "Yeaas," and produced a wet grin before he lost balance and back-pedaled away, waving like a silly flag.

The driver said, "I curse them to Hades."

He whipped past a jitney and forced a truck twice his size onto the sidewalk. "I am Methodist, and this night we made our parade amidst despicable drunkenness and lewd behavior."

Montgomery lived in urban St. Thomas. "Oh not so bad, eh? In Charlotte Amalie is all drugs and poncey boys."

"Oh we got them here, too," the driver asserted. He jerked his head assertively. He thumped his horn and a bicyclist vanished off the shoulder. "This year the Methodist float greater than the Catholic. Every year, Catholic float unchanged: Virgin and child. Virgin and child. They don't paint Virgin every year, neither, just cover her feet with frangipani flowers so it look like her crossin' the Red Sea."

"Them Catholics wild all right," Montgomery noted.

West of Roadtown, the road narrows and clings to sea cliffs, dipping down to the beaches and lifting suddenly, like a gull soars over the headland. Oncoming jitneys and pickups were standing-room-only with Carnival revelers who waved and hollered, but the cab driver clamped his hands to the wheel and eyes to the road.

"Nanny Cay," Montgomery sighed. "I remember when no condos in the islands."

Bougainvillea Road jumped off the main road and climbed, about as steep as a road can, and in the rainy season must be a torrent not a road. It leveled and traversed above the rooftops before dropping again. The villa at the bottom of the hill had an orange Spanish-style tiled roof. The stucco wall was interrupted by arched porticoes barred with wrought iron. The iron gate was overbearingly tall—like a mausoleum gate—and the sign beside it said, in Gothic type: THE FIFTH ESTATE.

"Home of Mr. Courtney-Brown," the driver announced. "I wait?"

Montgomery climbed out of the cab gratefully. "No, man. You too hurry to get to heaven."

When the cab lunged back up the hill, its tail pipe dragged, which pleased Montgomery.

"This fellow supposed to have boat?"

"Is what I hear. Courtney-Brown's son owned the boat but he killed now in road accident."

An enameled sign was bolted into the gate pillar. It advised: PRESS BELL FIRMLY!

They couldn't hear the buzzer. They could hear the swoosh of the ocean, somewhere below. The brick walkway curved away behind a screen of pale young mango trees.

The white man who came to the gate wore a thin silver neck chain and a brief black bikini. Bushy white hair on his head and a clump on his chest. You could count his ribs. His tan was dark, splotched with yellow. His feet splayed like he didn't often wear shoes. His eyes were gray.

"We come about the boat," Montgomery said. He added, "Good-afternoon, sir. Looks like gala Carnival in the town."

Wordlessly, the white man opened the gate. Click, he locked it behind them.

The villa was lovely, low and cool. The white man skirted it on a descending brick pathway.

Montgomery loved orchids like he loved white girls. "Oh man. You got some fine Stanhopea, here. *Bucephalus?*"

"Stanhopea *lusignis*," the man corrected.

The bricks gave way to steps of blue-bitch granite. An immortelle dropped scarlet blossoms into the murky green water of a lotus pond, where gnarled boulders were islands in a miniature sea. In the depths a carp flashed gold, like a dropped wristwatch.

The bottom step was drifted over by sand.

Winston's eyes were on the boat.

The white man stopped on the step, like he didn't want to track up his beach. Driftwood branches were tangled in seaweed pods, linked plastic fishing floats, half buried under sand curves and recurves, sculpted by wind and waves. Men didn't walk this beach often.

The boat had a green hull and red superstructure. It's trunk cabin was dotted with modest portholes. Anchored, fore and aft, the anchor cables were thick green with seaweed.

The white man pointed. "His," he said. "He thought he could sail the Atlantic." He snorted. "The Atlan-tic."

Montgomery said, "I'm sorry."

The white man said, "Vultures got to it, already. My son not in the ground two weeks. I absolutely must sell, you do see?"

Neither brother spoke. They looked out to sea, like that's where answers might be.

"I won't be cheated. I'll get a fair price for it, by God, I will."

Winston said, "Yes. We'd like to go aboard. That the dinghy?"

It was fastened to a palm tree with a chain heavier than itself.

"Just yank the lock," the white man said. "The padlock's a bluff. One of my son's wee bravadoes."

The brothers left their shoes beside the palm tree, toes pointing neatly out to sea. Montgomery waded out to hold the cockleshell-dinghy. Winston took the oars. Digging in the oars felt good. Winston'd been away from the sea too long.

"John Alden boat?" Winston asked.

"You know more about these things than me, man."

They clambered over the stern counter into the cockpit. "She what? Thirty?"

"Thirty-two feet. She old, man. They don't make the bronze porthole covers like that no more."

The green paint was bubbled on the hatch. When Montgomery picked at it, he exposed bare wood. He sighed. "These wooden boats look fine but they devilish hard to keep right." He jerked a steel halyard, bent to inspect the halyard block. "Man, I wouldn't want to go tightening this. This one so corroded, she break before she turn."

"Radio," Montgomery pointed to the insulated radio blocks in the rigging.

But Montgomery was wrong. The hatch had been crowbarred open and the shattered top board lay on the cabin floor below. "This coaming high enough." Winston got on the ladder. "Hard for sea get down this hatchway."

"It awkward like hell," Montgomery complained, dropping after his brother into the gloom.

They lifted the midships hatch and broke those portholes open that would. Almost half of them.

The cabin was musty, and stank of sweet dry rot. The chart table cabinet had been visited by the crowbar and shredded radio leads dangled where the radio had been. Drawers had been dumped and kicked over the floor, crockery shattered against the gimbaled stove and the steel sink.

Montgomery extracted the top of a glass bong. "They was lookin' for the ganja."

"They find it," Winston guessed. "Some drawers not pulled out like the rest."

On hands and knees Winston crept back to inspect the motor. It was a four-cylinder Atomic, foul with oil. The plug insulation crumbled in his fingers. "Oh my," he said.

Montgomery was rustling through the sail locker. "New sails, Winston."

The vultures had stolen the mattress pads off the rail bunks. Winston looked his puzzlement.

"They float, man," Montgomery said. "Those dumb niggers usin' them as surfboards."

The bilge held just a few inches of water, which was better than Winston had dared hope. The water was littered with cigarette packs, soggy can labels, and wooden matches. "Damn fool sweep his floor in here," Winston said.

The bilge pump was oversized, a manual piston pump that bore the legend: AFTEN WERKE, GHENT 1924.

"That she age."

The hull was mahogany over oak.

"It you boat, man," Montgomery said. "You go overside."

Winston stripped and dove into the green transparent water. Like a pilot fish cruising a whale, he circled the hull. She would have been a disaster as a charter boat: too deep, too narrow, too much keel. Most charters are glass boats, practically idiot proof. This one might draw six and a half feet.

Influenced by the 12-meter racers and IOR (International Ocean Racing) rules, modern cruising-racing yachts don't put much below the waterline and many count on the crew as movable ballast. Such boats are minimally faster (fractions of a knot) than older designs but can take worse knockdowns and some, in a rollover, cannot self-right.

Winston blew out his air and dogpaddled. "Man, she foul. I seldom seen so many barnacles."

Montgomery had his feet propped up on the transom. "So what, man? You in no hurry."

"Work the tiller."

Winston stuck his head back under to check the rudder action. He swam the waterline, looking for bad planks. Painted on the prow was a God's Eye in peacock colors: red, blue, and gold. The boat was named the *Bamboo Cannon*.

The bow anchor was new, a Danforth.

Winston heaved himself over the transom, found a musty towel, and patted himself dry.

As Winston rowed them into shore, Montgomery said, "Maybe I go with you, Winston. Ocean voyage good for the heart. Warm breezes, flying fishes, sunsets . . ."

"The tugboats coming to pull you off the rocks. . . ."

Montgomery gave Winston a look.

They found the white man raking woodchips around a tree fern.

Montgomery said, "I didn't know these ferns grew so near the sea."

The white man tidied a border, *scritch, scritch*.

Winston said, "Plenty dry rot in that boat, mister."

The white man said, "You people already have the radio and depth finder out of it, you saying you don't want the boat?"

Winston's lips narrowed, "Not me, man. I didn't thief them."

The white man inspected the fronds of his tree fern. "My son, Eric, was a gentle soul. The Negro who forced him off the road was so drunk he couldn't talk—three hours after!"

Winston said, "I sorry, mister."

"Eric loved that ugly boat. He repainted it himself, bought new sails. October, he meant to try the Atlantic." His eyes welled with tears and he turned away and the brothers watched his scrawny old back heaving in and out. When he steadied he faced them again. He hadn't bothered to wipe his eyes. "Five thousand dollars," he said. "U.S."

Winston said, "It not in good shape, that boat."

"It would have made it across the entire goddamned Atlantic."

"Forty-five hundred," Winston said, and the man put out his hand. Winston counted out forty-five hundreds, one at a time, licking his thumb so they wouldn't stick.

The white man rolled Winston's money in his fist and stared out to sea. "Get it out of here," he said.

Montgomery said, "Man, I ain't sure she ready to sail."

"You do it."

Montgomery said, *"Tout bête jene mode."* (Any animal in trouble bites.)

Winston said, "Okay."

The engine wouldn't start so they raised the mainsail and while it luffed noisily, Montgomery lifted the anchor, hand over hand. The main filled and the tiller came alive. They beat around the point of Buck Island into Sir Francis Drake Channel.

The boat's prow hissed through gentle swells. Montgomery at the tiller grinning like a fool while Winston checked the standing rigging. Overhead, the jib stay clattered against the mast.

Montgomery called, "Winston!" Winston ducked as Montgomery let out the jib and the *Bamboo Cannon* clipped down the channel, both sails bellying, wing and wing.

Winston clambered back into the cockpit. Montgomery said, "This fine boat. You and Rosemary could live on her better than a house."

"Help me provision in Roadtown before you go to Carnival. I want to be in the Anegada Passage by tomorrow noon."

"Where I take a girl if I find her? The hotels be jammed."

"I know these Atomic 4s. When the wiring rot they hell to keep going."

Montgomery said, "He got two sets storm trysails. That boy was ready for a blow. Winston, you think this right? This my type of foolishness, not you."

"She point pretty good, but boat she slow. I want you tell Rosemary. Tell her I gone Puerto Rico. Tell her DMS Airways business."

"I tell Rosemary that?" Montgomery leaned over the side where the pale foamy water splashed by. "I have told some fine stories, Winston. But to Rosemary . . . ?"

"It is business overdue," Winston said fiercely. "Me and Mal Esprit."

The bow slapped the green swell. Crystalline drops flew.

The masthead bobbed and circled in the blue, blue sky like the finger of someone arguing with God.

7

"Too much fête never kill a man yet!"
ALPHONSE CASSELL

"Carly, he's going to knock me unconscious and slash my face with a scalpel. While I'm unconscious, he's going to work his will with me."

Carly drawled, "I thought he already did that."

"Bitch!" The hiss came from the couch where Magdellana lay, cold washcloth over her eyes, window drapes pulled to kill the last rays of the afternoon sun.

"Mother, it's a minor operation." Carly was trying to read about a double murder in St. Thomas but her hands shook and the newsprint jittered.

"Minor! A sharp blade inches from my jugular vein! Minor! Helpless, in the hands of a guinea butcher who probably cheated and cribbed his way through medical school, Carly! You are so unsympathetic!"

Her wail hung in the gathering twilight. "You want me to read the paper to you, Mother?"

"Yes, please, dear." Magdellana folded her hands beneath her breasts like a good girl.

Carly quoted with relish. "'Police are puzzled by the apparently motiveless death of two U.S. citizens, Harry Brown and Mel Anderson. Brown (age 44) is a dentist from Wilkes-Barre, Pennsylvania, and Anderson (29) is a commercial pilot. "It must have been drugs," Captain Bunting of St. Thomas police said. "This was a particularly brutal execution-type slaying . . .'"

"Dear! Please, that's so depressing!"

"Mother, all news is depressing. If it was happy, they wouldn't call it news."

Magdellana crossed one foot over the other. "I go into surgery, first thing tomorrow morning, and what do I get from you? Smart-alecky remarks."

Carly stole a look at her Swatch. Where was Ringo?

"At least you could stay here this evening." Magdellana wailed, "I can't even eat a tiny bite. And that Dr. Dragotti, he—"

"The Dragotis are creeps, Mother. A-s-s-h-o-l-e: creeps."

"So why are you letting him squire you tonight?"

"Squire me?"

Magdallena moaned. "I'm so hungry!"

Carly studied the newspaper picture of the murder house. A property owned by a Canadian couple who would be displeased to learn that two strangers had broken in, used the place for several days, and repainted the living room walls with their hearts' blood, red. Carly took up a fashion magazine.

"Mother, what do you think about these tango dresses? Do you think I'd look good in a tango?"

"Too retro, dear, far too retro. If you don't like Ringo why go out with him?"

"He has good drugs."

"Carly! Tomorrow morning, I go 'on the table' and you torment me while my resistance is low. When I was your age, we didn't do all these drugs. A little pot. L.S.D., psilocybin—all organic of course—"

"At least, Mother, we don't use body paint."

"Body paint! Oh, my God!" her mother shrieked.

Softly, Carly shut her bedroom door on her mother's memories. She emptied her purse on the bed; perhaps she'd missed something, but no little green pill, no fragment. She wet her finger and ran it around the plastic vial and her finger tasted bitter when she sucked on it. Not even the hint of a buzz.

She inspected herself in the full-length mirror. Silver-lavender lamé blouse, with the midlength sleeve. Blue jeans rolled up above her ankles. Red leather Reeboks. Swatch. She touched her mascara and created a smudge. Her hands weren't right; what was she doing! How she hated her face.

Thirty-five minutes late, Ringo stood in the doorway, wearing a Hawaiian shirt, white drawstring pants, and a petty smile.

From the couch, Carly's mother called, "Is that you, Ringo? Tomorrow I shall be at your father's mercy. I shall dress myself in white, head to toe, like a virgin sacrifice."

Sweetly, Carly said, "Tomorrow morning, Mother, you'll be wearing a hospital gown, and your ass will be hanging out."

She got the door closed but her mother's "Bitch!" clattered against it like a thrown shoe.

Ringo said, "You're so lucky to have her for a mother."

"What do you know?"

"I know we're going to Roadtown for Carnival. I know we're going to have one terrific time."

"Yeah. You bring the drugs?"

"Carly, Carly . . . you have such a limited imagination."

"Buster, I already done most of the things you're still trying to think up."

His eyes sparkled. "We'll see, Carly. We'll see. . . ."

It was probably coincidence that Gerry—the kitchen boy, part-time ganja salesman—was at the helm of the Cris-Craft runabout. Graciously, Ringo helped her aboard. Without waiting to be asked, Carly went into the chest for a split of champagne.

The boat had to be cast off and the boatman given instructions, and, course set, burbling away from Sandpiper Cay before Ringo got around to opening her bottle. "Do you want a glass?"

"Sure, I want a glass. What do you think?"

His smile let her know what he thought. He opened his hand and four tablets were revealed. "Ah-ah. One at a time."

Ringo put his arm around her shoulders just like she was his. He wasn't the first man to think that.

First time she'd run away, she'd gone with Billy, the organic gardener and communard. Forty acres of waterless scrub on the Oregon high plains, weeks of weeding a garden plot that would never sprout anything but weeds and when the sun went down Carly did all the cooking and, if she didn't make an issue out of it, she'd do the dishes too. After three months of it, when Mother came to fetch her, Carly was ready to go.

Next time out, she'd picked Butchie, with his great sense of

humor. Second-rate bass guitarist with a fourth-rate punk band—
The Whistling Warthogs. Cockney Butchie with his pink hair and
pimples and unpleasant sex habits. Carly had made the bookings,
lugged the instruments, cleaned up after them, made all the apologies, somehow found money for Butchie's growing habit. And
when Carly's mother sent her a ticket (one way, London/New
York/LAX) she'd used it.

What if it had worked, Carly wondered. What if she'd got clear?

When Ringo took his arm away, she felt lighter. The boat
creamed through the swell. He went up front to sit with the
driver.

The trim runabout sped past old Fort Burt and wove through
the big yachts anchored well offshore. They looked like floating
motels. Several had stern helicopter platforms and Carly watched
a two-seater whuffle aloft, pivot on its axis, and race importantly
to shore.

The marinas lining Roadtown Harbour were ablaze with light.
Figures danced on the jettys. Boat people stood about on deck
with plastic glasses in their hands and called out jokes and songs
to one another. When Carly looked behind her, the sea was coal
black.

Shore smelled like spiced grease and iodine. The many steel
drums on shore settled into one rhythm, one relentless, overbear-
ing thuddity, thuddity, thuddity. Some other instruments went
ching ching ching and, for the first time, she heard this Carnival
chant:

> *Joshua gone Barbados*
> *Stayin' in big hotel.*
> *People on St. Vincent*
> *Got many sad tale to tell.*

Meant what? What right did these people have, imposing their
world on her? Did her mother know anybody in the big steel
yachts? Did her father know where his beloved daughter was tonight?

Poor girl, on her own, poor girl.

Ringo leaped onto the dock to make fast.

Carly thought Ringo probably cut a very dashing figure and that
some nicer girl would have a fine time with him. A second
thought: Honey, he is an a-s-s-h-...

"Don't let go of my hand," he said. Under her feet the dock was swaying worse than the runabout had. She wondered if she could get another pill.

"We'll be leaving for Sandpiper in the morning."

The kitchen boy—ganja dealer blushed to his earlobes. He stared down at his jogging shoes. "Right, Skip," he said. He didn't look at Carly at all.

"Hey, hey, welcome to Carnival!" A white man weaving on the deck of his white plastic and chrome sloop. The white man had pale blond hair and a flushed face and a blond moustache.

Carly said, "Thank you," lowered her head, hurried by. As she did, a woman stuck her head out of the companionway and said, "Harry, stop ogling the pussy!"

Ringo walked along slow, hands deep in his pockets, grinning at some life joke known only to himself.

Most of the tied-up boats were vacant and most of them were white Fiberglas, though they did pass a wicked-looking mahogany ketch and a green-and-red sloop where two black men were cleaning the cabin, oblivious of the festivities around them.

Downtown Roadtown was a minstrel show, the touring company of *Porgy and Bess,* so animated were the revelers, so sticklike, so hellishly black. As if they were onstage, they danced —two, four, six couples jumped to that steel band, whirled, broke into fragments. Jokes in incomprehensible patois, shouts and joys. But they were on the far side of a one-way glass and Carly couldn't be harmed, no matter what. A bearded black blocked them. His festive shirt was splotched and torn. His wire-rimmed glasses were wrapped at the nose piece with black electrician's tape. Wordlessly he pushed a bottle in Carly's face. "You goan' need this," he said.

He had a deep dent in his broad nose and, through his glasses, one eye seemed bigger than the other.

She took the bottle but, before she could drink, Ringo snatched it away. "Thanks, old man, but no thanks. Happy Carnival." Carly didn't understand the deep sadness in the black man's face. It wasn't the sadness of drink.

"Here," Ringo had another pill in his hand and pressed his palm against hers like he was trying to mark her flesh.

A few cars crept through the packed throng, people on the hood and back bumpers. The cars rode with snoots in the air and down on their back springs. On the street corner a powder blue paddy wagon waited, rear doors gaping open and six constables, sober as judges, arms folded, not joking.

"Come on," Ringo said. Ahead, a steel marching band was assembling. Faces laughed, with broken teeth, laughed. Faces that woke this morning impoverished, told a joke. Pockmarked faces, ugly faces, that fathered or bore hungry children, still laughed. Ringo took one hand and a black man, unknown to her, snatched the other, and the drums led them around the corner and the hands held her fast so she had to dance, had to, and the dancers snaked up the cobblestoned street, winding through stalled cars, horns honking.

"JOSHUA GONE BARBADOS," the anthem thundered. Just a few white faces, and Carly was surprised to find that Ringo's grip on her hand was much harsher, asked more of her, than the black hand holding her other hand. And the voices roared: "LIVIN' IN A BIG HOTEL," like there was something wrong with that, like a person was guilty for living in a big hotel, like they'd tear him limb from limb. The line moved sideways, swiftly, like a snake slithers. Across a low stoop, down into a broad storm gutter—the drums banged and banged, so primitive—downhill again, around the corner beside the harbor and no idea how long the line was behind her but she wished she could let go, just get loose. Three kids on short stilts and the line weaved around them too, laughing and joking, and two of the stilt kids were okay but the third balanced precariously and the sweat beads stood out on his forehead. His smile was about as wide as it could be. His smile was his balance pole.

Along the wharf, along the cold water's edge, they danced, and Carly's eyes stung with sweat. She was squinting and her heart was louder than the drum and she was afraid she'd fall and everyone would fall over her—little white girl at the bottom of a black heap, like chocolate-covered vanilla.

They surrounded the policemen and their paddy wagon, wound around them like a snake winds, the constables chatting to each other unruffled, and then the band was off down the street and one of Carly's hands came free and then the other, and the line segmented into hurrying blacks racing after the other dancers.

Ringo said, "Wasn't that fun?"

Her head spun, and she looked around for somewhere to sit.

Almost sat on the bumper of the paddy wagon but foolish, foolish! She slipped into an alcove behind a paté wagon and the momma woman offered a meat pie. The aroma kissed Carly and she backed off, waving her hands in front of her face like moth wings fluttering. Then she bumped into Ringo, his hands went right around her. Hoarsely, she whispered, "I need more medicine."

He looked at her, with the knowing expression of a man who has dissimilar vices: "You got a strong head," he said.

"Goddamn right," she choked.

He paid for a meat paté. He took a big bite and dabbed, inadequately, at the edge of his mouth. The juice was pale yellow and glistened. He said, "You got a great ass, you know that?"

A great thundering down the street announced the Carnival road march and the street cleared of people, pressing Carly between Ringo and the paté wagon. She pressed her face into his back so she wouldn't smell the cooking and wouldn't get sick. She began to sob. "Those poor men. Those poor American men."

"Huh?"

The stickmen followed the first steel band, tall figures like praying mantises, some with top hats to exaggerate their height; some would bend too, impossibly low, to shake a hand or pat the top of a child's head.

Mental pictures swept through her head: the murdered dentist, the murdered pilot. The newspaper hadn't described the murder room but Carly'd seen enough movies: walls dripping with Technicolor and dreadful gashes on the bloodless white bodies. Tears sprang to her eyes. Carly often wept for people she didn't know.

Ringo's face was a kaleidoscope of disgust, apathy, weariness. He said, "Sweetheart, you sure know how to have a good time."

The Virgin's ankles disappeared under bright red flowers. She was pulled by black men in neat dark trousers and short-sleeved white shirts. Priests scattered blessings.

How could anyone live in this world?

In Ringo's open palm were three old familiars, her Valium pals. Another steel band came whirling by, their costumes so gay.

"No, I don't . . ."

"Oh, come on. You know you love them. Here, wash them down." He produced a hammered silver flask. "There, that's better now, isn't it?"

"Oh, look at the children."

On the children's float, they pretended they were sitting in a classroom and their little desks were real and the teacher at the blackboard was real too, but the kids couldn't pretend to study while waving at everyone they knew.

"Teenage pregnancy is about 80 percent in these islands. They fuck like rabbits." Ringo's voice was a steel needle that slipped through her clamped-down ears to pierce her eardrums. The drugs had reduced her protections instead of increasing them. "I'm feeling rabbity myself," he said. "Back in a sec."

He dodged across the street, shirt billowing through the stick dancers. He ducked into the Mariner's Inn, a newish hotel whose upstairs balconies were packed with people watching the parade —white people.

Carly hoped they were full up. Her mouth was dry as a dying man's whisper. Her stomach felt hollow and bad. Her eyes were jammed open and she could probably stay awake until she died.

"You take this now," the black man said. The man with the taped glasses and the dented nose.

She said, "I've had so much already."

"Ah, yes," he said, "but them meant to harm."

The bottle he offered her was so cheap it didn't have a label. In island snack bars they make incredibly strong rum-and-Cokes because the rum costs less than the Coca-Cola. "Please," she said.

"You take some now," he said.

The Methodist float was passing. Stem to stern it glittered with gold and silver tinsel ropes. Ropes tethered a floral replica of the Methodist church, as if without them the building might soar off into heaven.

The bottle had a screw-on cap. She tilted it, intending to take the tiniest mouthful, but the bottle had a will of its own and she swallowed once, twice, the most horrible stuff she ever drank. It dropped to her stomach and crashed around. It drained her sinuses right out of her nostrils. It trickled into her eye canals and she could taste her eye fluids. "Aw," she said. "Aw."

He said, "Where white boy?"

She said, "Gone to get a room. What was that? Stuff?"

His cracked face smiled. He shook his head.

She said, "I never tasted anything like that before."

He said, "Carnival, she life. Not supposed to be for dyin'." He turned then and shuffled off through the crowd. She thought the word *Voodoo*. She thought the word *Obeah* and though a modest nimbus surrounded each word, nothing more occurred to her.

Ringo didn't come out of the Mariner's Inn so she edged through the crowd, "Excuse me, excuse me please," like the polite little girl she was. Her fingertips had gone numb and she was afraid the numbness would spread.

"Excuse me," she came between mothers and their kids, divided lovers, stepped into the street, blocking the view of those trying to spot relatives in the road march. The cobblestones were gray and treacherous.

She wanted to be out of sight. She wanted to be a stranger.

Drunken bad johns split at her approach and gave her plenty of room. One, crazy with drink, cried, "You white meat, that all. White meat!" and halfheartedly shook his fist but didn't pursue.

She had to pass through the stick men without slipping on the cobblestones. She charted their erratic course in her mind and leaned forward all at once to rush across the street.

And her legs weren't working right. The drum beats were no longer distinct; they were continuous, like thunder.

The dense crowd parted bit by bit, like rope fraying, until her back was to their backs and their black bodies were a wall against the drums. She tottered on. If Ringo finds me, she thought, he'll kill me.

She headed for the sea because the sea was big enough to forgive her failures, her meannesses, her not being complete like other women were.

White yachts bobbed at the dock, but she couldn't stand to look at them.

She wondered if she was going to get sick and worry was the mother of the deed. She dropped to her knees and crawled. She threw up everything she had, in heart-racking gushes. Oh, her hot stomach hurt.

She yearned for the runabout but Ringo would find her. He'd take her to the deepest part of the channel and work his will upon her. She wouldn't resist. She never had.

The dock planks hurt her knees.

Nobody on the yachts. Everyone was in town, watching the Carnival.

The planks were wider than her outstretched palms. Here and there, nailheads showed through.

She crawled toward the green-and-red boat because it looked like a bassinet. She puzzled how to get over its thwarts, which were two feet higher than the dock. She feared she'd slip between boat and dock where she'd be crushed, for sure.

She thought about Ringo. He made her laugh. Her mother made her laugh. Everybody! And, so! she'd made it over the thwart.

A dim electric light burned in the cabin. It was neat, like a house trailer. All the dishes were in the tiny dishrack beside the tiny steel sink.

She opened a cabinet amidships where sails were stored. She was so sleepy. The sails were stowed in long rolled bags. There was room in the locker for one very tired girl. She pulled the door closed behind her, stuck her thumb in her mouth, and slept.

PART TWO

HURRICANE

August, she mus'

WEST INDIES PROVERB

8

18° 21′ N, 64° 7′ W: The Anegada Passage

In the pale, metallic light of predawn, Winston Riviere stood in the cockpit of the *Bamboo Cannon*, a happy man. How could he have forgotten how the light sculpted the squat green binnacle, how the halyards quivered, how the mainsail stretched overhead, taut as a baby's belly. The bow crashed into the chop, Tortola on his stern quarter, the Salt Island light—every five seconds—on the starboard beam, Fallen Jerusalem dead ahead. He'd correct after he was past Round Rock Passage. Round Rock Passage was the direct route to Dominica, but by no means the swiftest or easiest. Current runs strongly westward in the Anegada Passage and Winston wanted to get as far east as he could within sheltered waters.

The *Bamboo Cannon* pointed well but was very slow.

Above the masthead, above the dark earth, cirrus clouds were faintly kissed by the sun. They were cold and very pretty, like white girls at a fête.

It was going to be a sharp and brilliant dawn.

Winston never had been the natural sailor Montgomery was. Once, on a wager, Montgomery had sailed a Windsurfer from St. John to St. Croix and that's a long haul over open water for a lone man on a bit of Fiberglas with a wishbone sail. What Montgomery did instinctively on a boat took Winston months to learn. If only Montgomery hadn't been so careless!

Give Montgomery credit for charm. When they tied up in Roadtown last night, it took all Montgomery's charm and bantering to convince the grocery-store owner to open on Carnival night. Shopkeeper already in his costume, too. Dressed like Blackbeard, with a fuzzy beard, triangular hat, and one hell of a cutlass.

"Man, you hurry now," he'd said, opening the back door.

Racing, they scooped items off the shelf—baked beans, Spam, canned tomatoes, green beans—and tossed them into cardboard boxes.

"Here, man." Montgomery picked foot-long loaves of French bread from the counter. Winston plucked orange drinks from the cooler, three gallons, and Montgomery found a bottle of rum. They counted out cash on the spot and Winston added a canned Danish ham because the owner didn't want to open his register for change. Three days' provisions for one man: thirty dollars.

And give Montgomery credit for pumping the brackish water out of the *Bamboo Cannon*'s scuttlebutt and hosing in twenty gallons of fresh. "No ice, man," Montgomery said. "The ice machine locked up."

Winston looked up from the carburetor he had disassembled. "What for I need ice? Think how it was when me and Leon sailed that Carib canoe off Dominica—dried fish and cooked rice and a jerrycan of warm water. This boat a fancy boat, white man's boat, white man's blue-water cruiser."

Montgomery said, "Well, there ain't no ice."

White man and white girl walked by and gave them a wave, which neither brother answered.

"This Atomic motor too bad," Winston said. "Wiring worthless. I goin' down island, sail alone."

Montgomery shrugged. Motors were for men willing to get grease under their fingernails.

Winston said, "Man, why you not go to Carnival? Find somebody warm. It is what you are wanting to do."

Montgomery put on a funereal face. "Winston, you sailing tomorrow into grave danger and you my brother, so . . ."

"You want to help, ask about the weather. Talk to one of them fellows from the big boats with the weather radio. Go."

And Montgomery retained his solemn expression but when he went below to comb his hair, Winston could hear his whistling.

That was last night. This morning, the sun was just a bulge on the sea. It touched the masthead, transforming the gray sail into a pink one. The binnacle became ordinary as the sun washed it into flats and shadows. The sun's road glimmered around the *Bamboo Cannon* and Winston felt his eye pupils narrow. Cormorants bombing a school of alewives—just a sparkle on the surface.

Winston thought about the passages he'd made on the big yachts. Puerto Rico to Trinidad, Monserrat to Chile—that was a long one, ferrying a gaff-rigged schooner south to its owner, Senor De Los Arivale.

What a mad time. After Senor Arivale inspected his purchase, he'd been so pleased he invited them, Captain Winston and the crew, to his estate on a hilltop west of Santiago. It was a soft June night and new Chilean wine and dark-haired young girls.

Of course, as Rosemary pointed out, Winston had only been a "Hired-Boat Driver."

Still, this morning, as the sun brushed his shoulders with light and silhouetted Virgin Gorda ahead, Winston smiled his memories.

The deck under his bare feet. The air, laden with iodine and salt. A phosphorescent streak off the port side, jellyfish maybe. There were some damn peculiar things living in this tropical sea. Winston had a sudden mental picture of the Obeah man guarding his house. Obeah man enjoying this sunrise too. Winston rapped his knuckles on the wooden taffrail: respect.

He looped a line over the tiller and slipped down into the cabin he and Montgomery had spent hours cleaning up. Though crowbar marks still marred the cabinets, they'd been jammed shut and the gear was neatly stowed. The gimbaled stove had two burners and an oven large enough for a modest casserole. Winston struck a match and filled the blackened aluminum tea kettle.

The cabin seemed somber after the vast horizon topside, the sun tipping the swells with flashes of red.

The barometer was steady at 1025 millibars. He noted that and the time in the log. Winston took his tea to the cockpit and adjusted the heading up a few points to miss Collision Point.

He hadn't sailed without a radio since he was a boy. Not having RDF to fix his position made him uneasy, but he did have a sextant and his wristwatch. He'd need to be particularly attentive to the sea's weather signs.

Maybe he'd just forget about Mal Esprit and sail on. Surely there were plenty of places in the world for a man who could sail boats, fix or fly airplanes. But as soon as he had that lighthearted thought a coldness like gall descended down his sternum, and struck his stomach like the pod of the cannonball tree.

Mal Esprit. How Winston had shunned that connection. He'd stayed away from his home island because Dominica was tainted by Mal Esprit's living presence. On St. Thomas he'd avoided Dominicans because they might mention Mal's name.

So today, his heart said, "Sail on. There are many worlds that do not contain Mal Esprit. Fine worlds, many of them. Sail on."

Winston could see Mal's mocking smile, same as when they'd been good friends. That smile seemed to say, "You may avoid me, run to the end of the earth. But you will never have roots anywhere in these islands for I will find you, trample those roots until you flee again."

Winston threw his tea dregs over the side.

Three A.M. last night, Montgomery returned from Carnival and poked his head down the hatch. Montgomery wore a smug grin.

"You find yourself a bird," Winston said, wiping his hands on a rag.

Montgomery's grin grew. "Gillian, from the north. A waitress. She's having a ma-vel-ous time at Carnival. Only Montgomery can make it better."

"Sure thing, brother. Have a memorable time."

"It will be my tourist bird that will have a memorable time, man. I think I don't see you tonight no more. The weather for the next days, she fine. I pray you get through, Winston."

"No depressions, no fronts?"

"I talk to skipper off a hundred-footer. He got the weather fax machine, got everything."

"You tell Rosemary I in Puerto Rico for a week."

Montgomery said, "I give Rosemary a big kiss."

Winston said, "Not so big a kiss. That girl already likes you too much."

Montgomery smiled and was gone.

Later when Winston cleaned up and went to the Carnival himself, he didn't see Montgomery, no white tourist lady either. Just revelers, drunk steel bands losing their tempo. Constables politely helped an old man aboard the paddy wagon, where he joined others on wooden benches waiting for the truck to fill.

Although Carnival was dying, Winston stayed for a bit, seeking human company before his days of solitude and danger. He leaned against a storefront and watched the dancers (only one or two bands still playing, only a dozen dancers still kicking up their heels). A handsome brown-skinned woman came right up to him boldly and said, "You want some rum, man?"

Winston smiled and shook his head.

She said, "I have too much rum." Then, vaguely, she said, "I looking..." and walked off.

Quietly, Winston said, "We all doin' that, darlin'."

Next morning, almost eleven, Winston rounded Virgin Gorda between Anguilla Point and Mosquito Island, on jib alone because this was shoal water and under the surface he could see coral heads flitting by, groping for his keel. He beat to windward across the calm water of Gorda Sound and, by noon, was through the Necker Island Passage. Waves come a long way across the Atlantic to surge through the islands.

Winston set his course, east-southeast, to compensate for the current.

When Virgin Gorda was just the faintest smudge on the horizon, he tied the tiller and went below again. The barometer was 1020 millibars, which he noted in the log. He opened the tinned Danish ham and made himself a sandwich. He opened a bottle of orange drink.

He stripped off his T-shirt, pants, and underpants. He folded his clothes into a neat bundle and stored them with the rest of his duffle.

On deck, the wind touched his groin and leg hairs shied from the breeze. His cock sprang away from his body like it had been imprisoned too long.

He patrolled his boat, shaking the rigging. He tightened the jib halyard turnbuckle. The sun beat down on his shoulder blades. The sea was thick gray swells. A couple of dolphins flashed their black humps off the port beam.

When he perched on the transom, his cock brushed the cold wood and right away, retracted. It was like a baby animal let loose for the first time, alert to every danger. Black hair on a dark brown body against mahogany weathered white. The brass stanchions were dull green where they gripped the rail.

Winston leaned the tiller against his leg and yawned.

Carly feared she wasn't dead. Black and cramped and smells like vomit. Oh, Carly. How could her eyes hurt when there wasn't any light and what was she lying on, so harsh against her bare arms, abrading her cheek?

Carly felt movement, rolling, like she'd been swallowed by some beast. Her mouth was dry, her lips cracked. Her nose was stopped with crust and her smell was appalling.

She lay in the darkness feeling sorry. She'd never had a fair chance, had she? And had she ever learned to spot opportunities when they came? Everybody told her she wasn't worth much, and everybody had it right.

Her bladder sent urgent messages. One nice thing about being dead is not having to pee. She tried hard to remember where she was. She remembered landing at Roadtown. She had fragmentary memories of street dancing; she attuned to her body and learned that her shins hurt. There wasn't room for her to uncurl with her knees against her chest. Had that bastard Ringo fucked her and buried her alive? HAD HE?

"No, I am moving up and down and rolling side to side, like a passenger in the gondola of a scary amusement-park ride."

Her hands patted overhead, left and right. Slick something, not metal, not concrete. Wood, then. Okay, she was in a packing crate. *Her head . . .* made her want to throw up. *Don't think about it.* Where was her mother now and why did she hate Carly so? She pushed on the wood roof, the LID? until her arms ached but no give at all. Oh boy.

A boom, a shudder ran through her prison. What was this stuff underneath? Canvas? Stiff as old tarpaulins. Bracing her arms straight out on either side she pushed until her head thudded and her eyes ached.

And it sprang open.

So good. Band of light at the bottom of the door (cupboard door?) so fresh and inviting. Carly rolled out onto the cabin floor, under the midships hatch, which swayed and danced above her. She put her arm across her eyes.

A boat. She almost remembered . . . something. It'd come to

her. Her knees hurt too. They'd got scuffed somehow. She crawled onto a settee and lowered her head into her hands. When she squeezed her temples the pain became bearable. Across the room (cabin?) she saw a minisink with a minitap and, in a moment, she'd make it across the floor and get a drink of water.

Was this Ringo's boat? It smelled.

She clamped her bladder down. She wiped her forehead. It felt greasy. If she had codeine. Just a quarter-gram of codeine.

Unsteadily she got to the sink and trickled water into her cupped hands, it tasted dull, it tasted wonderful. She splashed water on her sore cheeks and it ran down and tickled her neck. The boat lurched and she gripped the sink edge for support.

Did she want to know where she was? Did she want to start over?

"Come on, Carly," she muttered. She gripped the rails of the companionway and hauled her tattered body into the light.

A black man stood at the tiller, buck naked except for a silly cap. The hair around his groin was vigorous and curly. His thing hung down like this was a porn flick or something.

She pulled herself up the ladder, "Excuse me," she said, went to the rail and threw up a cup of green bile, which whipped back onto her pants legs. She rubbed her mouth with the back of her hand. As she turned, she ran a hand through her mussed hair. She jerked a smile into place, not a terribly big one.

The black man didn't have the decency to cover himself or anything. He pointed a finger at her. "You?"

"Me Carly. Who you?" Couldn't help herself. The boat suddenly heeled over so the water was hissing by not very far from her feet, and Carly grabbed for the companionway ladder so she wouldn't fall. She said politely, "I'm afraid there's been a terrible mistake."

"You?" This black seemed to have a limited vocabulary. At least he didn't drool. Maybe, in an hour or so, he'd think to cover himself.

Patiently, speaking distinctly, as if each syllable hurt her (each did), Carly said, "I am Carly Hollander. Pleased to meet you."

The black man looked up at the sky and shouted at the top of his lungs, "SHIT!" Then he fastened a rope over the tiller and stomped over the cabin to the very front of the boat where he stood, like a black figurehead, glowering at the ocean ahead. He had nice tight buns. Black, of course. He spun his head around to take another gander, like maybe, hopefully, she'd just been some voodoo fiction or something. "Got any Tylenol?" she called. "Tyle-nol?"

He turned back to looking at whatever he was looking at, in the monotonous ugly sea.

There wasn't anything to see. Ocean all around. A few clouds in the west. Their sails. The tip of the mast was swaying so wildly, Carly swallowed and looked away. The wooden tiller strained against a rope and the boat tilted, and once again she was looking right at the water hissing by and, by God, shouldn't somebody be driving this thing?

When he came back, she kept her eyes on his chest because she didn't want to watch his thing wiggling. "Excedrin? Bayer? Bufferin?" When he stepped down off the cabin roof, he passed so close she flinched and that flinch hurt her too. Her stomach cramped and she went to the rail again, this time downwind, and retched again.

The black man's brown eyes studied her, head to toe, and though it wasn't a sexual appraisal it was extremely personal.

She said, "I suppose you wouldn't mind putting on a pair of pants."

He glanced at an oversized compass set in an iron post and adjusted his steering. He studied the low clouds like they were important, like the *Los Angeles Times*.

In a little voice, she asked, "Where's the ladies room?"

He jabbed a finger at the companionway. "Forward. Below."

The toilet was tiny—much smaller than an airplane toilet. Carly tucked up her knees. The flush handle was just a valve on a standpipe. No regular toilet paper, just folded newspaper. Did newsprint come off on moist parts?

At the sink, she washed her face thoroughly, taking her sweet time, splashing water over her wrists. She snatched a towel, wet it, and dabbed, not very effectively, at the bile stain on her blue jeans. Wadded the towel and dropped it.

Took a deep breath, straightened her blouse, and started back up the ladder. Thank God, the black man had on a pair of shorts. His chest was big and black and she wished he'd had the decency to cover that too. He watched the horizon.

"Say, where are we?"

He jabbed a thumb behind. "Virgins." His forefinger flicked to the left. "St. Martin. Anguilla." He pointed to the front of the boat. "Saba," he said.

"When can you put me ashore? God, I feel like shit."

The black man shrugged.

"How the fuck far is Saba?"

Again, infuriatingly, his shoulder raised and dipped. "If rough seas, we can't land Saba."

Carly addressed him one syllable at a time.

"Perhaps you don't get the picture. I wish to go home. My mother is very, very sick. She is having an operation. My place is at her side." A hot dumb pain crashed through her head and she licked her lips. "Jesus," she muttered.

The damn black just looked at her.

"Look, I'm sorry I'm on your boat. I didn't exactly plan to go sailing today. I was a little smashed, okay?"

Just like he hadn't heard a word he shinnied right up the mast, like a damn monkey, made her ill just to look at him, swaying on the crossbars peering to the east.

He was just showing off. That's what boys do.

When he hit the deck again, he had a distracted expression on his puss. Carly put her hands on her hips. "Are you a fisherman? I'll pay for the fish you don't catch."

The black man drummed his fingers on the cabin roof. This bozo was not swift to get the point. "I said I'd pay..."

"You steer boat?"

"Well, ... I ... uh ... Jimmy Proffit used to let me drive his runabout on Tahoe. We'd all run down to the casinos and Jimmy'd get sooo wrecked..."

"Sit."

Carly didn't want to but sat. She took the thick wooden tiller when he pushed it at her.

"Steady at 110 degrees. Don't make no big moves, darlin'. When the bow falls off, bring she back slow."

"I wanna go home!"

"You've got the helm."

Carly felt the boat through her wrist, like it was some kind of bulgy aquatic animal, more alive than wood, canvas, brass. She overcorrected at first, because she was used to driving a car but gradually slowed her reflexes to match the animal she was driving.

The black man perched on the rail, not too close, and never took his eyes off her hands.

"It's worth five hundred dollars if you turn this boat around."

The black man moved to the companionway and—well, he didn't climb down—he sort of scootered down on his arms. They're more agile than we are. That's why they make such fantastic basketball players. He banged around below.

The sails billowed like picture postcards. Pretty. Carly thought about her mother, how pissed she'd be. Stupid gray canvas. Primitive. Carly shoved the tiller hard over so the boat would go back the way it had come. The bow dipped into a wave and sprayed and there was a heavy gurgling sound at the stern and the tiller got very stiff, but she braced her feet and pushed hard as she could. Carly's life was all behind her and if it wasn't the best life, it was hers.

The big sail trembled. As the wind fell out of it, it flapped and shook. The wooden boom lost tension and the rope arrangement that held it sagged and the boom bounced as the sail collected one more modest gust of air. Carly stood. She wondered if she should push the boom back or let it pivot. Maybe, somehow she could retie it differently. Oh damn.

She bent to the companionway. "Hey," she called, "there's something funny..."

The black man looked up. He carried a long bundle in his arms. His eyes met hers.

The deck dropped away under her feet as the mainsail caught the wind on the wrong side and the boom swooshed across the boat. Passed over Carly's head so fast, and so close, the spar brushed her brown hair. Her human brain cowered inside her skull, wincing.

The black man came up like a jack-in-the-box. The boom crashed against its stop and that's where he was looking, not at Carly. Quickly he grabbed the ropes and set his big feet against the deck and heaved and whipped the rope end around a cleat while with his free hand he snatched the tiller and brought her around, to her original heading. The sail cracked and filled. The black man hopped up on the cabin roof to inspect the boom hinge. He wriggled something. He ran fingers through his tight, kinky hair.

Carly's arm hurt and she rubbed the sore place. The black was breathing pretty fast, in and out, in and out. His eyes were hot and nonwhite. "You know where we are?"

"How," she drawled, "the hell should I know?"

Dramatically he pointed at the dark water behind them. "Barracuda Bank. You don't do what I say, you go for swim."

The flush started at her neck and went right to her ears. She clamped her mouth shut so her teeth wouldn't chatter. "You ever hear of the kidnapping law, buddy? That fucking sail could have torn my head off and then where would you be? Then where would you be?"

The bastard began to smile. A smile spread across his face from cheek to cheek. He had demonstrably orderly teeth. "Steer 110 degrees. Don't get up or walk around. Nothin' like that. Don't let go the helm."

"Aye, aye," she saluted. "Sir."

Still grinning, he went back below. Carly listened to her heartbeat. She shook her head furiously from side to side, loosening her vertebrae. Christ, if her neck had been longer, one of those swanlike necks. . . . Her fingertips touched her skull lovingly.

The awful water whooshed by on either side. One at a time, the black brought up three canvas bundles, which he lashed to the bow rail.

He rose up on his tiptoes, his worried eyes scanning the east. "Barometer gone crazy," he said, including Carly in.

She said, "Okay, six hundred bucks if you'll take me home. This isn't exactly my idea of a good time."

He said, "I take helm. Go below and cook something."

She said, "I'm not hungry."

He sighed, "You don't want to be cooking in a blow."

She said, "What's your handle, partner? Your *name*—what's your *name*?"

He closed his mouth firmly. He said, "You not need to know."

Sweetly she said, "Then you won't mind if I call you Rastus?"

He said, "Go fix the food."

Carly was so pissed. Kidnapped by a nigger version of John Wayne—Rastus Wayne. Oh, whoopee!

She slammed the blackened kettle onto the stove and scratched a wooden match, which went out before she found the gas bottle

and cracked the valve. Though she scrabbled through every cupboard she couldn't find coffee. "Hey," she shouted, "where's the
damn coffee?"

"No coffee, tea."

She unscrewed the rum she found but her nose wrinkled at the
smell; she didn't want any damn rum. When the kettle boiled, she
made herself a mug of tea, plenty of milk, plenty of sugar. It
wasn't coffee, for sure.

Carly could scramble an egg or make French toast but there
didn't seem to be any eggs. She cut up chunks of canned Spam
and dropped them in a frying pan. She opened cans of green
beans and tomatoes and slopped those on top. She added salt,
couldn't find pepper.

When it was burbling she called through the hatch, "Soup's on!"
So fricking cheerful: Doris Day.

The black sniffed her concoction but didn't say anything nasty.
He spooned a big helping onto a tin plate and ripped a hunk off
the loaf of bread. The smell reminded Carly's stomach. "Uuuuck,"
she said.

He looked surprised, "You cook it," he noted.

"Rastus, if it's alright with you, I don't want to eat it."

He tapped the barometer with his fingernail. Just gave it a flick.
"Goddamn that Montgomery," he said.

He started shoveling it in, aided by bread he used to push stuff
onto his fork. The boat lurched and Carly backpedaled until she
smacked against the gas bottle. That *really* hurt. She whimpered,
"I wanna go home."

Now he was dabbing his bread right into the green-and-red
mess and chowing down.

Sometimes, a girl's gotta do what a girl's gotta do. Carly took a
breath and unbuttoned her blouse, two buttons in the middle.
She said hoarsely, "I can be very accommodating."

He scraped his fork against the cheap tin plate. Scritch, clatter.

When you've got nothing, you've got nothing to lose. Carly
peeled off her blouse. She got a whiff of herself when the air
touched her bare skin and flipped the blouse onto the settee. She
peeled off her pants and underpants together because she didn't
want him to see her in her panties.

His fork dangled forgotten in his hand. He swallowed. It's hard to be seductive when your breasts are goosepimpled but Carly tried. "If you'll take me to shore, I'll accommodate you."

"*Ac-com-mo-date?* Who you? Some hotel?" He pushed his plate aside and stood up. He was probably unaware how he looked working his tongue around his teeth.

Carly had to move, *now*, she was so chilled. "I'm sure you'll be happy to get your pants off again," she said.

He pointed at the companionway. "Go above," he said.

"Love in the open air. How 'au naturale.'"

The sea was splashier than it had been. The eastern clouds stretched from horizon to horizon. Carly hoped he wasn't one of those lovers who take hours trying to juice you up. Just a little in-out and ashore—that was Carly's plan.

"You black boys make love with your pants on?" she inquired, delicately.

He scooped up a coil of rope. He said, "This safety line," and looped it around her waist and his finger flew at the knot.

"Oh, Christ, I didn't know you were one of THOSE. What ever happened to the old missionary position?"

He looked at her eyes then, first time. And though his face was solemn, she saw laughter gleaming there. He said, "*Touni pa eopze begne*," and before she could ask what the hell he meant, he bent and scooped her up under the knees and flung her into the sea.

Her mouth was open in an O of surprise and she came up gagging salt water. The stern was just ten feet away. A swell flicked Carly in the mouth. He watched, arms crossed, like a Mameluke.

"You assho—" She choked on her scream and spit and paddled and kicked her way to the top of the next swell and there the boat was, but the black man was gone, like he was going to leave her and she churned ahead with a strong stroke and didn't raise her face out of the water because that's what she'd learned in the pool at Miss Porter's. Don't look up or you'll lose the race, and when, after three minutes of desperate swimming, she did look, she couldn't see the boat at all.

Carly was so afraid, she peed. Her pee was so much warmer than the gray water.

The next swell lifted her high enough so she could see the boat, smaller still. She waved feebly. She had plenty of strength but her arm didn't know that.

The rope snapped taut, jumped right out of the water and tears sprang to Carly's eyes. So scared. So scared. *Barracuda Banks?* That bastard was trolling her like a scrap of bait. The sky reeled overhead and the line bit into the water. She dragged herself up the line, hand over hand, and it was harder than you might think. The boat was going at a fairly good clip and she had to drag her entire body weight forward each time she took a new hitch. The water smacked her and when she saw a wave coming she closed her eyes and held her breath. The red-and-green stern of the boat seemed like everything Carly ever wanted: every drug, every father, mommy, every love rolled into one.

Bamboo Cannon. She rested in the shelter of the stern. "Help," she cried. At first she said "help" in a conversational tone, maintaining dignity, but on the fourth repetition she got into the terrified spirit of the thing.

On the short line, the wake kicked her about and she was swallowing water but nobody came.

Like always, nobody came.

So poor Carly wrapped the rope around one arm and lunged up and took another bight and wrapped it again and pushed her feet against the slippery wood and walked right over the *on* in *Cannon* until she could see all the boat laid out before her, even the black man in the bow where he was attaching a new sail to the forward mast. Carly dragged herself from the acute angle and stepped right onto the cockpit cushion and down to the deckboards like it was something she did every day.

The black man hoisted the sail. It was much narrower than the sail it had replaced. He was, damn him, whistling. Carly wished she had a gun.

Her fingers picked at the knot, picked at it, and the damn thing was so tight she broke a fingernail before she got one loop loose. Water streamed from her hair down her bare back as she marched forward. Her jaw was set like the prow of an ice-breaker. He bent to cleat a rope.

"We pick up speed without you draggin' behind," he said.

"Bastard," she said. But suddenly her fists loosened and a great breath of air came into her and, quick as it had come, her hatred drained out of her. She shivered. Her legs felt weak.

He nodded (agreeing that he *was* a bastard?). "I think it gonna be goddamn bad. You go below and eat and when you wash up, spare the water. I didn't provision for passengers this voyage."

Even as Carly said, "I'm not hungry," she realized it wasn't true, that she was starving, had never been more ravenous in her life. As she made her way aft, she held her head high and her legs didn't tremble, not once. Carly wasn't easy.

She took her fork directly to the frying pan and the green-and-red mess tasted wonderful, like she was ingesting warm life itself.

After her belly was full, Carly toweled herself dry and got back into her blouse and jeans. She washed out her undies and clamped them in a cabinet drawer to dry. She collected towels and clamped them too. She scrubbed out her fork and frying pan and upended them in the plastic dishrack.

Each time the boat heeled, Carly grabbed the sink lip. One of the cabinet doors started to flap and she couldn't fasten it because somebody had destroyed the latch with a hammer or something.

Maybe this was a stolen boat. Maybe that's why the black man wouldn't turn around.

The bow boomed and dug into a wave and shook itself and Carly banged her elbow against the chart table. Where's the seat-belt when you finally need one?

Back topside, her heart paused a beat. Off to the east, not far, she saw a gray wall of clouds, floor to ceiling, unbroken. To the west was overcast sun, not very much light, just enough to see. The clouds rolling toward them promised the dark smothering of a dark blanket. The seas were higher and whiter and there was spray in the air; her face dampened right away. He sat halfcocked at the tiller.

"Good," he said, like he was waiting for her. "Take the helm. You got to steer 100 degrees."

"I thought it was 110."

"Wind's up, darlin'."

She knew he didn't mean anything by it. It was just a word. The helmsman's position seemed exposed to her, too near the wild water and, once, the stern dropped into a trough formed by two crossing waves and spray splattered into the cockpit and over Carly's hair. She didn't turn loose of the tiller though.

He hurried up the ladder with a couple bright orange vests. "Here."

She buckled the lifejacket on as tight as the buckles allowed. It was awful bulky but warm. With a short line, he snubbed her to the binnacle.

"You like black leather boots too?" Carly asked. At his look, she added hastily, "Just joking."

"Keep your course," he said.

"Get out of my light," she said.

The boat was tighter in her hands than it had been before. Probably they were going faster.

Rows of canvas ribbons dangled across the sail. He lowered the sail a bit and tied the unused part against the boom. The sail he created was smaller and, Carly thought, funny looking. They'd lost half their sail area in the last hour. That thought didn't do to dwell on so Carly rested her eyes in the west where the sun was a pale coin settling into the rumpled sea.

The black man retied a knot and eyed the remaining sail, dubiously.

"Watch your heading," he shouted.

"Sorry," and Carly brought the bow back.

With the tip of her tongue protruding through set lips, fully attentive, she kept the compass heading within three degrees.

The black man removed vent caps from their housings and carried them below. Somewhere he found hammer and nails and some plywood scraps and Carly didn't watch as he tacked those makeshift covers over the vent openings because she didn't feel it was right to drive common stupid nails into the skin of her boat. She felt every blow.

The midships hatch dropped and was dogged shut. Next he placed a high board in a slot in the companionway. The wall of clouds was fifty feet away and closing. The air went dead and cold.

"I've got the helm," he said. "Hang on."

As the cloud wall hit them, the *Bamboo Cannon* heeled over. The sea rushed past, swift and awful.

When the boat shook back to level, the sun had disappeared and they were inside an opaque wet mess of wind and water. Everywhere inside that cloud waves were breaking. Because of the whitecaps it was hard to tell one wave from another.

The boat surged forward like it was happy to be in this wild water, and the bow slapped and the spray flew the length of the boat and Carly squeezed her eyes.

It was dim light inside that cloud, and night couldn't be far off.

"Take the helm," and surprised, she did. Though the waves rolled the boat from one rail to the other, she wasn't hard to steer. Carly brushed her wet hair out of her eyes.

Hand over hand, the black man followed the safety rail, checking and pulling at it. Carly saw a nasty wave coming and, instinctively, she steered away from it and it broke over the bow rail and it should have been funny; a stooped man hanging on grimly with both hands as the heavy water sluiced off him; it should have been funny.

Carly said, "I'm sorry," but he probably didn't hear her.

He went into a locker for a line he snubbed around cleats to make a rope X across the cockpit. Then, with a pocketknife, he cut a piece off the bitter end, fashioned a lifeline for himself. He touched the tiller, like a doctor takes a pulse. The sinews stood out in the backs of his hands.

The boat hissed and grumbled and squeaked through the waves. The telltales were flat and stiff.

"Too quick for this old bird." Again he jumped to his feet and this time he lowered the mainsail completely and lashed it to the boom. He swung the boom amidships and cleated it fast. Now the only canvas was the tiny storm sail on the jib. The boat stopped its trembling.

He said, "Be glad she dirty. *Bamboo Cannon* fouled with barnacles. Make her slow."

Carly nodded.

He retrieved the sails he'd lashed to the bow rail and stowed them below. Finally he took the tiller. He didn't do much different that Carly could see but their ride smoothed.

"Got to strike them wave trains properly," he said.

"It's getting dark."

"Oh yes, going to be wild night tonight." He seemed pleased about it.

It got dark. The wind was howling and spray lashed from every side. Carly pointed at a huge wave off their port bow and he nodded and the boat slid up the face of it, like climbing a great sand dune and down the other side—with a lurch that slammed Carly's stomach against her rib cage.

It got dark, but never so dark Carly couldn't see the whitecaps outlining the waves—longer waves, and taller. Sometimes one end of the boat, stern or bow, came free of the water. When the bow fell it was like a child patting a flat palm into a puddle. The wind was too loud for speech, but that didn't matter. Side by side, separated only by the tiller, they didn't need to say anything. Carly would spot a bad wave and point. Most times he'd keep his course and the wave would crest astern or they'd slide softly up the backside before it broke. Sometimes he adjusted the tiller in response to her warning and when Carly's wave slipped past with no worse than a dip and shake, she felt proud.

Once a wave crested beneath the stern and it felt to Carly like some great hand held them, ready to hurl, but the hand relaxed, the stern settled with a lurch and the danger passed as spray.

Carly wondered what time it was.

They met one wave after another, the storm staysail rock hard in the wind. So this was what it was like. Carly yawned, but her yawn turned into uncontrollable shivering.

"Go below." His shout was faint as words spoken at the far end of a wind tunnel.

"Here. I stay here."

Maybe he didn't hear. He gestured peremptorily at the hatch.

Carly's pride was overwhelmed by a picture of how snug it must be below, how homey.

She picked at the knot that attached her to the binnacle but her fingers were too cold. Black fingertips flitted at her and she was free. She clenched one of the ropes that crisscrossed the cockpit. He nodded like—now you're catching on—but Carly was too cold to care. He scanned a quick 360 and his head jerked, *Go*, and she never released one rope until she had a grip on the next, scuttling crabwise to the companionway.

Lifted one slick leg onto the ladder, in a square wooden tube, enclosed on all sides. Spray slashed at her cheeks and hair.

He kept one leg cocked, one hand on the tiller, black as a wet basalt statue. Every ten seconds or so, he swiveled his eyes to spy rogue waves astern and muscles roped his back. With his free hand he made motions meaning, "Go below" and "Close the hatch."

The ladder rungs were wet and the hatch slot was swollen but Carly jammed her shoulders against the back of the wooden tube, ducked, and chunked it home.

It was like stepping into the belly of Jonah's whale. Faint light from the portholes. Because of the rolling, Carly clung for dear life.

No wind, no waves, no spray. Just groans from aggravated timbers, the "wheek" of rubbing fittings, thuds, crashes, and sighs.

At the foot of the ladder she groped for a handhold, but it wasn't too bad. It wasn't too bad.

She groped until she had a grip on the sink, turned loose of the ladder and was promptly pitched into the sink as the boat heeled to starboard. Her hand patted the bulkhead until she found the fluted plastic fitting, located the push switch at the base of the light. Ahh.

Floor and walls tilted this way and that. Carly rushed across the boat and tucked herself into the settee behind the chart table.

Wrecked cabinet doors banged and banged. The shadow of the stove lengthened and shrank with each roll. Dishes from the evening meal were on the floor, dishrack too. The teakettle and a box of tea bags lay against the far bunk, leaking tea water and package dye.

Planning every dash, Carly lunged around the cabin gathering utensils. She found Winston's hammer and crumpled bag of nails.

She shut the locker on the dishes and, on hands and knees, she toenailed nails into the broken doors so they'd stay shut. She ripped her thumb, bent two nails for each one she set, and once, when the boat whipsawed, she rolled and smacked her head. This boat has changed from one thing into another, she thought. After she put the hammer and nails away she felt rather pleased with herself.

The stove shadow swayed. Sometimes it was a blunt arrow tilting up the bulkhead, sometimes it lunged across the room at her but always drew up short.

Her body was dead weary, but her mind was flitting along, keen as a warbler. She'd make tea. No sense wasting good tea bags.

One hand clamped to the sink, she filled the kettle.

It was child's play to keep the kettle under the spout when the boat was heeled to starboard, much harder when it came to port. She didn't want to waste water but didn't have an extra hand to turn the petcock on and off.

Once the kettle was heavy she set it on the stove, back burner. On the gimbaled stove it was safe as an airplane on an aircraft carrier. It rode level.

Carly hooked her little finger around the stove rail to keep her match steady. It glowed blue-white with ordinary efficiency but Carly was proud of her century.

The boat tipped and she jammed one hand against the stove and defeated the gimbals and the teakettle slid against the back-stop as Carly gripped for dear life. When the floor was level, she snatched the kettle into place and let the next roll retire her to the settee.

It was unusual for Carly to sit still, which she did for fifteen minutes until steam appeared at the spout of the kettle. Steam: "Now what?"

Make the tea. Find a container.

Sure. She lurched to the sink and with the help of her death grip, dropped four tea bags into the kettle and cut the gas. The boat went briefly crazy, diving, thundering, shaking, and bobbing, while Carly held on with both hands. She opened the cup locker but the crockery started to tumble and she closed it fast. Another locker held fishing gear, net, fishing rods, and spare coils of line. The next locker had a fire extinguisher and books packed solid: *On the Road, Trout Fishing in America, The Electric Kool-Aid Acid Test, Caleb Who Is Hotter than a $2 Pistol, Sometimes a Great Notion.* Funny stuff, Carly thought, for a black man to read. Made her smile. Maybe when this was over, Rastus might play her some old Janis Joplin tapes. In the next locker beside a flashlight, hatchet, toolbox, boat paints, and caulks, she found a steel Thermos.

Handhold over handhold she returned to the stove.

"It's all relative," she said. The boat never stopped rolling. If it wasn't heeling to starboard it was heeling to port, yawing and pitching. Usually these motions flowed one into another, recombining constantly. She waited until the boat surged (climbing a wave) before she let go of her handholds, snatched up the hot teakettle, extracted her Thermos—it had been clamped in her armpit—and poured a thin stream of tea. When the boat stopped rising, she set the kettle down and clung with one hand.

It took five tries and twenty minutes before she had the Thermos mostly full but she didn't pour scalding water on her hand, not once. Screwed the cap on, tucked it under her arm, and hung on.

She remembered the bottle of rum.

Did she have to?

No, Carly, you can do a half-assed job, it won't make any difference. When did *you* ever make a difference?

Carly tucked the rum bottle under her chin. The rum was easier to pour into the Thermos than hot water had been.

The kettle swayed wildly on the stove and the stove was at the limit of its gimbals, clanking against the bulkhead. Its shadow darted here and there like a frightened bat.

Nothing she could do about it. Her mind was wonderfully concentrated. She abandoned that kettle, knifed her fingers through the Thermos strap and gripped the ladder. When she was high enough, she braced her shoulders against the back of the wooden tube and tugged until the hatchway slid back.

Carly raised her head into black madness. Sheets of spray, like gauze curtains, sluiced across the stern. On all sides, waves towered higher than her head. She had to lift her eyes to their long, rolling crests. The *Bamboo Cannon* skidded through a heaving plain.

If, when it slept, the desert had nightmares, this would be one.

Foam blew streaks across the face of the ocean, like the waves were carbonated, charged with air.

The black man sat where he'd sat, the sea streaming off his rock arms, his stone shoulders, his hard black neck and head.

He lifted a thumb and jabbed, meaning, "Stay below."

She held up the Thermos, meaning, "Something hot to drink?"

He leaned forward, puzzled, "Who, you?"

A wave smacked amidships and kicked tons of water in the air, which had to land somewhere. For a second, it was like Carly was underwater, like a fire hose was driving her below. When her knees buckled she hooked herself on the hatchway with her elbows. So, this is what it's like.

He was motioning at her, meaning, "Close the hatch," and she took a deep breath and jerked the hatch closed and hand over hand, rope to rope, crossed the long distance that separated them. She looped the safety line around her waist and once again his fingers flew at her like he was a steamstress sewing her in place. Carly clamped the Thermos between her knees.

A wave thundered behind, gurgled under the stern, and the boat hung like a reluctant surfboard before letting the ride go without it.

When he drank, his eyes found hers, and his mouth flashed a grin of appreciation.

They shared that Thermos all the long night, and once it was empty Carly kept it between her knees.

The waves came, the spray, the wind. Carly twisted her head into her shoulder to breathe. There was always a foot of water in the self-bailing cockpit, never less. Her white, pale toes were down there somewhere.

The stormsail exploded like a rifle shot. It became a fringe of canvas tatters.

Sometime later, the helmsman miscalculated and as the boat slid off one wave, it dug its nose deep into another and Carly felt the stern lifting, lifting, until looking down at the bow was like looking down a wall. The bow emerged from that wave, straining with effort, like a tired prizefighter getting off the canvas, and Carly waited for the boat to snap in the middle, but it didn't. Three feet of water smashed her and when it passed she was dangling over the transom.

Sheet lightning. It was impossible to tell how far away the lightning was. Bright glows and dim glows, like they were sailing through a great naval battle, rival fleets destroying each other on either side.

The black man wasn't steering 110 degrees. He was steering the waves, keeping the worst of them on his stern quarter. He let all the surfer waves slip past. Foam flew and the water in the cockpit rose above Carly's shins. When her bladder hurt, she relaxed and her own waters joined the others.

The sea was white and luminescent. It shook.

It was getting light, near dawn, when the rogue wave hit them.

Hundreds of yards long, towering above the others, like a mother wave gathering her children—the *Bamboo Cannon* slid up her face, through hissing water, and broke through the crest. Tons of water smashed down, and when Carly opened her eyes, the dinghy was gone.

That great wave was the hurricane's last effort and, in the very next moment, they sailed into paradise.

The wind died, dead. They emerged from a steep wall of black clouds into the blueness of God. Far above them, impossibly far, like the small end of a telescope was a pure circle of darkest blue.

Carly's ears rang. The black man used his left hand to pry stiffened fingers off the tiller and, loose jointed as a puppet, he wobbled to his feet.

"Lucky," he said. His voice was rusty. As water burbled out of the cockpit Carly's wrinkled toes emerged. Her head felt light—flimsy as a balloon.

"Oh," she said. "This is what it's like."

"Yes, darlin'. This the eye of the hurricane."

Driftwood, white and brown, bobbled in the waves. Uprooted trees floated by. A brown seabird thunked onto the cabin roof where the dinghy had been. Wearily it tucked its wings and preened.

"Steer 245," he said.

"245?"

"We been pushed and we been shoved and we driftin' onto Saba Bank and we need sea room."

"Could you take this Thermos downstairs . . . below?"

He took the bottle like it was a practical joke, a fake that might blow up in his face. "You hang on to this thing through that?"

"We might need it again."

He laughed, deep and hearty, and the seabird fluttered in protest.

"Don't hit no tree or nothing," he said. "Don't you go punching holes in our boat."

Without wind, the *Bamboo Cannon* drifted in the current and answered her helm sluggishly. Despite Carly's best efforts, the compass needle swung thirty degrees to either side.

The black man returned with a sandwich in each hand. "Very messy down there," he said. "You one hell of a housekeeper."

And Carly laughed too, and the laughter freed her from the exhaustion that had chained her body. She bit into her sandwich, which was a chunk of Spam between slices of stale French bread.

Everything in that sandwich had been alive at one time, as Carly was—her living teeth and strong jaw and the faint rumble deep behind her tonsils might have been a growl.

"Shoal water over Saba Bank," he said. "If we get driven onto Saba, we break up."

Somewhere the sun was rising over the lip of the earth, tinting the air.

"You come below and bail. We not out of this thing yet."

"Sure." When she called on her knees to straighten, they said, "Who me?" and bounced with pain as the blood returned. She grabbed a halyard and wiped salt-hardened hair out of her eyes. She stared into the bright black eyes of the seabird. She said, "As one stowaway to another, this isn't exactly the QE Two." She laid the last crumb of her sandwich where the bird could reach it. The bird stuck his head under its wing so Carly ate it herself.

"Come below," he hollered.

"Good luck," Carly said solemnly to the bird, who kept its own counsel.

The ladder's last rung was underwater.

"Over here."

The black man had screwed a handle onto a pivot mechanism. "This is the bilge pump. Up and down, up and down." He demonstrated. Ka-lunk, whoosh. Carly took the handle and felt the resistance but it wasn't bad. He watched her through half a dozen strokes. With his foot he sloshed a circle near the pump base. "The intake is in the bilge and there's plenty trash floatin' around to get stuck in she screen. When she get plugged you unplug her, keep on pumping."

"How long should I pump?"

"You bilge pump quit, you use this." The yellow plastic bucket looked like a child's beach toy.

"And where do I throw the water?"

"Out the hatch."

"You've got to be kidding."

Carly pushed and pulled. The black man went topside.

On the locker doors she could see the waterline drop. Encouraged, she pumped harder. She tried to think about that seabird, how far it had flown, but her mind was too tired to keep hold of the thought.

With a thunk, the hatch closed. Ten seconds later, the boat heeled way over, and they were in trouble again.

It was like before except the water rushed back and forth, and sometimes her feet were dry and sometimes water slapped her shins. Push and drag. Hang on. Push, drag. Her arms got tired, tireder, and she pumped whenever she wasn't hanging from the pump handle like an ornament. Push and drag. The handle got harder to push and some strokes later, Carly couldn't budge it. She knelt in the water and felt for the circular intake, a two-inch pipe covered with screen. It was clotted with stuff: cigarette wrappers, filters, hair. *Stuff* and she brought up a wet fistful of it.

Abruptly the boat dove and Carly slid forward, still clenching the *stuff*. "Christ!" she howled.

For the next hours, she sloshed through that water, pumped when she had balance, cleaned that screen. Her goal: to get the water below the floor. She lowered it so she could see floor planks (even when the boat was dead level) but she never dropped it into the bilge no matter how she tried.

The boat heeled over, over, until the floor was at 45 degrees, and the crockery lockers gave way and the plates and cups, blue, green, white, rained and a pot cut Carly's knuckles as she covered her skull. She stared stupidly at her numb hand as the blood welled, formed a trickle, dropped. The boat groaned back to horizontal and some cups floated but most sank. Carly kicked or crushed them underfoot. The locker door banged open, and banged closed.

There was more water now; the floorboards were deeper under. Gray light gleamed at the portholes and the electric light shone yellow and Carly brought up another handful of *stuff* and there was broken glass in it and she cut herself again.

The blisters on her palm broke and when seawater washed them, you bet that hurt.

Pump, drag, pump, drag, and the world turned around her head but she couldn't faint, not now.

Once again the boat heeled way over and Carly gripped, fingers and thumbs, and her feet fell away and she hung directly above the starboard bulkhead. She sobbed. She fell. Beside her a porthole burst and a column of water shot upward into the cabin, like a summer fire hydrant. She touched the column of water, disbelieving.

The *Bamboo Cannon* lay on her side and did not right herself.

Banging, like a giant's fist on the cabin roof.

The companionway ladder lay sideways like a picket fence. She dragged herself into the wooden tunnel and jerked the hatch open.

So this is what it's like. Waves bigger than cruise ships rolling serenely by. Blinding lightning, the hard stink of ozone. You could drown just breathing.

Where is he? The tiller in the air like an unused broom.

Oh, he is drowned.

In crazy water behind the stern she saw something—his head, tinier than she would have imagined. She crawled into the tilted cockpit and balanced on the rail.

The mast and steel rigging lay broken in the water, banging into the boat. Oh. Carly hauled his lifeline hand over hand thinking he was probably dead and pretty soon she would be too.

A great flash of lightning. Oh. She couldn't believe it. Off to her left, not very far away, she saw a shore. Dark rocks and foamy whitecaps behind a camelback hump of water, which was great waves crashing. Hand over hand she hauled until a black arm lopped over the transom and he dragged himself aboard. His eyes were mad.

"Why you not pumping?" he cried, like it was her that had got them into this.

"The pump's on the ceiling!"

He jerked at the knot of his safety line but there was no dexterity in his fingers anymore. "You steer."

Crazy. She stared helplessly at the tiller over her head. If she jumped she could just touch it.

Broached, the *Bamboo Cannon* lay dead in the water and though the lightning threatened and wave trains followed each other like freight cars onto the rocks of Saba Bank, no rogue wave struck her as she bobbled in a tangle of her own wreckage.

Winston snatched a hatchet and without benefit of safety line danced along the starboard rail. Every time he came to a line he chopped through it.

The mast had snapped six feet above the cabin roof. The ragged end had punched a big hole in the cabin, and was rubbing another one. As Winston chopped, the mast spun like a drill bit, wrapping its lines around itself.

Dead as a rotten mattress, they weren't 500 yards from shoal water. Winston went to his knees and took that mast in his forearms. With a groan he heaved it over the side.

The cabin lifted then, and the portholes. The broken mast drifted, attached at the bow by a jib halyard.

The current was westerly.

One foot on the stanchion and the other braced against the anchor pulpit, Winston whacked at the halyard, banging through one strand after another. The halyard lay across the rail and the severing blow gashed the rail two inches deep.

Like a weary dancer asked for one more—please, one more waltz—the *Bamboo Cannon* righted herself.

That woman had the helm and when Winston pointed west by north, angling away from the banks, for a wonder she understood. He saw the helm come over.

Too late, a wave crashed onto the deck and Winston hooked both arms under the rail and concentrated himself. When he straightened, water was sluicing through the roof hole into the cabin below.

Belowdecks was not encouraging. Seawater waist high, and some damn fool had nailed the sea locker shut. Winston used his fingers as steel claws to open it. The empty sail bag floated under the surface, white as a drowned tourist. With his lanyard knife, Winston whacked squares of canvas and before the next wave struck the foundering vessel, he had canvas tacked across the ragged hole. The swell piled up on Saba Bank. Noise beat against his eardrums, hard white noise.

He kicked the porthole mostly closed and covered it with canvas.

Belowdecks was dim and filthy and the water filmed with engine oil. He hated to ask the woman here; but either they would both live or neither.

Winston took the helm, seeking every advantage of wind and current. They were doing four or five knots westerly, no farther from Saba Bank but no closer. The *Bamboo Cannon* was heavy in the water.

A bucketful of water sloshed out of the hatch. Another. The bilge pump must have quit. Winston cheated the *Bamboo Cannon* northerly as breakers tugged him toward the shoals. The lightning had stopped, the wind backed off ten or twenty knots.

Surely, this would pass.

A couple hours later, sometime after 10 A.M., Saba Bank fell behind and they eased into deep water.

Sa Bo-die, were pou-ou, lavalas pajam brotel. (What God has laid up for you, water will not carry away.) The hurricane shrank into a mere gale; twenty foot waves and puny winds of fifty miles an hour or so.

Winston dropped down below.

She didn't pay him much attention,. She bent, scooped, shifted weight to get a palm under her bucket and hurled. The water was knee deep. How many tons had she moved? She bent, scooped, set her hand, hurled.

The fumes made Winston sneeze.

While she bailed, Winston cleaned crud out of the bilge pump screen. A bent aluminum kitchen colander floated by and he pressed that over the intake as a makeshift prescreen. He bent to the pump, th-wock, ka-whosh, th-wock, ka-whosh.

Thirty minutes later, the floor was dry and the woman dropped onto the settee, her head in her blistered, bleeding hands. Soon after, the bilge pump drew air and Winston quit. He straightened and arched his back.

He'd have to jury-rig a sail. Most of their food was ruined; their cooking gear was scattered. He'd have to shoot a position.

Golden sunlight streamed down the companionway, a wash of warm sweet air. Her face was marked with blood prints where her hands had been.

"Come above," he said. "We goin' to live more days after this."

She said, "What's your name?"

"Winston," he said. After a second he added, "My mamma, she like those grand British gentlemen."

"Hello," she said, and they climbed out of that foul cabin into the light of day.

9

15° 52′ N, 61° 19′ W

The Grand Bourg light flashes twice green at 6 sec. intervals. Alt. 8M, Geographic range, 5.6 mi—Light list: Defense Mapping Agency 1964 (rev: 1973)

Winston untangled the lines and stays streaming from the broken mast while Carly mucked out below. She found four undamaged tin plates and one porcelain one. All the cups were gone except for the metal cup on the Thermos. One of the six cans she found was labeled Del Monte French-Style Green Beans, one unlabeled can—from its shape—had to be Spam, and four shiny labelless cans might be anything. The heel of bread dribbled through her hands. Three bottles of orange drink were unbroken. Already there was fresh seawater sloshing in the bilge.

Carly set cans and bottles on the wooden settee and stared at them, hoping for inspiration. She blinked. Where were the cushions? Surely this hard wooden bench would be more comfortable with cushions. She curled up behind her rescued provisions because it seemed such an easy thing to do.

With a halyard, Winston attached a spinnaker stay to the mast stub. He ran the halyard ends through a common turnbuckle and snubbed them tight. He lashed the storm jib to this makeshift mast and the *Bamboo Cannon,* which had been rolling sluggishly in the billows, came taut, shook, was alive.

The seas were still high but winds were light and easterly—the hurricane's final backspin. Current was running against them at less than a knot. Winston set the helm southeast and went for the sextant.

The woman was sleeping behind a frail palisade of tin cans and bottles. She snored—a snort and sigh. While Winston pumped she didn't stir.

It would be great good luck, Winston thought, if the scuttlebutt hadn't got seawater in it. He dipped a finger under the spigot but they hadn't been lucky. He wrapped the bottles of orange drink in a soaked towel and stuffed them overhead.

Although its mahogany case had been underwater, the sextant was undamaged. His watch was still working too. Winston took his sunsight, and set his course a few points more southerly. His dead reckoning hadn't been too far off.

He found himself staring at the compass like it just might, suddenly, flash significant messages. Wearily he shook his head. What he must do is stretch a canvas canopy over the cockpit.

Since the port rail and two of its stanchions had disappeared, Winston's canvas made quite a dramatic angle. He located a musty kapok cushion and was inordinately pleased with himself for doing so. He laid down beside the tiller on a cushion soft as eiderdown.

Five hours later, he woke hungry, took another sunsight, and brought her back up ten degrees.

One of the unlabeled cans turned out to be tomatoes. Winston forked up half the tomatoes and drank half the juice. When he set the can down his stomach complained.

The bilge water was almost at the cabin sole but pumping soon had it clean. Though the girl rolled away from the kawhooshing noise, she didn't awake. Carly who? Hollander? Like them Dutchmen on St. Maarten maybe. She looked like a child sleeping. She'd used her body hard fighting against the sea.

Luckily the chart locker had stayed dry. Winston unrolled the blue-and-green ImRay-Iolaire chart and put his finger on their position. They were making about three knots. He laid a light line on the chart. He rolled the chart, clipped it. His mind thought since he was twice the girl's weight he should eat twice as much. His will said, "Stop, thief. It's just a half can of tomatoes."

Shamed, Winston climbed into the sun and took the tiller.

The sun was far over in the western ocean when Carly came above. The dark blue sky hadn't a trace of haze, the yellow-red sun poured its benison upon the ocean road. The sea was scarcely less blue than the sky, a light chop, 2- and 3-foot waves. She walked to the bow and stood, hands on hips, looking around. She shrugged off her clothes and laid them on the foredeck. Her buttocks and thighs were raw where her salt-encrusted pants had chafed.

Light as a bird, she perched on the companionway and looked around the world. Winston felt like saying, "It's always this way after the hurricane, the storm scrubs the air," but didn't. He didn't own this beautiful world and didn't have to sell it to anybody.

Her breasts were small and high on her chest. They had the swollen look young breasts get when they first fill with milk. Her hands were drawn-up fists, cracked and raw. Her knees were scabbed and had sores. Her pubic triangle was the same light brown as her eyelashes.

"Where we going?"

"Dominica."

"When will we get there?"

"Two, three days."

She was quiet then for a long time, while the sun tiptoed into the sea, cautious as a gentlewoman in a hot bath.

"Why are we going to Dominica?"

"Man stole my airplane. I steal it back."

"Oh."

"Mal Esprit, him."

"What a funny name."

"He born as Leon Balla but he change when he become bad john."

She went for the tomatoes. Cross-legged on the coaming, she slurped them down and drank the liquid, every drop. Winston had to look away.

He said, "You can telephone your mother from Dominica. Many telephones in Dominica. Don't say nothing about me. Say you got picked up by a fishing boat, don't know who. Brown men, Spanish turtle fishers."

"Okay." She ran her finger inside the can and licked it. "You ever eat those fresh tomatoes, the first ones of the season? Stiff on the outside, not a bit squishy, but tart inside and the juice . . ."

"Stop talking that."

"We're on short rations, huh?"

"How you happen on this boat?"

The evening star was an inch and a half above the horizon. It was flanked by satellites that outgleamed it.

"I was so fucked up," she said.

Winston blinked.

"Sorry. Just a habit of speech. What time is it?"

"'Bout nine."

She counted on her fingers. "Forty-two hours."

The tiller squeaked softly in the hole. "What?"

"I haven't had any drugs in forty-two hours." She laughed. She used a voice—not her own—a gravelly man's voice, "How sweet it is," she said.

"Drugs?"

"Downs, mostly." She looked at the frail stars. "Nothing can hurt you if you're stoned. I mean, even if something did, you sure wouldn't know about it."

"Sometime I smoke some of that ganja . . ."

Scornfully, "Ganja!"

"Mal Esprit. Him and the Dreads growin' ganja in the bush. Bales and bales of ganja, they exporting."

"Dreads? Like dreadlocks? Bob Marley? Reggae?"

"Not them musical fellas, no."

After Winston pumped the bilge again, he said, "Boat sprung some planks, maybe. Tomorrow I swim around, see."

"When you heaved me overboard, you said something. What'd you say?"

Winston grinned. "You was marvelously astonished, darlin'."

"*Doubi ubi* something . . ."

He opened his hands like his missing memory might be contained there.

"I 'spose I wasn't very appealing?"

"You married?"

"No. You?"

"Soon . . ."

The wind shifted so it was blowing south to north and Winston set a course of long, slow tacks. With no boom, Winston had to relash the makeshift sail each time the *Bamboo Cannon* jibed.

The sky was ablaze and aglitter. Horizons glowed like great cities lay just beyond.

"What's she like?"

"Who?"

"Your fiancée."

"Rosemary, she good. Rosemary says two and two is four and no mistake." He chuckled.

"She pretty?"

"She most pretty, oh yes. When we walk downtown, her on my arm, all the dudes turn their heads."

"She good in bed?"

Pause. Then, too quickly, "Fine, yes, miss."

"I never liked sex very much. What's that star?"

"Next to those three little stars? That the Dog Star."

"Don't you think we should come about?"

"Keep on sailing. We jibe, little bit."

When he pumped again he thought the water was coming in faster but couldn't be sure. He unlashed the sail and they came about.

"What's Dominica like?"

A shrug. "Little island, not much."

"Isn't it part of Haiti or something?"

"No, darlin'. That the Dominican Republic. Way north." Winston pointed." Dominica all by herself. Used to be British. Independent now."

"I never heard of it."

"Nobody heard of it. Roseau, the capital. Rose's lime juice got big plantation, Dominica. Plenty mountains there."

"Why didn't you call the police?"

"For what?"

"When Mal Whosis stole your airplane."

"Law no good there, darlin'."

Next time Winston looked at his watch it was midnight, time to come about again.

She said, "I never knew it could be this light without the moon."

When he had them set on a new course they shared an orange drink precisely one swallow at a time.

She said, "This ain't exactly your Pear-i-eh."

"They bottle in Tortola. Why your mother sick?"

"Shit."

"That's extremely rude."

"Fuck you."

He tchupsed her with his lips and she knew real rudeness when she heard it.

"Mother was getting a facelift."

"Plastic surgery?"

"Yeah. Second time for her. First time, they did her snoot."

"Snoot?"

"Snout, her honker, her nose."

"They do that work, Roadtown?"

"Sandpiper Cay, that's where the clinic is."

Winston eyed her suspiciously. "You ever had one of them facial lifts?"

"Oh, Christ! I'm twenty-three. Look, my father divorced my mother twelve years ago. This bimbo from the office, his private executive secretary, got in his pants, and Daddy split. Ever since, Mama has been trying to land another one. I hate her."

"You hate your mamma?"

"Yeah."

"Why you still livin' with her?"

"You know, that's a good question." Another long pause and the prideful anger in Carly's voice dwindled. Softly, she said, "I don't know how to do anything."

"You got no education?"

"I went to Swarthmore for one year but I flunked out. Stupid place!"

"Oh yes, I see. Girls on St. Thomas with high school education they go to work in the hotels and motels. Serve the drinks or be maids."

She drawled, "That isn't exactly the kind of work I had in mind."

"Pay not so good but honest work."

"Yeah? How much?"

"Maybe three hundred dollars a week and tips."

"Terrific. I spend that much every week on drugs."

Winston found this revelation shocking. "If you not spending so much on drugs you could buy your own food and have an apartment."

"Screw that. Every month I draw from an escrow account at Wells Fargo Bank, San Mateo branch. It was in the separation agreement."

"They payin' you to be her daughter?"

"Why don't you steer for a while? My butt is getting sore."

She leaned against the cabin, arms crossed. "What chance we get rescued?"

"We far out of the sea lanes. Nobody come here but fishermen to fish Gibbs Seamount. Fishermen be in home port now, lickin' they wounds."

"You sound cheerful about it."

He shrugged.

"If we got picked up by a freighter, I could radio my mother and let her know I'm safe."

"I put you off in Dominica. That soon enough."

"And who are you to say?"

After they changed tack, Winston pumped again. The water was coming in steadily, but nothing the pump couldn't handle.

"Mal Esprit one of the worst fellows in Antilles. Mal my friend when we was boys, but we enemies now. Mal Esprit went away to school and learned about that Rastafarianism, from them Jamaican hairy men and Mal brought it back to Dominica. Rastas, they want to keep their body clean and eat clean food they grow themselves and they don't want nobody too near when they grow ganja and smoke it. So they take up land back in the bush and grow vegetables and ganja and nobody bother with them. Plenty bush on Dominica and nobody live back there since the Maroons."

"Maroons?"

"Oh, they escaped slaves, darlin'. In the olden times. Nobody live in the bush in modern times. Too steep to grow nothin', no donkey roads or footpaths even. Sometimes the Rastas come to the market in Roseau to sell produce, but not many people buy from them because nobody like their looks."

"But it's wrong to judge a man like that!"

"Maybe. Some of them Rastas get to be Dreads. Dreads are

convicts and bad johns from all the island come to Dominica, help Mal Esprit, they grow their hair funny and don't take no bath and murder people. Other Rastas not too bad but the Dreads . . ."

"Can't you ask the Dominican police to get your plane back?"

"Darlin', Mal Esprit *is* the police."

"You didn't have insurance?"

"No insurance, no. Why don't you stop vexing me, woman?"

"I got no downs. I got to do something with my mouth." She grinned. "You and this Mal Esprit used to be tight?"

Stars rolled lazily overhead, the makeshift sail strained against its cordage, the *Bamboo Cannon* splashed eastward.

"I know Mal when he was Leon Balla," Winston said. "Oh my, yes."

Winston rarely thought about events before he and Rosemary got together. For Winston, life began in the hospital bed when he first looked up and saw Rosemary's quiet face. Why now? Why was the past floating up in his mind, like an unwelcome mystery?

The day he and Leon Balla first met, they were playing at cricket—not enough boys for a real game, just a few of them fooling around after school.

There was Michael Lockridge and Lenox Beattie and Jack Lewis. Jean Hubbell held the bat, the handle wrapped with black tape and the paddle painted with three dramatic V's—red, green, and black, the colors of the West Indian cricket. Winston couldn't remember how he must have looked. Surely he was wearing shorts like the others—clean khaki shorts and tennis shoes, ragged shoes perhaps. How can you see into the past if you can't even see what you were wearing?

The new boy had his hands in his pockets. His eyes kept to a point some distance above their heads. Perhaps if they were suddenly to grow taller, he would notice them.

Jean Hubbell, a white boy, was their captain. Jean's father was a cousin to the Hubbells of Bedminister Estate and Morne Patates. Already the Hubbells were bottling the fruit juice and hot sauces that were to prove such a good business for them in later years.

"What you lookin' at so?" Jean demanded.

The stranger said, "I lookin' at you, what you think?"

"You got a name?"

The boy smiled, as if Jean's question was so foolish. His shorts were green linen dress-up pants, cut off at the thigh. His yellow shirt was clean but three sizes too big.

Most boys' fathers were estate workers, though Jack Lewis's was overseer at Gran Coulibre Estate—the dairy—and Winston's mother was housekeeper for Father Lamertine in Soufriere. Michael Lockridge's family were fishermen.

The boys shared the usual anxieties of their age. Some already had sparse pubic hair, others not. Voices cracked or did not. Most touched themselves at night and wondered why nobody had told them about the shameful flooding pleasure that came then.

Their village, Soufriere, rose from the narrow crescent of its deep bay to brutally steep mountains immediately behind. Estates—200- and 300-hundred-acre farms—nourished it. The school grounds had been donated by Soufriere Estate and behind the batter's crease, lime trees grew and tethered cattle grazed. The narrow track that fronted the school continued into the highlands: Palmiste Estate, Gran and Petit Coulibre, Morne Rouge. In the morning their fathers would leave the boys at school on their way to work—gangs of joking, gossiping men, how the boys envied them!

Jean Hubbell's face was free of blemishes that troubled most of his friends. Jean had the reasonable manner of someone who knows others will come around to his point of view, given sufficient time. Jean's father was active in the Dominican United People's Party. "You that Roseau boy?"

"Who askin' me?"

Everybody knew about them already. They'd arrived on the Geest boat, mother and boy ferried ashore with twenty new grapefruit seedlings from the Botanical Station and three young Barbados Blackbelly sheep, flour for Michele's bakery, Soylo's books, tinned goods, and powdered milk for Jacques Whitsun's store.

The boys would dearly have loved to watch the newcomers' arrival but were trapped in school. Whatever you might say about Maurice Soylo, however you joked about his thick spectacles, he never missed a truant no matter how sly.

By nightfall, the woman and her son were settled in Whitsun's cocoa-drying shed, below the Scotts Head road. When men asked Whitsun about her, he laughed. "She my 'outside wife,'" he said, with a shrug that dismissed her past, family, birthplace, everything about her. She didn't come out of the shed often. Every third day she hung her laundry up: dress, underthings, boy's shorts, and yellow shirt. On these days Leon didn't come out of the shack.

Her name was Veronica. Someone got the idea she had come from Venezuela and soon everybody had that idea. She went about her business with head lowered and though she would exchange greetings, more complex communication seemed too much for her. "Why you askin'? What you lookin' at? Who asked you to stare?"

Father Lamertine paid his call and came away shaking his head. Mr. MacIntosh of the Methodist church in Scotts Head visited but fared no better. She was like that snake they got in Martinique, the fer-de-lance. Better not step too near.

Soufriere is near the southern tip of Dominica. The island is so narrow here the boys could walk across to the Atlantic (the windward) side in an afternoon and sometimes they climbed down the steep cliffs that guarded the cold beaches below.

Soufriere Bay was too deep for good anchorage. Portsmouth, in the far north, had a fine harbor and since the seventeenth century warships of all nations anchored there because of plentiful water and shelter from gales. Portsmouth is where Winston had been born. Montgomery too.

Although it wasn't ten miles from Soufriere to the capital, Roseau, it was bad traveling. The track hugged sea cliffs and hurried across the beaches, but sometimes landslides plucked it from the cliffs and sometimes the seas removed the beaches. In those days Soufriere was most reliably served by the Geest boats that came for bananas. Bananas that would travel across the Atlantic to the tables of London. Mr. Maurice Soylo had studied in London. London! Mr. Soylo would tilt his head back and close his dim eyes as he spoke of that so great city.

Winston had never even been to Roseau. He had an idea of it though: cricket games and cockfights every day (except Sunday) and hundreds of technical manuals in the Carnegie library Mr. Soylo had told them about. Winston envisioned that library bulging with manuals for the Aga Cooker (all models), the Norge kerosene freezer, the Cummings diesel electric generator (10 hp), the Fordson hammer mill, and many more.

Dominicans treasured the manuals they had but it sometimes happened that rats ate the bindings, or hurricanes removed a roof and rain poured in, or a machine changed ownership while its manual did not.

Winston had never seen a library but he dearly wished to. With a library, he thought, a man could fix anything!

The schoolhouse at Soufriere was a low stucco one-room building with deep, shaded verandas. In fine weather, Mr. Soylo would take the older boys outside for school under the banyan tree.

Under that same tree, Leon Balla first met the boys of Soufriere.

"You from the capital, I am told," Jean Hubbell persisted. The bat spun on the toe of his sneakers. An irritated spin.

"Roseau? Oh yeah, I been hearin' about that place. Bad johns on the streets there."

"I do hope you are not among their number. It is peaceful and quite pleasant here." Again the bat spun.

The tall, skinny, extremely black boy took a step toward the stocky batsman. His laugh was sharp, brief, and quite unpleasant.

"Now look here . . ." Jean said. His bat was still.

Winston came right over then and said, "Hello, my name is Winston Riviere. Good-afternoon. This is Soufriere that you have come to and we are welcoming you. Magnanimously. You be comin' to the school?"

Because of its ironical edge the boy's grin was no more pleasant than his laugh had been. "I take all the school that is free to me," he said.

Winston had interposed himself, pushing Jean Hubbell aside, and such was that young man's surprise he let Winston get away with it.

"Well," Jean said, rather at a loss, "I believe we have four outs remaining," and marched stiffly back to the wicket. The other boys—save Winston—followed. The game resumed with occasional sideways looks at the pair under the tree.

"I seen Greyson Shillingford in Roseau," Leon said. "Augustus Gregoria too. Great cricketers."

"I can fix what don't run," Winston said.

When the new boy took his right hand out of his pocket he had a length of steel—an automobile wrist pin—wrapped in a grubby rag.

"That boy's bat—if it jump up, he be sad and sorry," Leon said.

Winston was stunned. He didn't plan to switch sides or oppose the other boys, the words just came to him because he was stunned and had nothing else to say: *"Bato gomie pase me vid"* (even a poor weapon is better than bare hands).

And the new boy smiled a bright smile so fine and full of life it was almost more welcome then Winston could stand.

Twenty years later, he still remembered what he'd said, remembered Leon's complicitous smile. Perhaps we are never innocent. Perhaps the young only lack power to do the evil in their hearts.

Winston stretched his neck and eyeballed the misshapen stubby mast. Doing okay. He switched buttocks on the hard wooden seat. Steady at south-southeast, talking to a girl he'd just met, talking about things he'd never mentioned to Rosemary.

"Me and Leon got to be closer than brothers. Little Montgomery tried to tag after me, like young brothers do, but me and Leon'd give him the slip and laugh when he went home cryin' tears in his eyes. Leon was so free. His mamma was a great bitch and all the people knew it. Her mouth was worse than blows. Leon used to stay away from home, sleep under the overturned fishing boats or on the school veranda. Me, I was not so free. Every morning my mamma fed me food and at night I sleep in the bed with Montgomery. The storekeeper, Mr. Whitsun, wearied of Leon's mother and she walked up to Gran Coulibre and got job there, maid. Pretty soon, her and the overseer were together. Leon moved back into that cocoa shed and I guess Whitsun felt sad for him because he never asked him to leave. Dominica a lush land and there bananas and grapefruits and village gardens in the bush. Leon went out with the fishermen some days and they paid him a little. Hard to get rich in Dominica, hard to starve."

"How about the other boys?"

"First they laugh at him and snub him. But soon enough, they get curious and before long, everybody want to be Leon's friend. He funny, you see, tell a joke or quip and soon the whole village saying it. He gave people names, "Sensay," that the old masquerade costume with cow horns, he called Maxwell Cooper Sensay because his wife was goin' around with other men. "Dog ears," that's what he named the priest because his ears were pointy, and got so I couldn't see Father Lamertine's face without the name coming to me. Might be that's why all the boys laughed with Leon; they afraid to get a name."

The Soufriere Roman Catholic church was square-cut stone, and the rectory was stone too. On slow, sunny afternoons Winston would sit inside doing homework, scents and sunlight streaming through the windows and boys' calls and street cries . . . Winston wasn't a talented scholar but he was dogged. Montgomery never had to work at school, him and Leon Balla were the same in that respect, they could play while others stayed inside on fine days, flogging their brains.

"That priest was my mother's uncle, hired my mamma when my father sailed away and didn't come back. When the allotment stopped coming, Father Lamertine wrote the United States navy and got it started again. I don't remember nothing about him. When I was in the army, outside of Munich in 1969, I met a navy petty officer said he'd known my father. A chief messman he was."

"You go to Vietnam?"

"They trained me to fly helicopters but when they found out I born in Dominica I couldn't get me a security clearance."

"You're a U.S. citizen?"

"Oh yes, ma'am. My father married my mother, legal. That was me. Visited Dominica again two years later, that was Montgomery. Leon mother, she never bothered to marry. 'Outside wife,' one man after another. Maybe she was a whore in Roseau, like they say. She could curse, yes, my. You got a lady-mouth on you compared to Leon's mother."

"Thanks a lot."

"Leon glad when his mother gone to Gran Coulibre. She why we out in the boat that day they try to land the bull at Soufriere." Winston laughed. "My, oh my."

They watched the stars. They listened to the lap of the waves, the flutter of the sail, the faint swish of the boat through the water.

"Leon used to go out with the fisherman, some days, and Jimmy Lockridge, the old man, gave Leon a Carib sailing canoe, he didn't have no more use for. There ain't much freeboard on those canoes but in old days them Caribs sailed all over the ocean conquerin' people and eatin' them. Ain't many Caribs left since the white man came. The mast step so worn on that boat we had to jam wooden chocks in the hole so she'd stay right, chocks thick as the sole of your shoe. So many rudder tholes drilled in her transom it looked like a honeycomb. We painted it the brightest purple you ever saw.

"One Saturday they was going to lighter in a bull for Gran Coulibre, for the dairy, you know, and we went out in the canoe to watch. Leon afraid his mother would come to town with the overseer, do her shopping, give Leon some licks. So we was out plenty early that morning when the packet boat came into Soufriere Bay. There ain't hardly no bottom in Soufriere for anchorin'. The crash boat goes out to meet her, Jimmy Hynan showin' off, like always, and the overseer from Gran Coulibre aboard.

"The bull calling and shouting but we can't see him from our canoe, there's so many people surrounding him on the packet boat foredeck, we just see the people, can't see the bull at all.

"All the village on the beach, gonna catch the bull when he come ashore. Me and Leon the only boat out, except the crash boat, and we ain't got no mast up, we just paddlin' around. Sea calm. No swell.

"The bull he get vex when they sling him and lower him over the side. Bull brown and white but most parts brown and he got all his feet hangin' out of that sling and, oh, he cursin' and mooing all the time.

"Five hundred pounds, that bull cost Gran Coulibre. The overseer and Miss Napier, shouting and crying their directions, 'lower him here, lower him there, don't hurt him,' oh my.

"The crash boat, plan to herd him onto shore like Roy Rogers and his cowboy horse. But the same as the bull hit the water, crash boat motor die. Vapor lock completely. The bull gonna drown if they don't loose the sling, so they loose it and he start to swimmin'. Bull see that beach and all them people and it decide 'the Hell.' It turn and gonna swim out to sea.

"Everybody on shore running to and fro and they yelling on the crash boat but ain't nobody can do a thing, except me and Leon. We the only ones can keep that bull from swimmin' to South America, where they be greatly surprised to see him.

"Well we paddle to that bull and we splash our paddles in the water before his face but he snort and keep coming. Head out of the water pretty good and he eyes bugging out—Leon strike him on the face with his paddle, and we splash water smack, smack, for to scare him away. He close his eyes, treadin' water, thinkin' it over, and then he open his bulgy eyes again and proceed. Leon smack bull's head and me, I smack too, and he put his chin on the gunwhale of our canoe and his head heavy as lead shot and the canoe roll. Our purple canoe stove in and go to the bottom and never no good no more. Leon Balla laugh like crazy and he climb onto that bull's back and twist his ear until that beast swimming for shore. I grab onto he tail and I am towed like a fruit barge through the water and Leon laughing and yelling and the villagers on the beach cheering because we have saved the 500-pound bull from drowning. That was the best day me and Leon ever had."

There were bad days too. Some small item would come up missing in the village—a kerosene lantern, a mattock, the new propeller for the crash boat's Evinrude—and everybody would look at Leon. After a while, the villagers started looking funny at Winston too.

On September 5, in the morning early, the fifth form boys from Soufriere gathered at the school where the priest blessed them and the schoolmaster gave each a handshake and wished them good luck.

For most of the boys, this was pure lark. Most boys would go to work on the estates or the fishing boats before they even got their results back from Oxford, England, where the examiners graded —as the schoolmaster reminded them—papers from all the British Caribbean and India, and the Falklands, everywhere. "Think of it, boys. In all the world today, boys will be sitting for the same comprehensive examination. And there will be scholarships for some. Oh, yes."

The boys smirked. Leon Balla elbowed Winston like this was a joke. Winston didn't think so. He had studied hard for this moment, long hours of jamming facts and dates through resistant brain tissue. Leon didn't have to study. Although Winston was Leon's equal in mathematics and bested him in science, Leon always took the literature prize (a certificate and book personally selected by the schoolmaster). One year Leon was awarded *Turn Again Tiger* by Sam Selvon and the next year, *Miguel Street* by V. S. Naipul. Leon Balla was the only student who could argue the pluses and minuses of West Indian Federation with the schoolmaster (Jamaica had just pulled out and the Federation's future was moot). Sometimes in the late afternoon, all the teaching under the banyan tree was the dialogue between the two of them, the passionate dogmatic schoolteacher and the brilliant, sardonic boy.

Although the schoolmaster used to tutor Winston extra hours after school, he never offered to do the same with Leon.

Winston was no great reader. Impatient with fiction, indifferent to history—even West Indian history—he loved science. Winston memorized the chemical tables, valances, and bondings and wondered if, one day, he might discover a new element. "Emilian," he'd name it, after his mother.

Schoolmaster Soylo was of that generation of West Indian teachers whose faith in education was strong. Education would "lift us by our bootstraps, boys." He was terribly keen on Federation. Dominica is a small island: twenty-seven miles from Scott's Head to Capuchin. "We must hang together with the other islands, don't you see? If the black races cannot learn this, it will be to our sorrow."

The schoolmaster welcomed the outpouring of new Trinidadian writers and poets, as proud of them as if they'd been his own. "That Mr. Naipul, boys, what a master of the written word. He show the black man and the white man, boys. Don't you forget it."

Few boys ever asked to borrow books he'd imported at such difficulty except for Leon Balla, who read everything.

The road from Soufriere to the capital had been recently repaired and it was hoped that by starting early the truck of Soufriere students would arrive at the examination place before noon. What with blessings and exhortations and family advice, it was eight o'clock before they finally started the climb out of the valley. The driver was cautious and approached the narrow turns like they were deadly peril. Two boys would jump out with flags to warn oncoming vehicles, although they saw none until they were halfway to the capital.

The driver had a cousin ran the bakery in Pointe Michel so there he stopped the truck in the middle of the road and jumped out for a quick gossip and a snack. The boys from Soufriere climbed down, and stood around, ogling, but local boys ogled right back and a black-and-tan dog barked.

One of the Pointe Michel boys said, "We got a telephone here in our town."

Leon Balla, who until now had taken no interest, draped himself against the tailgate and picked his teeth and said, "What's a telephone to us? Just make it easier for policeman to catch hold of you."

The driver came and abused them for getting out of the truck. "I responsible for your examination," he said, wiping crumbs from his mouth. The driver didn't stop at Loubiere, just hurried through, scattering chickens and dogs.

When they entered the outskirts of Roseau, the boys pressed close to the tailgate so they could see. Only Leon Balla stayed back in the dim interior like he didn't care. Like Soufriere, the homes were one-story wood, bright greens and pinks and blues, with shutters painted in contrasting colors. Like Soufriere, most of the paint was peeling but the boys didn't notice that.

The Roseau boys wore long pants, so the Soufriere boys felt ashamed of their short pants. The Roseau boys wore colored T-shirts. The Soufriere boys wore starched dress shirts. The Roseau boys were shoeless and the Soufriere boys wished they were.

Street boys hollered and shouted and pointed at the truckload like its cargo was stupid and peculiar. The Soufriere boys dropped their smiles and became indifferent to urban wonders.

They passed the Methodist graveyard and the brightest flamboyant tree Winston had ever seen. The cathedral was three times the size of the church in Soufriere but built of the same implacable stone. There were dogs, but no chickens in the streets. When they rumbled past the Fort Young Hotel, three white women were getting into a taxicab. The white women were dressed like women in British magazines.

The Soufriere truck pulled in at the end of a line of trucks and buses from all over the island.

"You all stay right here until they come for you," the driver said. "I responsible." Then he went off to visit a rum shop. After a bit other boys, looking defiant, disappeared too.

The examination was held in a big room at St. Mary's Academy. Nuns monitored and gave out pencils and examinations "Do not turn these over until we give the signal, please."

Winston laid his cool hand on the thick stack of stapled white paper. His fingers trembled.

Name and Post Office box, Parish, Town, Dominica, B.W.I. Winston didn't understand the first question. The question seemed like it was written in a foreign language. He felt blood rush to his forehead. He heard the scratching of pencils, the ruffle of paper. Without meaning to, his eyes strayed to the desk next to him where Leon Balla sat.

Leon was marking his answer, an X in the second box. Winston jerked his eyes back. A brush of Leon's elbow, might have been accidental but wasn't. It was an invitation. Winston's neck stiffened like wrought iron. He marked his examination, the same as Leon had.

He didn't cheat again. He didn't cheat even when he came to questions he couldn't answer.

When Leon Balla finished, he laid his cheek down on his closed examination like a sleepy child. When Winston finished, he went back over as many answers as he could.

Outside, waiting for their driver, Leon stretched and grinned at Winston like they'd thiefed something together, as indeed they had.

Months later, the results came back from England. Both Winston and Leon had passed, Leon with honors. The schoolmaster threw a fête for Winston and invited the priest and Winston's mother and Jean Hubbell's father, from Morne Patates estate. Mr. Hubbell sent congratulations and regrets. He'd just heard from his son who was doing fine at the Lodge School in Barbados, thank-you. The schoolmaster drank too many rum and jelly waters. "I am as proud of this boy," he announced, "as if he my own son. Men like Winston are men like Dominica need."

Nobody threw a party for Leon. Since he had no money, everybody expected him to give up the scholarship his high marks had won. The scholarship covered school fees but nothing for board and room. The schoolmaster, priest, and Winston's mother paid Winston's fees and found a family in Roseau who'd board him in exchange for two hours work after school and all day Saturday. Until Leon and Winston actually boarded the Jeep that would take them back to Roseau, the schoolmaster thought Leon would go to work on the fishing boats and forfeit his scholarship, but, in ill-fitting clothes that smelled of fish, Leon Balla set off on his life's adventure, same as Winston.

As Winston talked, it got light. The sun came up, pushing scattered stars from the field of blue. Winston yawned. "I go pump some more," he said. "You hungry, yes?"

"You bet. Whatever happened after you went off to school?"

"I see Leon, not so much. I mus' go pump."

There was more water in the bilge than before but the pump handled it. Light enough for him to seek the problem. Topside, he unfastened the staysail and waited until the *Bamboo Cannon* lost way before he slipped over the side.

The hurricane had stripped clots of barnacles off the hull, leaving her polished in yard-long patches but it had sprung her sheathing too, above the keel. Winston surfaced, breathed, kicked down the green-blue hull again. He'd hoped to find a hole he could patch with canvas. This long narrow separation was unpatchable. Probably happened when she broached, keel and hull pulling apart. Two cracks ran fore and aft on the portside, the length of the keel.

He came up sputtering. "She need dry dock to fix her," he called to the girl. When he clambered over the rudder, the sun struck the water streaming off him and his chest glinted golden.

He fetched cold Spam and applesauce. Not much Spam but plenty applesauce.

"We headin' south of Marie-Galante, come around to the windward side, Dominica. Nobody see us, maybe."

When Carly asked why he was being so careful, Winston told her some of the things Mal Esprit had done. "He got murderers be his friends," Winston said.

"Schoolmaster Soylo, I believe, he knew what Leon Balla would become. I couldn't see the man in the boy. He quicker in school at first, though he slowed after the first year. I was living with the Faradays, you know, and they had that Land-Rover distributorship and the Poulan chainsaws, them things. I'd man the parts counter or fix broken saws that came in and the Faradays took me to their family table and treated me like I was their own. Mr. and Mrs. Faraday, they old." He dabbed a finger at a grease spot on his plate. "Leon had his scholarship and he kept it too, though in his last years they threatened to take it from him. If they'd known what Leon doing to stay alive, they would have. St. Mary's run by Canadian priests, Christian Brothers, and they easy for Leon to fool. Leon work cockfights, taking bets, raking the sand. Girl named Flora Walcott falls in love with Leon, and she do everything Leon say. Leon live with Flora. Nobody catch Leon for no burglary, but constables catch Leon's friends breaking into the LaBelle warehouse, stealin' bonded whiskey. Leon come to school every single day but he look like hell, clothes dirty and his eyes rimmed with red and sometimes he sleeps in the classroom and the priests take cane to him for that. He don't do good in his recitations no more, just bluff his way through. He so much quicker than the rest of us he can almost do it. Outside school I didn't hardly see him no more. Once I saw him helping a drunken white man—I was coming back from my girlfriend house at three in the morning—and I see Leon steering this fat white man into the Fort Young Hotel. That a fancy hotel too. Fanciest in Dominica. Later, man complained that somebody picked his pocket but nobody proved Leon done it. Some say Leon involved smuggling liquor at Anse Du Me, but some say he never.

"In his classes, Leon falling behind. He cheating his exams. The priests never know, but he crawl through a basement window into the school at night and thief questions for the examinations."

"He must have really wanted an education."

"Oh, indeed. Yes, indeed. The good jobs on Dominica, job with the government, you need the sixth form matriculation. And in those years they start something new; they start scholarships to the University of the West Indies, in Kingston, Jamaica, you know. One scholarship for each island. Scholarships pay school fees, and the board too. Oh, that's a big prize they award."

Carly took the helm while Winston brought the boat about.

She said, "I don't think I ever wanted anything."

"Yes? I want that scholarship and I thought I have the prime chance. The Faradays are coming to depend on me for Land-Rover repairs but they let me take half Saturdays for my study. Oh, I study incessantly. That's all I remember about that year is the studying."

Carly had coasted through her year of college before she flunked out. For the first time in her life, that fact embarrassed her. She could feel the lightening in the boat whenever Winston pumped. She wished he'd been able to plug the leaks—when the *Bamboo Cannon* got heavy, the tiller felt sick and unhappy in her hands.

"What's a bamboo cannon?" she asked.

"Oh that." With a wave, Winston dismissed it. "For holidays we make bamboo section filled with kerosene and mud or a rock to cap the end. Bamboo make a frightful bang and everybody be gay. Why you never want nothing?"

She shook her head. "Where are the birds?" she asked.

"Oh, we be seein' them pretty soon now. Plenty birds on the Cabrits headland. Frigates, spoonbills, all them birds."

"So what happened at the examination?"

"Examination began at nine sharp, we break for nooner, conclude five P.M. Science, math, English, history, each subject until we wear that subject out. Twenty boys sitting. Some worried but me, I felt prepared, oh yes. I did not write a perfect examination: 'Describe the French Revolution as William Blake saw it.' My, my. But the science and the maths, they were elementary.

"The science was the final part and I first one finished. I laid down my pencil then and I got a big lump in my throat, I so happy. All the other boys' heads bent over their exams. Leon, he starin' up at the ceiling like maybe his answer gonna be written on the plaster. He look at me and I give him a fat wink. The monitor announced we finish and thanked us since we was obedient to his commands. 'Tomorrow noon,' he said, 'your papers fly on Liat Airlines from Dominica to Barbados and London, England, and then when examiners see them they gonna know how the Dominican boys are tops in the Windward Islands.' Me, I was proud of all of us. I knew them examiners be surprised and pleased to see how well we'd done. We'd all studied hard—the library crowded with scholars these final weeks and even Leon, yes, Leon, coming in to try compress four years learning into four weeks.

"The Faradays meet me outside. They wish to take me out for a night on the town. They are relieved when they see how happy I am. As I am accepting their heartfelt congratulations I see Leon on the steps, looking defeated and alone. I am sorry for him but we haven't been friends since we are boys and the Faradays don't know him. What am I to do, invite him to our fête? Why don't you fetch another bottle of orange water while I steer. We fallin' off a point."

They divided the orange water in measured sips. "We pass south of Grand Isle, the Saintes, 'bout six hours now."

"I never felt good after taking a quiz. Not once," she said. "I always felt sort of dirtied."

"Oh yes?"

"Everybody was making me do what I never wanted."

Fat clouds floated overhead. A pair of frigate birds clipped by, twenty feet above the blue eaves. At noon, Winston took a sighting and marked the chart. The current had been about a knot more favorable than he thought. When he sat down beside her again, Winston continued like he'd never been interrupted. "The Faradays they take me out to dinner. La Robe Creole is the best for fancy dining in Roseau. Right across the street from the Fort Young Hotel so they get many white tourists and them fellows spend money like water. I never eat there before tonight so it's a special treat for me. There was old Mr. Faraday and he wife, and their granddaughter, Soublette. Soublette, she just eight years old, but already turnin' men's heads, she so winning. Oh, we had a charming evening. Very charming. I eat the Mountain Chicken —that Dominican frog's legs—you know. And I have some of their red wine there, which is so good, and I feel so excited, I tell two, three jokes and everybody laughs, and I tell about the examination and have more red wine. Mr. Faraday, he too old to drink his share and Soublette drinking Coca-Colas so most of them two bottles of wine, is me drink. And I talking and telling how excited they gonna be in Soufriere when I come back from the University of the West Indies, dressed like the white administrator, British accent, because that's what they speak in Jamaica, you know. Not French Patois like Dominicans. The Faradays they smiling and nodding, but I so thrilled with my prowess I can't let them talk. Mr. Faraday's got a shipload of parts coming into Portsmouth and he worried how he gonna get it ashore from that bunch of thieves but my soon-to-be white suit seems great big to me, and his whole shipload of parts not big enough to fill one tiny pocket. We drink our coffee and Mr. Faraday asks me to taste some Cognac and I have had rum but never this, it is so smelly it makes me sneeze and they laugh and I laugh too because it seems fine to be a young man and drinking such whiskey first time.

"After dinner they say they go home now and I say not me, not yet. It just dusky, sun low in Roseau Harbor and the whole town full of smells from people cookin' their food and the charcoal smoke. The owner of La Robe Creole he come outside with us and he congratulates me on taking my examination and we all agree that education a fine thing, yes, indeed. 'Education,' he say, 'gives you wings to fly!' And that makes Mr. Faraday sad because most Dominican graduates leave the island, never come back. I promise I not be like that. I promise to come back." A gloomy look fell over Winston's face.

"Well here you are," she said.

"Oh yes," he said, but his face didn't lighten. He sighed. "That night of the examination I excited like a young boy and I walk all about Roseau, down by the post office jetty, listen to the sea slap the pilings. I walk through the market, which is empty now except for banana leaves and paper scraps blowing on the pavement. The sun sinks like a stone and all my excitement is falling away and I start to feel chills on my arms. This rum shop near, just a block from the harbor, next door to Falconer's house where they used to hold political meetings in the old days. Now I know about this rum shop and it is not a place for me to go into. But this is a night I can go anywhere and nothing can touch me. I feel strong. The rum shop?" He laughed. "There isn't anything to it. Shutters closed but electric bulb hangin' there and another bulb over the counter where the owner serves drinks. I get to talking to the owner, who didn't ever get so much education as he wanted, and I am drinking and the rum shop fills up and about midnight there is some women come in and one of them is the woman Flora that is Leon's. She sits alone, by herself. She is wearing makeup so her face is more white and her eyes are most unhappy. I think about going to her. I think of thiefing her from Leon that night."

"Leon?"

"Not until two o'clock in the morning do we see Leon. He startled to see me. He startled to see me sitting with his woman, too, but does not mention it. 'Leon, how you been, man?'

"'*Neg timalisie trop, pakon of yo neg.*' (That's the old patois for 'A man can be so smart he doesn't know the man he's talking to.')

"'Leon,' I say, 'I just sitting here havin' a fête. I glad to see you.'

"Leon get himself a glass of rum, this little"—Winston held thumb and forefinger two inches apart—"I say, 'Leon, how 'bout that exam.'

"He say how difficult exam was."

"I say I don't find it so difficult. I also say that if I'd known he had such a fancy girlfriend I would have visited him more often. I say to the girl how me and Leon grew up together. I try to say how the bull tried to climb in our canoe, but I drunk and she say to Leon she has a headache and wants to go home. He not even drink his little glass of rum. After they gone, I drink it.

"Before Leon leave, he say one thing. He say, 'You and me. Today, we be changing places.' I didn't know what that meant. I think and think about it and pretty soon nobody left in the rum shop. So the owner turns off the lights and puts me in the street."

Winston jibed again. He climbed out to the cabin roof, peering. "Plenty of boat traffic off the Saintes," he explained. "Them weekend yachtsmen from Guadeloupe come down. Got beachhouses all over them islands. You see a boat, sing out."

"Why?"

"We give them a wide berth, is why. Don't want nobody coming and giving us tow or getting friendly, no. When we land in Dominica, you make your phone call. Remember what I told you. Was Spanish picked you up."

She shrugged. "What happened after the examination?"

For a long time he didn't speak. "I go to work full time for Faradays fixing the Rovers what break down. When I get my examination results, I quit and go off island, join the United States army. My mother see me off at Melville Hall. She die when I was in Germany so that the last time I see her. Priest die too. I never see him again. I pass the exam but Leon pass very much higher and the Christian Brothers, oh they vex, but they must award Leon the scholarship. What the Christian Brothers don't know is that night, Leon break into the school and he creep into the headmaster's office and find those British exams and he take my first page with my name and exchanges it for his own first page. That's how Leon cheat me out of my scholarship. Next day police summoned because a basement window broken and the window latch too. Police ask questions but nobody speak out. Police don't care. They say it vandals done it."

She said, "And now he stole your airplane."

"That is correct, yes." He coughed. They'd be coming up on Marie-Galante after nightfall, he said, but they'd see Dominica first, because Dominica was so much bigger. "Them Dominican mountains got their head in the clouds."

When Carly went below, oily water was creeping out of the bilges. Just looking at it, her hands ached. She wrapped rags around her hands and pumped. She tried to think what would happen if they couldn't keep up with the water. They'd do something. She was very tired. Something, she thought. She lay on the hard bunk, her head resting on her shoes. When she woke, darkness filled the cabin beneath the oblong portholes and wicked water slickered across the cabin floor. Carly hated to put her feet in it.

Sluggishly, the *Bamboo Cannon* met the swell.

She said, "She needs pumping."

"Yes," he said. "I didn't want to wake you." He pointed.

"Oh," she said.

"Dominica. That is Morne au Diable. Below is Capuchin, the village there."

Silver mist belted the shore where the glossy sea met the dark mountain. Mist slithered up the corrugated flanks of the mountain and no sign of humans, no road scars, jettys, shacks, no lights of men (where *was* this Capuchin?), just green and mist, like Columbus must have first seen it.

Carly felt lonely. There's been a world longer than there's been men and this ocean had slapped the uncaring shore millennia before the first Carib fisherman set sail, before his children first made tracks in the sand. She shivered. "I don't see any village," she said.

"They not showing any lights. Electricity out, because they are striking."

"What strike?"

Winston told her about the turmoil on the island.

"Terrific," she said.

"Most nights from sea, we see many lights. Lights at Capuchin and Clifton, lights ahead at Pointe Jaquet. Most nights, this island lit up like a Christmas tree."

As the brooding mass slipped by, Carly tried to imagine it lit up and welcoming.

"There. Grand Bourg!" Winston called. Off the port bow, very faint, a pop of green light. Gone like it had never been . . . Again!

"Grand Bourg light, darlin'. On Marie-Galante."

"I don't see any island."

"Marie-Galante very flat. Next time light flashes, try count. Six seconds it flashes. Every morning the fishermen, they sail out of Grand Bourg. Windward of Marie-Galante, nothin' but ocean, all the way to Africa. Them fishermen put small boats into a very big ocean. I hear they drunk all the time."

Carly watched the flash hopefully, like if she stared long enough, it'd bear a more complicated message. When would she see another newspaper, a fashion magazine?

"I go pump the bilge now," he said. "Keep her at 95 heading, best you can."

In this passage, current ran from the Atlantic so the *Bamboo Cannon* made laborious headway. The tiller was sluggish in Carly's hand. The Grand Bourg light flashed like it didn't give a damn.

A little dope would sure make this loneliness bearable. The thought made Carly's stomach cramp—she'd be so helpless! How had she ever allowed herself to take such chances, be so stoned trusting in a world that required all her strength, every bit of her ingenuity?

The bow smacked a heavier swell. When they overtook a black snag—a broken treetrunk—Carly gave it plenty of room. The pump went ka-thunk-whoosh, ka-thunk-whoosh.

Two birds passed overhead, homing on the island. Flights of smaller ones swooped over the passage, taking insects. Absently, Carly scratched her arm. She felt like her bum'd been on this seat, her arm looped over this tiller, forever.

When they rounded Pointe Jaquet, they lost the Grand Bourg light aft.

Winston hugged the shore, to catch the wind flowing down the mountainside. The light air smelled of cinnamon. They were in the Atlantic now and the boat crashed through the swell. At midnight, they passed Crompton Point to starboard and the moon came out. It lit the spine of the island, far above them, above a thick skirt of mist. Later, Winston brought the boat too close to breaking waves at Captain Scott Rock, but Carly was below pumping and didn't know about it.

One or the other was at the pump constantly, until they abandoned the *Bamboo Cannon* below the cliffs of Pointe de Fous at three o'clock in a Dominican morning.

PART THREE

UPRISING

I'm just a red nigger who love the sea,
I had a sound colonial education,
I have Dutch, nigger, and English in me,
and either I'm nobody, or I'm a nation.
DEREK WALCOTT

10

The Volcanic Caribbees

"The Post is unreliable since Independence," Mrs. Chapman complained and none of her companions demurred. Mrs. Malouf fanned herself with a strike bulletin. Postmaster Robertson might have noted that the only service still functioning in Dominica during these days of strikes and uprisings was the very same Postal Bureau, but he held his tongue.

Mrs. Chapman's companions clucked sympathetically, said, "Oh my, yes," and "That's the truth, surely," though none of the three liked Mrs. Chapman and, under more normal circumstances, Mrs. Malouf wouldn't have given her the time of day.

Though it wasn't ten in the morning, it was quite warm. The little stone Postal Bureau concentrated the heat.

Mrs. Chapman was widely disliked for the manner that elevated her to the presidency of the Leeward Botanical and Floral Club. Mrs. Chapman gave with one hand and took with the other:

"What a lovely dress. I wouldn't have thought your husband could afford it."

"Your daughter is so good-looking. It's distressing about her complexion."

That sort of thing.

It was widely believed in St. Joseph village that Mrs. Chapman's aggressiveness and bad manners had propelled her husband, Neville, into his government slot—Minister of Fisheries and Tourism—a position, some whispered, Neville Chapman did not enjoy at all these days.

Mrs. Chapman's companions had accompanied her to the Post each morning since Neville had been detained, but the message they so greatly feared hadn't arrived.

A week ago the van had come to pick up the minister. The brightly painted van with no windows they called "the Dread Van." The man who actually came to the front door of the Chapmans' house was that white fellow, Mr. Bones.

The only level street in St. Joseph runs along the beach. The shops front this cobblestoned passage, which is just wide enough for two vehicles to pass. Residential St. Joseph clings to the steep bluff behind. The roads twist and turn back on themselves and it is steep going for any vehicle or an overweight fiftyish woman to descend and return up the hill every single morning even though she is accompanied by neighbors lending consolation and support.

Postmaster Robertson wished to be on strike too, but the Postal Workers Union had voted to stay on when the road and telephone and customs and hydro and school officials and even the constabulary went out. Although strikers dragged logs across the airstrip at Melville Hall and Liat planes quit landing at Canefield Airport although Dominica's postal links with the larger world were quite severed, at 9 A.M. daily, six days a week, postal workers opened their postal bureaus (at least as far north as Colihaut, 5 miles beyond St. Joseph, where strikers' logs blocked the coast road).

Daily, Postmaster Robertson felt a twinge as he unlocked his Postal Bureau, but he knew where his duty lay. Mr. James Edwards, from the Hydro Board, had made public remarks about "Some people's inadequate patriotism." Mr. Robertson, who'd fought with British forces at Dieppe and Arnheim, felt his patriotism should have been safe from question by any man who'd spent his war supplying the troops stationed on Dominica with girls and rum.

The Postal Bureau dangled over the beach, its thick concrete foundations eroded by past hurricanes' wash. It was two rooms, Mr. Robertson's office and the public room where citizens waited for mail. The public room was decorated with government bulletins: CHILDREN'S LITERACY: A NEW PROGRAM, FRESH WATER MAN-

AGEMENT PROPOSALS FOR DOMINICA, ADJUSTED HYDRO RATES, and so forth. More recent bulletins detailed antistrike legislation the Roseau government had passed but Mr. Robertson didn't bother to post these. They'd have been torn down in an instant.

Perhaps, if Mrs. Chapman hadn't pressured her husband, Neville Chapman would have kept his opposition to the new government more muffled than he did. Chapman wasn't an especially brave man—though he'd been brave enough to resign in protest with eight other ministers when President Rollo-Long Pre named that gang of dreadlocked exconvicts to head up the Defense Force. A week later, when the Dread van picked up Minister Bahnson (that was in Portsmouth) and did what they did, Neville Chapman wanted to mute his criticism but was more afraid of his wife than either Defense Force or Dreads. Also—as his wife had argued—Mrs. Olivia Macpherson (resigned minister of education) had been arrested by Mal Esprit himself and his "picked band" (those were Mrs. Chapman's very words), who questioned her politely in Mal Esprit's office in Government House, treated her courteously, and released her unharmed.

Minister Bahnson hadn't been so lucky. "It was what happened to Bahnson brought logs across the road above Colihaut so nobody can drive north no more," Neville Chapman said.

She said, "Neville, it's a matter of asserting your authority."

Easy for her to say.

It had been Neville who answered the sharp knock and confronted the sweaty white man in the white linen suit. It was Neville who had to think what to say as the white man wiped his forehead with his stained handkerchief and said, "When are you going to get some decent roads in this village?" Just like he himself wasn't powerful in the government, the very man to ask if you wanted a new road or some special dispensation.

Neville said, "Oh, sir, we've petitioned on high. We've written to the president himself. You know how old these streets are? Was the French built them when they occupied this island three hundred years ago and maybe they are fine for donkeys and oxen but not for modern vehicles like your fine van...."

Which was bumped up against the curb, two black fellows hanging out the windows, another, like he was deep in the bush, took a steaming piss.

"Neville, who's there?" his wife called from the kitchen.

She thought she had time. Time to finish basting her fish, time to set her oven timer. But the neighbors saw it all through their curtains; how the blacks got out of the brightly painted van (red lightnings and green earth and a black sun and, in yellow letters, *JAH* on each back door) and they took her husband firmly by the arms and lifted him free of the ground. Mr. Malouf said the minister's feet were walking through the air but never touched earth. Although Malouf had been distressed by the sight, some listeners, later, hearing his description thought the minister walking through the air was funny like a cartoon.

"They took all the time they needed." Mr. Malouf added, "Oh they was cocks of the walk." The white man looked up and around, all down the street like it and its occupants had been offered for sale, cheap sale, before he got in the van. Mrs. Chapman reached her doorstep as the van rounded the curve at the bottom of the hill and when she saw those gaudy doors, those *JAH*'s she let out a shriek that created supporters of people who'd scarcely been able to abide her before.

Mrs. Chapman begged several men, including Mr. James Edwards from the Hydro Board, to travel to Roseau and make inquiries but they all made excuses, and Mr. Edwards said, "Your husband go brave, see where it got him."

Although the postal lorry was a Land-Rover, it traveled from Roseau to the logs at Colihaut and no further.

"This island, she shrinking" the driver'd been heard to say, and the drive that once took him the best part of a day from Roseau to Portsmouth and return, he now finished by noon. Although he did only half as much work as before, the government hadn't thought to reduce his salary, busy as they were with more pressing matters.

As it passed the church, the postal lorry honked.

Mrs. Chapman straightened the sleeve of her blouse and stepped onto the street, wearing her most powerful face. Her friends remained inside.

Mr. Robertson slipped out his private door. He wore his Postmaster's jacket and cap. "Driver, how are you today?"

"Good-morning, Mr. Robertson. Yes. You are well I hope?"

"I am, for an old man, quite fit."

The postal driver laughed like this was a joke though the Postmaster was seventy. The postal driver said, "There has been a crash of jitneys into a royal palm at Hillsborough Estate and the government has not remove them though the jitneys were crashed yesterday morning when I pass."

The postmaster shook his head. "I am very much afraid, postal driver, that we Dominicans are no great shakes for governing ourselves."

The postal driver said, "They close up the Royal Canadian Bank tightly and pull down mesh screen over the doors. There is a note. 'Working in banks calls for a very high level of efficiency and at the present time Government has installed fear and suspicion in bank employees' minds. They are unable to work until a climate of normalcy is restored.'"

Mrs. Chapman said, "Efficiency not such a big matter in the Postal Bureau, eh? Two workers can go on chatting all morning without doing nothing about the mail?"

Postmaster Robertson hefted the canvas bag of mail, which still bore leather patches branded HRHM. His aged back bent under the strain but the driver knew better than to help. "It is not your job, mister, to assist a postmaster who has long served the commonwealth," Robertson had snapped when once he tried.

When Robertson dumped the bag, he spotted the package immediately but he carefully locked his door, removed and hung his jacket on the hook provided because routine protects us when we are afraid.

The package was slender and might have been a glove box. Among the litter of envelopes and government circulars it glowed. It was very light, much lighter than you'd think. The postmaster laid it softly on the counter.

Mrs. Chapman's body shook, from her toes to the top of her head. Only the hand that reached for the package did not shake.

She clasped the package to her breast.

"I am so sorry," Postmaster Robertson said. Another woman was saying the Rosary. The driver removed his cap as the women began their slow processional up the cobblestoned street to Mrs. Chapman's house. Others from the village of St. Joseph would follow them, more would arrive as the news flashed through the town on Radio Neg, and in her house the assembly would answer Mrs. Chapman's wail of discovery with a shout of wrath and fear. This! And brought to us by our own government!

* * *

Carly opened her eyes when a rough stinky *something* washed her cheek. She blinked her gummy eyelids. "Stop that," she said, but the fat dog wagged her tail and persisted.

Carly lay on the rough floor wrapped in a single cotton blanket and the sun streamed in through the cool air and she'd never felt so luxurious. "G'wan," she complained. The dog shifted attentions to Carly's hand, slurp, slurp, slurp. Carly squeezed one eye open. The dog had dark eyes, a gray muzzle, and worn-down yellow teeth. The dog worked down one side and up the other, like Carly's hand was a puppy. When Carly tried to retract her hand, the dog used a paw to hold it in place. In apology, the industrious dog wagged her tail twice, thump, thump, against the planks. Dust motes in the sun. It farted apologetically and a second later, Carly sat bolt upright. "Thank you so very much," Carly said.

The room was high-ceilinged and latticework above the walls. Nothing in this house to stop the air flow, no. Air could traipse right through the open window with the sunlight and roll the length of the living room and through the lattices into other parts of the house. Outside the window a bird chuckled, "Tek-tuk, ee-oo." The walls were dark wood, perhaps mahogany, Carly didn't know. The lattices, pale yellowish. Between the bright windows were three rows of photographs arranged precisely: photos of black dignitaries. Some unframed, faded, water streaked. Carly saw Marcus Garvey and Malcolm X and a gaunt angry face she seemed to remember from the American civil rights movement. The place of honor was Martin Luther King. The front cover of a *Life* magazine. "I have a dream," the magazine said.

The dog thumped her tail, and absently Carly petted her broad head. Carly's muscles felt loose, her hair flew from her head like Medusa's. Her blouse was salt stiff and uncomfortable.

Mr. Soylo's home was on a rise above the road and you could see the mountain across the way and the schoolhouse itself from his veranda. When Carly came to the window a chunky green tanager fluttered away from the mistletoe it had been feeding on.

The sky was swirling overcast; fog snaked through the lime orchard in the valley below.

Dog at her heels, Carly went outside onto the long shaded veranda that ran the full width of the modest house.

The sun was well up in the sky, the day long ago begun.

Leaning against the railing Carly saw three cows tethered singly beside the road and one calf. The cows were black and white, the calf brown, black, brindled like a Great Dane. The calf stretched its neck and bawled, the plaintive cry muffled by fog. Fog-colored goats were tethered among the lime trees. An old woman walked the road Carly and Winston had walked last night. She wore a long skirt and balanced a wicker basket on her head. The road was deeply rutted and for a bit she'd walk on one shoulder then, carefully, she'd cross to the other. Across the valley—half a mile as a bird might fly—was a great yellowish slash in the mountainside.

Rain pattered the tin roof and cool air splashed Carly's cheeks. The basket woman continued on, unconcerned. All around were trees Carly had never seen before: trees with funny-looking lurid leaves.

Winston had said there weren't any snakes. "Nothin' sting you Dominica except for Jack Spainard, they nasty bees."

The swim ashore hadn't been bad. Winston brought the boat in as close as he could and wrapped life jackets around his duffle, which held all their clothes, and kicked it over the side and Carly clamped her nose and followed.

Winston swam steadily, the dip of his shoulder, the spark of moonlight on his wrist as it dug into the dark water. He swam like he could swim forever.

The sea cliffs grew. The line Carly had fastened to the bundle jerked and fell slack, jerked and fell slack, regular as the working of her lungs. Outside the surfline she put her feet down. Football-size stones hurt her feet and Carly followed Winston limping, banging her toes. Whoosh and whisper, slap and chuckle of the waves.

Carly sat on a rock to put on shoes. There, much better.

He was staring out to sea, black and primitive as the first man who ever stood on this beach, the sea at his feet.

"Good boat," he said, like perhaps the poor broken thing could hear.

"The wind is taking her out."

The stern of the *Bamboo Cannon* was low in the water, but her single sail was full and she heeled over as the breeze took her.

"Maybe she won't sink," Carly said. "Maybe somebody will find her."

"Darlin', it's a big ocean." And he slung the duffle on his back.

When they found a broad ravine Winston started to climb like he'd been this way before. Carly took a deep breath.

The ravine was full of rubble, some of it big stuff. Vines hung from boxcar-size boulders, and bushes crowded the narrow chute they were ascending.

Winston climbed like he'd swum, steadily, but Carly slipped ahead leaping from boulder to boulder, finding footholds he thought were shadows.

They came upon a motorless wringer washing machine that had once been enameled green and Winston hauled himself along the moldering machine.

Fifty yards higher they found their next piece of junk, somebody's suitcase—a rather grand one.

"Welcome to civilization," she said.

"Watch your hands," he said. "Morne Rouge Estate fellows throw their junk over this cliff, since who knows when."

"How romantic. A moonlight climb through a garbage dump."

The moon was bright enough. The path skirted the sheer boulders, scrambled up crevices, traversed ledges a foot wide. Carly was carefree as a mountain goat. Winston came behind, one foot, next foot, hand against the wall. Carly hopped over broken glass. Winston hesitated, did the same.

Nearer the top, perhaps four hundred feet above the rocky beach, thick heaps of garbage: cans, bottles, bedsprings cluttered the path. There were rats in the garbage—Carly could see them and she could hear them. She shunned the thought: What if she should put her hand . . .

Winston was puffing and sweat stood out on his forehead. "Was easier when I was a boy," he said.

Carly let him go first. She pretended it was courtesy but it was because of the rats.

Thirty feet below the rim was garbage dump pure and simple, and they mushed through the bottles and cans and rotting matter. It didn't do to think about what Carly's feet were sinking into so she didn't. She kept her eyes straight ahead. She blanked out all skittering sounds.

On top, she stood well back from the rim because her legs felt funny—not frightened, but like the earth was lifting and tilting same as it had been aboard the boat.

The whole sea was laid out like a silver platter. The edge of the world was distinct. "What's that?" Carly asked.

"Where?"

"That light. There!"

"That Martinique. You can see Pointe de Macouba when it clear night like this."

The road was level and easy as it passed through the ruins of Bois Cotellette Estate. Winston wondered if Mr. Dubois had it. Of course not! Dubois had been eighty years old when last Winston saw him. The guinea grass was ragged where workers had chopped it for livestock. The mango trees were neatly pruned and royal palms still lined the dirt road like it was the Champs Elysées. Perhaps Dubois's sons had the estate.

While Winston's mind wandered his feet did a perfectly good job on the road he'd walked as a boy. When his mind took command, he found things subtly different, a switchback before he expected it and steeper, a new road that detoured the eroded gulley that had been the old one.

Winston worried about his airplane. He wondered what in the world he would do with this white girl. Island in turmoil ain't no place for white girl never been nowhere, done nothing. Made him smile, remembering her on that ravine that had been much *much* steeper than he'd remembered it, her scampering all over the place. And she hadn't been a hopeless sailor either. Winston wondered if she could bear children, all the drugs she'd used?

No houses along this road. At least that hadn't changed. The day workers lived below in Soufriere, walked up here to tend their gardens, work the estates. For some it was an hour uphill hike to the gardens they'd hacked out of the bush—many on estate land, and gardeners liable to be evicted without notice when the owners (British, American, Canadian) decided it would be a profitable idea to cut down everything and plant wall-to-wall vanilla or coffee trees.

Thick timber slabs formed stairs to Mr. Soylo's house. The house was so squat and the roof overhang so deep it seemed like an elf's house tucked into the hillside. At the door, they heard a growl.

"Yes?! Who's there? It is too late for boys to be playing the ass with an old blind man."

Another growl, more serious.

"Mr. Soylo, it is Winston Riviere."

As the sweat cooled on Carly's neck, she felt chilled. This was the tropics and she wasn't supposed to feel cold.

"Hush, Mrs. Polly. Now you lie still." Mr. Soylo's doorway yawed open like a dark mouth of a cave. *"Common ouye, Winston! Common ouye."*

And Winston embraced his old teacher. "Could we have a light, old friend? We can't find our way about as you do."

"Certainly! Winston Riviere, I would have wagered a hundred pounds I'd not see you again on Dominica. Splendid!"

Carly had expected a heftier man: a man with a 44-inch waistline. But when the match scratched at the kerosene lantern, Mr. Soylo's shadow was bigger than he was.

He was very black, blacker than Winston, with close-cropped salt-and-pepper hair. His head craned forward, his cheeks were pulled off his gums in a terrible squint. "Oh, Winston," he exulted.

At his feet a fat black Labrador retriever smiled, her tail all atremble. What fun! Unexpected guests in the night! The terrible smell that rose from the dog made Carly's eyes water.

Mr. Soylo wore a tattered Chinese robe—white-and-gold silk —with a grand dragon hissing across the shoulders. Carly wondered how it had come so far. "Sit down, Winston. You have heard of our troubles and come to help?"

The blind man's grin took most of the light in the room. The floor creaked under his feet.

Winston said, "We talk about that tomorrow, sir. We are without sleep for many nights. Please not to say to anyone we are here."

The fixed, puzzled grin. The pale pink gums in the cracked black face. "So many people will want to know you have returned to the island."

Winston sighed. "So too Mal Esprit. He also want to know. More than talk, we need sleep. The woman is very tired."

Carly resented that.

"I am so sorry, miss. You must forgive an old man his manners, eh? Here"—he indicated a gray-green armoire—"inside you will find blankets and you can take a bolster from the settee for pillow. My nieces sleep in here when they visit me so you will be quite comfortable. Winston, follow me."

Winston looked at her. "Good-night."

Her head was swimming and if she didn't lie down, she was going to fall down. "Nice climbing with you," she said, almost as jauntily as she had hoped.

The men left her the light and she heard them bedding down in the next room. She managed the blanket and meant to get the bolster but it seemed an awful lot of trouble. . . .

"Good-morning, good-morning. Up already, eh? I usually rise earlier but your arrival reset my internal clock."

He spoke as if the clock he spoke of was a mechanism with face and gears. "I shall prepare tea."

Carly had a powerful longing for a cup of coffee, milk and sweetener, fragrant and steaming.

"Unless you'd rather have coffee. Our Dominican coffee is excellent. It's a shame we don't export more of it."

"Yes, please. That would be very nice."

Carly had envisioned a cup of coffee where you pour boiling water in a cup and a spoonful of Maxim's Instant and the milk from a plastic gallon jug (2 percent low-fat) and Sweet 'n Low.

What happened was that the blind man put charcoal in his cooker, added curled-up bark, and struck a match. The bark blossomed into fire and he shut the cooker but not before a puff of smoke coughed back at them. Then he set the kettle on the grate. Moving with the ease of long practice, he found the proper jar and poured a child's handful of beans into the minute drawer of his coffee grinder and ground it, growl, growl, growl. He tapped the drawer into the top of a drip coffeepot and replaced everything exactly where it had been.

"Shall we wait on the veranda? It takes several minutes for the water to boil."

Carly wanted her morning coffee right now. She deserved her morning coffee and if she'd been in some sort of decent civilized place she would have it. She flashed on her mother's face like a face in an old snapshot. Her mother was fixed in time—she was what she would be. Carly relaxed. She could wait. She had her whole life ahead of her. "Dominica is very beautiful," she said.

"Oh we are a paradise here, it is long been our greatest problem."

Carly raised her eyebrows, realized he couldn't see. "Problem?"

"When I was young like yourself, all over the Antilles I travel.

Boat, no airplane in old times. I visit French islands and British islands, all alike. Trinidad, Jamaica, Grand Turk. And wherever life the hardest, the people have made a civilization. Here, on Dominica, man get hungry, he go back in the bush pick grape-fruit, mango, banana. His chickens they scratch in the dirt. You know what we say here when things go very badly: When the big wind takes your roof, another man is seen loving your wife, your children hold you in contempt we say, *Kai poule kwazi*. That means: The chicken house is falling down. That's the kind of peo-ple we are."

"In California, we say, 'Oh, shit!'"

"Ah," he said, looking up the valley. "California. You know Winston long time?"

Once again Carly had to catch up with his sightlessness. "Not long."

"You must be dear to him, to bring you with him when he come down here. Situation bad here."

Carly didn't answer. The blind man seemed okay but Carly fig-ured it was Winston's business to make explanations.

"You not hear much about Dominica in California?"

"Not so much, no."

"Well we hear about California because that's where your grape-fruit grows which is such a competition for us. Oh yes, we know all about California." He nodded solemnly. Carly had a flash: Har-bor Freeway at rush hour. She hid a smile.

"For many years we struggle for freedom and independence. Though the political parties change, they all the same. Dominican people want independence. 'We must rule our own affairs.'" As he spoke, Carly almost smelled the cigar smoke from ancient political meetings. The black men on his wall had been real men then, real as you and me.

The kettle began to hiss and, with economical movements, he filled the top portion of the pot. "Not be long," he assured her cheerfully.

The coffee smelled better than any coffee Carly had ever smelled. She salivated.

He continued. "Always a few men want everything for themself and their cronies." He found two coffee cups—Carly's had a han-dle. Hospitality. "I have the condensed milk, if you like."

"Great."

"Dominican sugar. See, it is brown."

It looked just like the sugar you buy in health food stores. A thump and grunt from the other room was Winston getting up. Carly stirred her coffee.

"Good-morning, good-morning, everyone." Winston was happy. "Oh, the coffee smells so fine."

Mr. Soylo said. "It is a two-cup pot only, but I will put more water on."

"Never mind," Winston said. "I'll have some of Carly's."

"You will not!"

He looked so astonished, Carly had to laugh and his own laugh caught up to hers. She pushed the cup at him and he put his palms in front of his body to defend himself against it.

Mr. Soylo said, "Oh, it is so long since I hear laughter in this house. Only when my nieces visit me from Portsmouth do we have jokes and laughter."

"Your sister's daughters?" Winston asked.

And as they talked about Mr. Soylo's family, Carly leaned against the rail, both elbows, and watched the soft life in the fog below. Again it rained, again it was just a sprinkle, again the sun came out to dry the leaves, the timber stairs.

Carly wondered why she felt at home here, on this faraway island, among a people not her own, when she'd never felt at home in her own country. Her coffee was delicious.

She said, "I'm making the next pot," and Mr. Soylo said, "Please to return everything back where you find it, just so. I'm afraid I don't see more than light and shadow. Shapes, when the sun is strong."

"You retired now?" Winston asked.

Carly went inside to make a second pot. She memorized the position of everything she used.

Mr. Soylo said, "Oh yes. I cannot work with the young childrens anymore. Some boys come to me for tutoring, that is all. Young Jimmy Rawle, he come up Tuesdays and Thursdays to read to me. Mrs. Polly here helps me get about."

Winston said, "She has an indelicate odor."

Mr. Soylo laughed. He stabbed his finger into Winston's chest. "You mean she stinks, oh she does, she does. You always were too polite, Winston. Polite and proud. Now that's a combination can get you in trouble. The pride get you into trouble and politeness makes it worse. Is the woman your wife?"

In the kitchen, Carly stopped. Her hand fell to her side. The two men faced each other, in profile.

"Sir," Winston said, "Carly is white."

Mr. Soylo craned toward him for the longest time, like he was waiting for more information. Then he tapped his bifocals and laughed, a high whinny. Carly faced away, her cheeks burning up.

"She is your master then?" Mr. Soylo asked and whinnied another laugh. The schoolmaster must know Carly was still within earshot. Surely he knew.

Stiffly Winston said, "She is a stowaway."

"A stowaway, oh my. A girl with a sense of adventure. How about you, Winston? Are you still cautious?"

"Ahhh."

"Cautious, proud, and polite. My, my. And have you done well for yourself in this world, Winston?"

"I am a pilot with DMS Airways. Three planes we have. I am the chief mechanic also."

"Oh that's a fine job, Winston. I am so pleased you set aside your fine job to come down and help us Dominicans in our hour of need."

The coffee water boiled. Carly put a handful of beans in the grinder and cranked them into dust.

"Not my struggle," Winston said. "It is an airplane I seek, that belonged to me before Mal Esprit thief it."

The schoolmaster cocked his ear like he wanted to catch every word. "What color this plane?"

Carly said, "Winston, what do you want in your coffee?"

The schoolmaster cried, "Oh our white stowaway has made coffee, Winston. She is already earning her passage."

Winston looked right at Carly. "She's earned her passage," he said.

Unaccountably, Carly was embarrassed again.

Winston said, "You must tell your students not to come today. I cannot be seen. Only you to know I am on Dominica."

"Yes?"

"The plane is black. Black Commanche with the Navaho engines."

"Ah. The bomber plane."

"Which?"

But the blind man turned to Carly. "You come with me, miss. Leave Winston Riviere here. He can hide in my house like a thief and if someone knock, he can lie on the floor, hide behind the couch."

Carly wished she could tell whether the schoolmaster was grinning or squinting. "Come with me, miss. Mrs. Polly and I will show you Soufriere."

"Which bomber plane?"

"But you are not interested in our struggle, Winston. What a shame and pity."

Outside, Mr. Soylo waited patiently until the black dog circled into position and his hand fell right onto the harness. He said, "I never thank Winston for Mrs. Polly." He chuckled, "I not thank him now. You follow me, miss. Mrs. Polly doesn't like anyone directly in front of her."

The two—blind man and guide dog—became one, a composite beast, as they progressed down the steps. Each move of the one flowed into the other. The dog, who'd been distant and vague, was all business now.

The schoolteacher summoned Carly to his side and jerked his head at a schoolhouse he couldn't see. "Many good years I teach here. I am educated in London, me."

They padded in silence past the banyan tree where so many had received their first schooling under its great branches.

Students in neat blue uniforms waved. Carly waved back. "I didn't wear uniforms to school," she said.

"Uniforms make all schoolchildren the same. Rich, poor, all the same."

"Uh-huh." Carly thought the uniforms were dowdy and she wouldn't have been caught dead wearing one.

He marched along at a pretty good clip. Below the school, around a turn, past other houses clinging to the hillsides, the valley opened up and she could see all Soufriere, its broad beaches, its bay.

The Crossroads Disco bore an advertisement—blue letters on pink:

WHERE THE DOODS MEET THEIR LOVERS

and perhaps it was true. Two agricultural workers (shorts and cutlasses) were chatting up a young girl. They removed their hats.

"Good-morning, schoolmaster."

"Ah, good-morning, Robert. Yes."

And three sets of eyes followed the blind man and his white companion as they descended into town.

Without preamble, Mr. Soylo said, "You must understand that we are a peaceful people who have recently attained independence from Great Britain. When our government thwarts the will of the Dominican people, it must resign. President of Dominica, he gone dim in his brain. He import Dreads and ruffians to run his government and they raise up amazing schemes which we are supposed to know nothing about, but we hear about them, indeed."

Firewood sticks were stacked beside the door of a modest stone house, and a delicious smell assaulted Carly's nostrils.

Inside, Mr. Soylo called out, "Good-morning, Carlos. I need some of your wonderful penny bread."

"Good-morning, schoolmaster." The baker wore a madras sport coat over his full body apron. Industrial black steel shelving held loaves of bread: round bread, flat bread, elongated French bread. Two teeth were missing from the center of the baker's smile.

"Good-morning," Carly said shyly.

"Good-morning, miss. I hope you taste my penny bread."

"Oh, it smells heavenly."

It was a small loaf, the size of a Pullman roll and she bit down, without butter or jam or anything. "Oh," she said. She didn't say that the warm bread was the best thing she'd ever tasted in her whole life, that the taste made her replete in a way no food ever had before. She turned away and sneezed. "Excuse me," she said.

The schoolmaster said, "It makes her sneeze this penny bread of yours. Perhaps it should be named, 'pepper bread' eh, Carlos."

And the baker smiled. "You here long time, miss?"

"No. Not long."

"You like Dominica? I from Trinidad," the baker confided. "Trinidad very modern island. Not like this place."

Printed fabric, eye high, hung across the interior doorway. The young woman behind it had hair in tight cornrows and wore jangly gold earrings. Her eyes were big and brown and she pretended the fabric made her invisible.

Carly said, "I was born in California."

"Imagine that."

Mrs. Polly led the way down the cobbled street. The chickens avoided her, the scrawny brown-and-red mongrels eyed her but kept their distance.

Carly said, "Is there a telephone in the village?"

"Oh my yes. Telephone in Catholic rectory. We have had phones in Soufriere since 1968."

"I wonder if I could make an international call."

Mr. Soylo showed his teeth. "Phones on strike, miss. Can't call nowhere. Oh, this government."

A Land-Rover eased along the narrow street, about the speed a man might walk. Five agricultural workers sat in back, white man at the wheel.

"Good-morning, schoolmaster," he said. "It is I, Jean Hubbell." He spoke too loudly, like Mr. Soylo was deaf as well as blind.

The agricultural workers murmured "Good-mornings" but didn't identify themselves.

Carly smiled. "Good-morning, yes."

"Ah, Mr. Hubbell. And the aloe vera, it is still promising?"

The white man was about thirty, wore a khaki shirt and well-worn short khaki pants. He never took his eyes off Carly. The workers rolled cigarettes and looked everywhere but directly at her.

"You have heard about the march?"

"Another, so soon?"

"Yes, schoolmaster. We gather at the church Friday, in the morning. It cannot continue like this."

"What about the bomber plane?"

"Now our government is selling rights to South African government, come Dominica build an oil refinery. It was broadcast last night, on the BBC. South Africans, come here, to a country which is ninety percent black. Imagine." The white man was as indignant as if he'd been black himself. To Carly he added, "I am Jean Hubbell, hello."

"Carly Hollander."

The white man waited expectantly but when Carly just smiled in a vague way, he started his Land-Rover and it jounced up the rough street.

"Winston told me about him," Carly said.

The schoolmaster laughed, "Oh yes. A good man, Mr. Hubbell, but so fiery. Another march on the government, oh my."

The churchyard fronted the beach and overturned fishing boats cluttered the alleyway beside the rectory. Mrs. Polly trotted briskly up the church's steep stone steps. The doors were weathered, and just as stern as the building.

The pews were massive and dark. Light streaming through the narrow windows was much whiter than the yellow sunlight that splashed the entryway. The altar mural depicted a colonial scene: Caribs on one side, British officers on the other, a Jesuit kneeling between.

Mr. Soylo perched on the altar step and Mrs. Polly lay beside him. When he slipped her a crumb of penny bread, she thumped her tail in gratitude. "Now, Miss Carly," the schoolmaster smiled his stretched smile, "tell me about yourself."

11

Kai Poule Quaze!

"That bomber plane flew at our heads and scattered us like we was chickens," Mr. Soylo said.

"What has that to do with me?" Winston said, and since he couldn't conceal the anger in his voice, Mrs. Polly growled.

The schoolmaster chuckled, "Mrs. Polly thinks I need protection from you, Winston, is that correct?"

Mrs. Polly yipped sharply.

"It's all right, darlin'," Mr. Soylo murmured. "He is the same foolish boy he always is. Just Winston." Carly sat outside on the darkened veranda thinking about her life. After she and the schoolmaster came back to the house she'd taken a nap while Mr. Soylo made supper: chicken, pigeon peas, tomatoes.

Through the meal, the schoolmaster lectured them about Dominican politics. He said: "One minister, Minister of Education Bahnson, was arrested by that white man Mr. Bones. He is well named, that devil. Three days after Minister Bahnson's abduction, the post delivered a package to his wife. Box contained Mr. Bahnson's wedding ring and the finger bones of his hand. Oh, an outcry people make then! Mr. Bahnson was a popular minister, quite able. Radio Neg—rumor—say they fed his body to the fish in

Pringle's Bay, but true or lie the minister vanished and is not seen again."

The schoolmaster said: "When we Dominicans march to Government House to lodge our protest, Defense Force shoot their rifles in the air and they hurl tear gas and one of they tear gas canisters flies through the window of a house where a baby is sleeping and baby he suffocate then. To top it off, the bomber plane fly over dropping paint on the citizens and perhaps we should be grateful it wasn't nothing more frightful than paint. We flee and we cannot breathe and some are marked with paint for the Dreads to take notice of them.

To which Winston had said, "When I find that plane it'll be one less vexation. Plane be gone."

"And you with it, Winston?"

Which was when Carly went out onto the porch. Carly was sick of quarreling.

Wind blowing down from the mountains swept the mosquitoes off the veranda. A pale moon silvered the road below. Lime tree leaves shivered like schools of tiny fish. What did she want? Was there anything she deserved? Carly had never troubled herself with these questions, not because she was thoughtless, but because she'd been afraid of the answers. In this faraway place where she had nothing but her life, she wasn't afraid anymore.

Earlier, that day in the church, she'd found it easy to talk to the schoolmaster, perhaps because the only eyes that saw her weakness were the dark, kind eyes of the blind man's dog. Carly talked about her mother and father. More about her mother.

When she started to speak about the drugs, she hesitated, but he was nodding and smiling like Stevie Wonder getting another Grammy award. Why do blind people smile so much?

He said, "Oh yes, drugs. Here, on Dominica, it is rum we reach for when we wish to be dead while alive."

Tears sprang to her eyes and these tears *hurt*. They scorched her cheeks like acid streams. The blind man's dog scriggled forward and licked her hand.

"So you stow away to Dominica."

"Thought I'd change my luck," she said bitterly.

"Oh you lucky, you young."

"I don't feel so young."

"Some people don't get to be children when they children, so they become children while everyone else becoming adults. They feel so foolish."

Carly wiped her cheeks. She asked the schoolmaster about his life, why he'd become a teacher, why he'd returned to Dominica from London.

"London fellows build that great city," he said. "In the Caribbean we have opportunity to build ourselves. Some the islands, like St. Barts, doin' good. Cuba and Grenada, oh my, they fearful object lessons, those two. Dominica can go either way. Give all the power to the government or keep it in our own hands."

The yellow sunlight was a warm triangle in the doorway. Carly shivered. "Do you come here often?"

"Most days, yes. This the house of God, miss. Sometimes he home and sometimes he down the road." He laughed.

"I haven't been in church since I was a kid."

"Could be a little warmer, eh?" Again he laughed, like goosebumps were the greatest joke in the world.

That night on the veranda, in a shadowed moonlight, Carly thought about what the old man had said. She wondered if he liked her. So what? Evidently, he liked Winston and listen to them! Winston's talk punctuated by occasional growls from the dog who hated having her charge abused, even verbally. They argued about politics, a citizen's responsibility, the airplane. Winston wanted the schoolmaster to send a boy to Roseau to the Canefield Airport and spy out the whereabouts of the black plane, how many guards were on it, so forth. Then Winston would fly the plane off the island.

"No more black bomber plane, and I would be out of your hair."

"Winston, it is too dangerous. To get to Canefield you must pass through Roseau, cross the river bridges. Many patrols of Dreads and Defense Forces on the lookout there. You want to steal the plane, you go steal it."

"If I am seen, Mal Esprit . . . I know what he will do!"

"Winston, no man can be invisible."

Words on top of words.

Winston said something angry, in patois, Mrs. Polly growled.

Carly pushed inside. "I'll go to the airport. I'll find out what you want," she said.

Well, that shut them up. Winston's brows dropped like bags of rocks. "I cannot let you."

"You got anybody else in mind?" she drawled.

Absently Mr. Soylo patted his dog. The kerosene lamp was bright on the table. The pantheon of black democrats was in shadow.

Carly said, "I'm not doing this for you. I'm doing it for me."

Winston said, "I suppose that makes things different."

"Yup."

"You a white girl, darlin'."

"So? Just another silly white tourist. I go to the airport to find out when I can get a flight out of this tropical paradise."

Winston groaned, *"Kai poule . . ."*

Well, he argued with her, the way men always argue when a woman has a smart idea they should have thought of themselves.

After some minutes, Winston said, "She could say she was the cousin of Jean Hubbell, visiting his estate."

After some further minutes, Mr. Soylo announced that it was late hour for an old man and preceded his dog into the other room. Winston put his hand on Carly's shoulder. "I did not think you would do this thing for me."

She took a step back and said, "What makes you think I'm doing it for you?"

He said, "You are a fine-looking woman."

She said, "My tits are too small and my hair is thin."

He said, "Darlin' you look fine to me."

She said, "I think you better take a good look at yourself, Winston. I think you're forgetting who you are."

He dropped his hands to his side. "Because I am black and you are white?"

"No. Because you are a Dominican."

Well, he tilted his head and his nostrils flared and he took a deep, deep breath. "And you are a woman who has ruined herself," he snapped.

"I used to think so," she said, hot and ashamed all at once.

He bowed stiffly, "I thank you, miss, for what you are doing for me."

Before dawn Mr. Soylo woke her. Rummaging through the dark armoire, he found a clean blouse and skirt his niece had forgotten on her last visit. Carly wore her own running shoes. No socks.

"To Roseau," the old man said, "is eleven miles by road, and you will pass through two villages on the way. Smile, say good-morning, and walk on. Nobody will bother you. You have a passport?"

"No. I left it on Sandpiper Cay."

"Probably better, so. You got no immigration stamp. You be careful!" His voice was so fierce! The old man gave her twenty-three E.C. dollars. "Nothing be open in Roseau, but you might get food in Pointe Michel or Loubiere."

Winston made her a cup of coffee. He looked like he had slept badly and his eyes were red with worry. He said, "I apologize."

She said, "Yes," and took the offered coffee and it was better than yesterday. Mortal peril has a way of putting a fresh bloom on things. She loved the worry in Winston's eyes.

Winston said, "Canefield Airport is three miles after you cross the Roseau River. The plane is twin engine, all black. Don't get so near they catch you."

"Sure."

"Carly, I did not mean for you to do this."

It was the first time he had used her first name.

Confidence ran riot in her veins like strong rum, and her feet were eager on the path. When she and Winston reached the crossroads above Soufriere, it was as if this dusty crossroads, above a sleeping West Indian village, was the crossroads of everything, the departure point for all the caravans of the soul. It was her idea to kiss, and the kiss was all hers too, giving everything, needing nothing in return. The arms he lifted to hug her, fell to his sides.

She wheeled then, onto the coast road, lifting a hand in careless salute and her feet glad to be going. At the first curve she turned around, walking backwards and blew him a kiss. Deep in the village, a sleepy cock crowed.

Not ten minutes later, she was revolted and badly scared. The downhill slope of that hill was blanketed with land crabs. Their claws sounded like dice clicking or small ivory bones and when she put her foot down they withdrew but not far enough.

"Ugh," she said. "Oh, yuck!" A dark moving carpet clicked across the road and the only ones that didn't ebb and flow were the carcasses the others were jerking apart for a meal. When she slapped her feet they retreated, but there was no way to tell whether they were going to rush, quivering on their stem legs.

The moon came out of a cloud. How they glittered! The ferns

beside the road were like two-edged swords. She stepped wide around the dead ones—those horribly active mounds. Her heart was beating double time. "Listen, fellas, you don't fuck with me, and I won't fuck with you. Deal?" They wriggled their antennas like little radar sets.

Then she was beyond them, climbing, badly shaken. If the crabs weren't now between her and Soufriere, she would have turned back.

For their own reasons, the crabs liked the road on north slopes. Uphill—no crabs, downhill—crabs all over the place though no patch quite so uninterrupted as that first; and now Carly was slapping her feet and saying, "Shoo! shoo!" Though if a crab had actually dashed at her and clamped on her leg she would have screamed.

She wondered if land crabs were good to eat. They certainly think so, ugh. When the road came down beside the beach, the land crabs disappeared. Carly worried about sea crabs.

The Caribbean surf hushed the moonpath. Why had she never walked night roads before? A memory came to her—of her father, Magdellana was there too—it must have been at Laguna, and the three of them were actually happy. Magdellana bought a hot dog and a blob of mustard dropped into her bathing suit and she just laughed. There are no monsters. It hurt Carly to realize that. When her tears quit she crossed the beach and knelt and splashed seawater on her cheeks. How far was it across this sea to California?

Her feet padded the road. If her pals could see her now. Oh my, they'd think I've gone native. A thought with a British accent.

The road crossed metal culverts where streams erupted onto the beach. Birds twittered in the bush. The sky lightened. Her right heel was feeling tender and she wished she had socks. Far ahead, dots on the beach—men were launching a narrow boat. They rushed forward until the prow was in the water and several clambered aboard, while others, waist deep, took it out deeper. As a sailor heaved himself over the gunwales, water sluiced off his back and caught the sunrise like a stream of white diamonds.

They mounted a simple sail, white with neat rectangular patches. The tiller was broad and clumsy. The boat had very little freeboard amidships and Carly thought they probably didn't take it out far. Carly, the boat expert. She waved and the men stopped to wave back. One fisherman—a youngster of fifteen or sixteen—whistled a long shrill blast and waved with both hands.

The best air in these islands is a scant pistol shot from shore, and sooner than Carly would have thought the boat scooted out of sight.

The beach was littered with wrecked trees, plastic stuff, oil blobs. Ahead, tin roofs shone in the sunrise and small boys whacked branches from a hurricane-tossed tree on the beach, its girth as thick as they were tall. One boy balanced fagots on his head, and he was quite surprised to meet a white woman so early in the morning, "Oh good-morning, miss."

"Good-morning. That's quite a load."

"This is a pittance, miss. More often I load more."

The boy was eight or nine years old and barefoot. He wore brief schoolboy shorts and a buttonless short-sleeved shirt. He smiled shyly. "What you doin' in this place?"

"Pointe Michel is your home?"

"Oh yes, miss. So long as I live. Where is your home?"

Carly found that question unexpectedly hard to answer. "The United States."

"What do you want with us here?"

"I don't know. Is there anywhere I can get breakfast?"

The beach below the village was fine white sand and boulder humps. Garbage, plastic jugs, and empty coconut hulls drifted out with the tide. Pointe Michel smelled of fish and charcoal and the sea.

"You can sometimes eat at the Pelican Lunchette. Mrs. Oregard, she cook."

Carly's stomach was growling.

"Below the church, ahead there..." and with a farewell wave he turned up the hill.

The women waiting at the standpipes for their morning wash water, how they stared. "Good-morning, miss. Nice day, yes."

The Pelican Lunchette had stools mended with black electrician's tape and an empty cake container on the counter. The wall poster showed an elegantly turned out black couple, smiling and smoking:

FOOLISH PEOPLE BELIEVE

The world is flat,
The moon is made of green cheese,

Expensive Imported Tobacco is superior
to Dominican tobacco.

TRY HILLSBOROUGH CIGARETTES AND TOBACCO PRODUCTS

A large woman wiped her hands on a scrap of dish towel.

"Good-morning, good-morning. I've just walked from Soufriere, and, oh my, what an appetite!"

"Soufriere?"

"Yes, I am walking to Roseau. . . ."

"Roseau?"

"Yes, I want to go to the airport."

"Very unsettled, miss."

"What can I have for breakfast?"

But the black woman was shaking her head. "This cursed strike," she said.

"Bacon? Pancakes? Sausage?"

"I can't get nothing, miss, on account of some stupid people blocked the roads and nobody offload the boats, so there is no provisions coming in. They will starve us to death, these trade unionists and rebel ministers." Grudgingly she added, "I have the passion-fruit juice, miss."

"I wouldn't want to deprive your family."

"Ain't no family, miss. Husband, dead. Son, in Roseau with the Defense Force."

"I've never tried passion-fruit juice," Carly said, for lack of anything else.

"Sergeant Oregard. He went into the Defense Force when it was formed, five years past, and is a noncommissioned officer."

"I hope he isn't, uh, in any danger."

The mother snorted, "Them? Oh no, miss. No danger them. They are communists. They think this island keep like the British days when all our produce and childrens go to Great Britain and the white governors tell us what to do. Miss, Dominica must modernize. We must make those alliances that are offer to us."

"And your son agrees."

"My son with the Defense Force of the government, going to put down mutineers."

Her words so fierce, her eyes so afraid.

"But what about Mal Esprit?"

"He Dominican, Mal Esprit. Born right on this island. Come to help us with new ideas, thoughts which are right for the times. Mal Esprit has Dominica's interests foremost and uppermost."

"I see." Carly got off the stool.

"Don't you want nothin' to eat? You got a long walk ahead of you."

"No trouble, boil an egg. Got cold grouper cooked yesterday and I squeeze some juice. Strike or no strike, nobody on this island gonna starve."

"If you're sure . . ."

"You sit down, miss. Please, the Pelican Lunchette don't turn any hungry person away."

As Carly ate her cold fish (which was quite nice with pepper and lemon), the cook spoke of her son.

"I don't know how he got into such a thing," she said. "Guns and troops and the Dreads and, I frighten for him sometime. Defense Force can't leave the capital now, now there's roadblocks across the roads. He used to drive right here, park in the street with his new vehicle, and say, 'Come on, Mamma, let go for a ride,' and right down on the beach we go, wind blowing and spray. My boy is raised decent."

"Sure," Carly said.

"You like the passion fruit?"

Carly paid two E.C. dollars for her meal and didn't leave a tip because she didn't think it would be courteous.

The road squeezed between cliffs and the beach and basketball-size rocks littered the road. Where the road was narrowest, broken trees had been dragged across, tree trunks intertangled, the crowns wedged against the cliff, the butt ends over the beach, here so narrow the longer trunks overhung deep water. The surf splatted and hissed. Carly clambered over the trees, following a trail of broken branches and bark scars where others had gone before. With some effort an agile human could climb the barricade but it'd take a tank to push through it. Fifty feet ahead, a second barricade loomed and Carly climbed that too.

Loubiere was smaller than Pointe Michel. Carly hadn't seen a single traffic sign. What had she expected: ROSEAU EXIT LEFT 2 MILES?

In Loubiere, she waved her good-mornings pleasantly though her heel was hurting her. It rained but the rain vanished as it touched the tarmac. Carly marched through Woodbridge and

Newtown, past brick and tin buildings that might have been factories.

She met her first soldiers below the Anglican cathedral, where the road becomes cobblestoned and divides, one fork dipping to the waterfront and the other continuing toward Government House.

Four soldiers, commanded by a young corporal. Their Toyota pickup was painted in camouflage pattern and emblazoned with the shield of the Commonwealth of Dominica. The soldiers wore camouflage pants, khaki shirts, and plum-colored berets. Ugly machine pistols dangled from their web gear.

"Good-morning," Carly said. "How are you this morning?" Her mouth was dry, bone dry.

Their silence was rude, official, and the corporal lit a cigarette.

And Carly said, "Oh my, some people bein' rude today!"

So one of the soldiers said, "Good-morning, miss, yes," and scratched his arm.

Carly's neck burned as she passed, walking just like she knew where she was going.

Postal lorrys outside the Main Post Office and loiterers sitting on the sea wall and she said "Good-morning" or nodded.

Roseau looked much like the smaller villages. Most buildings were wood, some stone. A few had second stories with covered balconies and iron filigree. Shuttered windows propped open and people sat on their stoops or leaned against the buildings or lingered in small groups, talking quietly. Dreadlocked men in green, black, and yellow cars—four, always four of them—drove too fast through the streets.

Supercentre was closed, shutters over the long windows. Pepiz Super Discount Centre closed too. Barclays Bank was shuttered. Except for Dread and Defense Force vehicles, no car moved. On Hanover Street, Carly saw other white people; they were dressed same as the black people.

A Dread van raced past.

She walked like she came here every day of her life, like this Caribbean capital was as familiar to her as the video store at Pacific Palisades Mall.

A bridge crossed a puny, stinking stream. She did too.

It rained and washed her hair into her eyes. She wiped her

forehead. The green-gray hills above Roseau danced with fog and rainbows.

She was limping. Whenever a Jeep whipped by, she concealed the limp.

She passed industrial yards surrounded by chainlink and a stone building that was Old Sugar Mill Cultural Centre. Carly would have stopped and rested but it was closed.

Canefield Airport was a single short runway and two Butler buildings beside the sea. Three planes parked at the end of the runway, one was black. Carly could see it from the road.

It was so quiet, just the soft pad of her shoes on the tarmac, the cries of sea birds. Somewhere a bump, bump, de-bump sound. The runway was bordered by sea oats, taller than a child's head, wavering in the light breeze.

Bump, de-bump, she turned in through the gate, passed the airport snack bar, which offered:

Fish Roti	$1.75
Ham Sand.	3.50
Pies, cakes	.75
Beer (Red Top)	2.00
Heineken	2.50
Fruit Juice	1.00

Also closed.

Bump, bump, bangety bump. When Carly came inside she badly startled five armed Dreads.

The Dread with the rifle jerked it at her. The Dread in the orange plastic chair dropped the spliff from his mouth. The Dread banging on the steel drum kept his eyes closed and rocked from side to side as his slender brown fingers tapped out a map of his brain waves.

The Dread with the white scarf uncurled from the head bench where he'd been reading—*Vanity Fair? Vanity Fair!* . . . "Yes, miss?"

His eyes were zoned out. His smile was too much, too wet. His scarf was fringed, six feet long.

The rifle pointed at Carly was like those cowboy rifles John Wayne used in his movies. The man holding it in one fist was so big he made it seem a toy. He wore his hair in tight cornrows, like small children do.

"Good-morning," Carly said. "Isn't it a wonderful morning and how are you today? I've come to see about a plane."

"You want a plane?" That was the big man. He poked his rifle like it was a pistol.

White Scarf said something in patois and the man with the spliff unbuttoned his holster before going to check outside.

"I can't stay on this wonderful island forever," Carly said.

The drummer had his eyes open. "Some do." He laughed. Bam de bam. "Oh my yes. Government ministers even. Are you the whore of Babylon?"

"No, I don't believe so. When's the next flight to Guadeloupe?"

The man with the gun relaxed but his gun didn't. It stayed aimed at Carly's navel.

The Dread came back sucking on his spliff. He shook his head.

The man with the scarf spoke dreamily. "I the only one flying on Dominica. You want to take a spin?"

"To Guadeloupe."

"Maboya, what you think Mal say to that?"

Maboya, the big man, giggled. "Mal, he, oh, my."

"When will regular service be resumed?" Carly said.

Everybody got a big laugh out of that one. "You hear that, man. Re-zoomed."

Maboya prodded Carly with his rifle. "You lookin' to buy a ticket out of this place. I sell you a ticket."

"Maboya. Don't be too bad," White Scarf said.

"Well," Carly said. "If you cannot help me, I'll just have to try elsewhere." And she stepped back from the gun like it was nothing and said, "Excuse me," and turned to go.

"No."

And her feet were so loose and so fast she almost fled. She told her trembling feet "stay" and faced them like whacked out, armed men were commonplace to her.

White Scarf said, "I take you to the government. If Mal say fly, I fly." He added, "You handsome for a white girl." He grinned forever. Bam, de bong bong, bam.

"Terrific," Carly said. "If I don't get off this island, I'm going to puke."

Their vehicle was parked out behind. "Alertly now," White Scarf said, and the Land-Rover jumped and heeled around the building, out the gate, and onto the main road. Click, he hit a gear, click, another, and Carly was scared but it beat walking.

White Scarf swerved around pedestrians like they were slalom gates and the blare of his horn hung in the air after he'd passed. On the narrow bridge he forced people onto the bridge railing. He swerved onto a wide boulevard and here were other vehicles. Land-Rovers and Dreads and pickups buzzing around a pre-stressed concrete building, like it was their hive.

He skidded to a stop. "Government House," he pointed. "Also police. Defense Force." He giggled. "Is everyone under one roof."

Like Government House, the courtyard gate was strong and gray. Brushed steel interstices you could almost poke an imploring arm through. The Defense Force soldier at the gate was a boy and his salute was precise and young.

Carly said, "Just a minute. I'm not sure . . ."

Her guide flipped his hand, "Oh, miss, not to worry. Everything is A-OK."

The courtyard was surrounded on three sides by hard walls and the Dreads had created a bush encampment here, fire circles, chickens, two tethered kids, several wooden clothes racks where ganja was drying.

"Hey, man, where you goin' with my fren'?"

The speaker was a stocky black with a heavy beard and round spectacles mended with a piece of black electrician's tape. His broad nose was dented. Carly knew him from somewhere.

"*Common ouye*, miss. How are you?"

Carly's "hello" was faint and her smile too as her mind whirled, trying to place him: Tortola?"

White Scarf said, "This pretty white lady want to fly off island so I go to Mal, get he okay."

Carly's friend (from Carnival?) wrinkled his face: no, no. "Don't want to vex Mal Esprit today," he said. "Bad business goin' on in the government today." And he smiled right into Carly's eyes, a toothy, fey smile that invited her to savor life's wonderful foolishness.

Petulantly, White Scarf pushed his hands into his pockets, got up on his tiptoes, and rocked. "I don't know these things, man. I just fly the aircraft. 'Rupert, fly Martinique,' I go Martinique; 'Rupert, fly Antigua,' I . . ."

"Turn her loose, man."

The courtyard smelled of wood smoke and exhaust smoke and the sharp, resinous stink of ganja. Carly felt a little faint. The bearded man had offered her a potion at Tortola Carnival and she'd taken it gratefully enough. Was he Winston's friend? How had he come here?

Rupert had almost made up his mind—Sure, turn the white girl free—when the Dread van pulled up, executed a swift one-eighty as the guard swung the courtyard gates open.

The Dreads in the courtyard rushed toward the van, like it was calling for help.

"Voilà."

Carly never did know who'd spoken, her friend or Rupert. Her stomach dropped so low in her gut she couldn't talk. The Dreads who weren't helping at the van were peering nervously around, fingering weapons.

The thing on the military stretcher was wrapped in garbage bags, head to toe—the bags lashed with clothesline, loose child's knots, two dozen of them.

When they dragged the stretcher out of the van, the man in the bags curled up his legs.

"Mercy," Carly's friend said.

The knees were bent, like the knees of a burn victim. The huddle of soldiers whisked the stretcher through the doors, out of sight.

The sight left a ringing in Carly's ears.

A white man sashayed from the van then; a white man wearing tropical linens and a Panama hat. He picked his way across the courtyard of Government House like it was littered with dog droppings, one precise step at a time, hands clasped behind his back, and at the door he turned and his eyes met hers and Carly felt bad, like there was no good reason to continue living. The pilot sawed his scarf back and forth.

With a queenly swirl, the white man disappeared and the courtyard let out its pent-up breath.

"My God," Carly said. The pilot had been frightened too, and Carly felt warmth for him which was instantly betrayed.

"Miss, I think we go see Mal Esprit. I think we talk to Mal."

She said, "I don't have to fly out. I can stay. The Hubbells, you know, in Soufriere, they are cousins—they've put me up."

"Come, miss."

With the resignation of a beast entering the charnal house, Carly followed him and the stocky man came too.

Like concrete fillets on steel skewers, steps curled out of the blank lobby. Carly's feet made no sound on them. Not a scuff.

Empty corridor to the left, another to the right. The partitions were steel and frosted glass. She heard a tape player: delicate romantic piano. Horowitz, Chopin, perhaps. Tinkled to a crescendo, crashed.

Hesitantly, Rupert turned left.

"No, man. Mr. Bones be busy just now. Take her to Mal Esprit."

A Dread poked his head out of Mr. Bones's office, looked left, looked right, retracted. Seconds later, they heard a *thump* like a luxury car door closing.

The pilot gripped Carly's arm.

An astonished sob was quickly muffled. An object tipped over, something slammed into Mr. Bones's door, which bulged in its frame. Through gritted teeth, someone said, *"Right!"*

Rupert's eyes were childishly wide. He tugged at her. "Here, miss. Mal Esprit the one you see."

Carly wondered where she could go if she had to throw up. The word *Passport*, in blue neon, popped into her mind. When her friend touched her elbow, warmth started there, like his touch was linament. She took a deep breath.

Rupert said, "Mr. Mal Esprit. Is you home?" And pressed his ear to the frosted glass.

Down the corridor came a curious sound—like the mewling of a hurt kitten. On it went. On and on.

So Rupert flipped his scarf around his neck and took his chances.

Wasn't anything on Mal Esprit's desk except a stoneware bowl of ganja and a bottle of Arthritis-Strength Excedrin. His pleated high-backed chair had been stylish in California car dealers' offices five or six years ago. He had it pulled sideways to the drapes so he could see out without anybody seeing him. A musty ganja smell clung to the drapes, curled through the air like grease. Carly pressed a finger against her nose so she wouldn't sneeze. Carly's friend pinched some ganja between his fingers and sniffed it like he was the Ganja Inspecter.

Mal's tired long eyes were perfectly reflective. "Close the door," he said.

Rupert said, "Mal, this white girl wants me fly her to Guadeloupe."

His uniform was crisply pressed but hung on him like he'd lost thirty pounds. There was a soiled spot on the drapes where he pulled them apart. "This the Department of the Interior, man," he said. "Why you come strollin' in here?"

Carly's friend's chuckle was juicy as an overripe breadfruit: "Because you the Boss Nigger in Paradise, man."

"Rollo-Long Pre, he president."

Carly's friend put the Excedrin bottle to his ear and gave it a shake. "She can go?"

Mal said, "Talk to that white man about that."

Carly's friend flipped the bottle in the air. "Mr. Bones"—he savored the name and Carly understood Mr. Bones was a taboo name here, rarely uttered—"Mr. Bones presently occupied."

Mal brought a large handkerchief from his desk drawer, spat, and delicately refolded it. "Passport?" he asked, the very model of the modern colonial officer.

Carly said, "I didn't think I'd need it. I left it in my room." Her lie was such a terrific rush. Why had she ever fooled with drugs? "I'm staying with my cousin, Jean Hubbell. Soufriere."

Mal took a small notepad from his desk, unclipped a pen. "Name?"

Carly told him.

"Place of birth?"

His pen circled that information. "Ah, American citizen."

"Good old U.S. of A."

When his pen hesitated, Carly rushed right in, "I didn't want to fly today, I mean. Tomorrow or next day. I mean, naturally, I've got to pack and say good-bye to Jean and bring my passport to get it stamped. . . ."

His eyes were disappointed. "I suppose you landed at Melville Hall, which is under striker control so we cannot verify your immigration record."

"It *was* Melville Hall," Carly said, just a little breathlessly.

Behind Mal Esprit's closed door were footsteps (one? two?) men, dragging something heavy. A garbage bag or something.

Mal whispered, "You see what we have come to on this island? On account of some people's ignorance?" He retrieved the Excedrin bottle. He shook a couple tablets into his mouth, rubbed his temples. "You fellows, you go now. Ain't you got work, keep you from fillin' up my office?"

The stocky man folded his arms like an armature completing its field of force. As he swelled, the office darkened like a brownout. His voice was precise as words etched on a tombstone and as cold. "This woman ain't doin' harm. Don't you harm her."

Like a man rising through mud, Mal Esprit stood. "Go now," he said. And they did.

Carly's mouth was moist and she felt common power return to her body. Whatever was to happen, she wasn't a victim. Mal crumpled his notes. "AID officials, Canadian observers, several investors from the States caught up in this strike and can't fly out. I got their passports in my desk here. Why I don't have yours?"

Carly shrugged foolishly.

"Maybe you CIA? Don't laugh. Couple those AID men, they CIA, I know it. And now you appear from nowhere, like Obeah sent you, like you a Jumbie." He rubbed his temples and pressed the blood vessels there.

He said, "I am turning you loose, Miss CIA. You tell your masters our president is senile and Mr. Bones is chief here in Dominica and," hissed, "he is white Idi Amin. You going to invade us, like Grenada?"

Carly met his eyes like she was CIA. "Anything's possible."

"Don't be captured no more."

Her escorts waited in the hall. Down the stairs, through the courtyard, Carly looked at nothing—absolutely nothing—and didn't turn until she was safely beyond Government House gate. When she turned, the stocky man wasn't with them anymore. The sunlight was hazy but bright and she blinked her eyes.

"Good-bye, miss. When it proper to fly, you look for me."

Carly had a brave thought and spoke, quick, before she could change her mind. "Those planes don't look very well-maintained to me."

"Those planes? I keep them up. Only me, I fly them and they in tip-top shape. Full of gas, ready to go. Tip-top, miss."

—— 187 ——

Carly pressed her luck. "If you can't fly me to Guadeloupe, maybe you can drive me back to the barricade at Pointe Michel. My feet hurt."

White Scarf hesitated. "Oh, miss. I don't think so, no." When he drove off, his scarf streamed behind him and Carly hoped he'd have the same luck Isadora Duncan had.

So, she walked. Limping openly. She nodded at loungers' "Good-afternoons," but didn't answer.

She limped past the Defense Force roadblocks. After she climbed the log obstacle at Pointe Michel, she took off her shoes and tied them around her neck. The air scalded her broken blisters, her eyes teared, but she felt better after the first mile.

In the late afternoon, on a rocky beach, Carly bathed her feet in the soft, stinging surf until she couldn't feel the hurt anymore. When she looked up and down the beach she couldn't see another mortal soul. She wondered how often lives changed like hers had. She was so afraid of crabs.

12

Winston Comes Home

Winston washed Carly's feet and prepared a poultice while the old schoolmaster fired questions: How many Dreads? Was the minister smiling or glum? Over and over he asked about the prisoner in the garbage bag—was she sure she hadn't heard his name?

"If she knew," Winston said quietly, "they fly her away all right. Over the Guadeloupe Channel and, 'This way to the exit, miss.' Carly have any good information, the sharks eat it by now." He wrapped oily leaves around her feet and taped them. "Don't you goin' around too much."

"Oh," she stretched her leg. "That feels wonderful."

"Herb a vers. My mamma use it."

The schoolmaster broke in impatiently, "This bearded man who befriended you? He did not say his name?"

So Carly told it all again, answering each careful, specific question. Yes, she was sure she'd seen the man at Tortola Carnival.

Finally Winston laughed, ha, ha. "Only man I know looks like that, made of wood. And he ain't said one word to me yet."

Carly stretched her legs across Winston's lap.

Mrs. Polly lay on a well-worried bath mat, one eye on her master.

"And who do those scalawags abduct now? Which minister? Unless they be stopped in their tracks, they muzzling dissent far south as Scotts Head. Truly, these black days for Dominica."

Mrs. Polly eyed his uplifted arm hopefully and thumped her tail: Perhaps he was going to throw a ball?

Carly yawned deeply. "Winston, let my legs down, my muscles are starting to cramp."

Instead, he took his hard hands and dug into her flesh, kneaded and rubbed the twitch that prefigures a cramp, out of the muscle. He worked her calf muscles, one, then the other.

Mr. Soylo took a deep breath. "Well, Winston?"

Winston didn't look up. "Well, what?"

"This brave girl, white girl, she has found out about your airplane. Armed men to guard it, five of them."

"Yes."

"Curse the dog, but admit his teeth are sharp."

"Yes." Winston's hands found more knotted muscle to loosen. She'd put on a few pounds since he first saw her climbing up the companionway on the *Bamboo Cannon*. Seemed like a lifetime ago. She'd had strength when she needed it and the news she'd brought back from Canefield Airport made both men happy: the schoolmaster because he was sure that Winston could not now steal the plane, and Winston, because he was sure he could. He'd creep onto the airstrip late at night—there'd be a curfew in Roseau—but one man, who'd been a schoolboy in that town, could slip past the patrols and lurk in the bush until the Dread guards fell asleep. Then he could fire up the plane and fly. He wouldn't have time for a preflight check or time to warm up his engines, but running rich mixture he could get off the ground before they could do much and three hours later he'd put down in Puerto Rico, just like he'd planned. Black plane wasn't worth any less money because it was captive of a government gone mad. Rosemary. At first he couldn't picture her face and when he did, it was scrinched up like when she vexed him about money.

Under his fingers, Carly's skin wasn't pale white, more like milk with a drop of coffee in it. White girls were more complicated than black girls, not in a good way—more worried, unclear about what they wanted today and tomorrow. And he couldn't get over the feeling that, to white girls he was a symbol—one they'd carry with them always. One or two girls had slept with Winston only because he was a pilot, but in Winston's eyes that seemed different.

Her skin roughened by salt and open air, her feet bruised and bloody, Carly was much prettier than the girl she'd been.

"Thanks, Winston," she said, and, wincing, set her feet on the floor. "Mr. Soylo, what can you do? Roseau is full of guys with guns and some of them are really whacked out. How can you fight men like that?"

The schoolmaster's face tightened and he aimed his chin like he could plow all the way to Roseau. "We are Dominicans," he said. "They Dominicans too. We will make them ashamed."

Mrs. Polly rose, passed gas, and gripped the old man's trouser cuff in her teeth. "So soon, Mrs. Polly? Well, if I must. Goodnight to you two. Mrs. Polly says it is time for bed."

After they'd left the room, Carly said, "What now, Winston? What's the plan, Stan?"

Winston shrugged. "Same plan."

She worked her tongue around her gums. "You're not going to help."

"Dominica where I born. I don't elect this island government. This not my home."

"When you gonna run out on us?"

Winston stood up. "Woman, do not speak to me that way. It is very rude."

"'Woman,' well at least it isn't 'white woman.' I suppose it's an improvement to have just sexism instead of racism and sexism. Winston, I don't understand you. Truly, I don't."

Winston had been wrong. White girl very ugly. "It not easy for me to make up my mind for this plan," he said.

"I'll bet not. I'll bet your life was a bed of roses until one morning you decide to up and steal a plane. It's hell when a good man goes bad."

"It wasn't me stealing. Mal Esprit, he steal..."

"Sure he did. You had a better right to that airplane than he did? Come on, Winston. Come on!"

They heard a growl from the next room.

"Shh," Winston said. "How can they rest with us quarreling?"

She grinned a sparky, unpleasant grin. "We can go outside."

"No. No." Winston stretched and yawned. "You must be very tired."

"Oh, I'm all beat to hell."

Winston slept lightly and badly. Once he got up and sat on the veranda for a half hour, worrying. He'd spent his savings and probably lost his job. He'd landed himself and a strange white girl in the middle of a bad situation. The moon threw indifferent light on sheer mountain and lime plantation alike. The pale road was empty.

When Winston finally did fall off in the cool morning air, he slept hard, and when he woke, the schoolmaster was gone and Mrs. Polly with him.

Carly's bedclothes were neatly put away and she was on the veranda beside a hot cup of coffee, reading C. L. R. James's great cricket book *Beyond a Boundary*.

"Good-morning," he said enthusiastically.

"Morning."

"You learnin' all about cricket, eh?"

She closed the book. "Learning about the West Indies."

"That book not all the West Indies: Trinidad. Oh, Trinidad, so rich island. Give us writers, sportsmen, the calypso, the soca-calypso. Very hot island, Trinidad."

She opened the book again, using her finger to mark her place on the page.

"I don't suppose there's a second cuppa in that pot?" he said cheerfully.

"No."

He drew back from the railing when two young agricultural laborers started up the road below.

She gave them a broad, happy wave.

"Don't you go bein' too friendly, now." Cricket! What could she know about cricket? Cricket was a disciplined game, an exact and haunting game—what could a white American know about it? He put water on the stove and prewarmed the two-cup teapot for three minutes before steeping his tea. Probably she didn't know how to make good tea, either. She probably drank tea from the little paper bags and used a cold cup and left the teabag in the tea until it was vile.

Probably had used so many drugs her brain was vile as her tea.

At the kitchen table Winston faced the schoolmaster's pantheon of black heroes. Tea tasted great. Just perfect! He put it down. He heard the rustle as she turned a page. Other men, he thought, had lives that were far less complicated than his own. He thought about such men—boat bums, young soldiers, Montgomery. What did Montgomery have to worry about? He heard the clatter of stones dislodged on the path. The back door was closed though not bolted. Winston slipped onto the veranda.

Bang, bang, bang. "Hello in there!"

"Say Mr. Soylo's not at home," Winston hissed to her.

"Good-morning. Good-morning. This is Jean Hubbell out here, payin' a call."

"Carly!"

"Winston Riviere! Damn it, man. It is your old school friend, Jean, aren't you going to let me in?"

Winston went blank. Literally didn't have a thought in his head. Carly opened the door.

"Winston, you crazy man, come here, say hello."

"Jean . . ." Because he didn't know what else to do, Winston put out his hand.

"How long you been in this place, man? How'd you get in?"

"Boat."

Carly said, "It was called the *Bamboo Cannon*."

Jean snorted. "You remember them damn things. How we used to fire them off on the Queen's birthday? You lucky miss that hurricane. Heard it passed just north of Guadeloupe."

"We lucky, yes."

"The schoolmaster told me you were here, goddamn, what a trick you play on us all."

"Yes. Goddamn."

Jean rubbed his hands together. "Aren't you going to offer me hospitality."

Carly said, "Mr. Soylo keeps rum in that cabinet there."

"That be fine. Rum, some jelly water, fine. We chat. What you think of us here on Dominica, Winston?"

Winston's old schoolmate wore tattered stained shorts and a short-sleeved shirt with frayed collar. Jean was white, his family big landowners, he was privileged. For the first time, Winston began to understand that Jean's privilege was not enormous or unintelligible. This Hubbell, who had always seemed so important, was a small farmer on a small Caribbean Island.

"What you growin' now?" he asked.

Jean described his experiment on Morne Patates. "I've got our land in limes and grapefruit, but we plant five thousand aloe vera plants last year and I have my fingers crossed."

Carly filled a pitcher with coconut jelly water and they took their ceremonial drinks to the veranda.

"Too early for me," Carly said. "I'll stick to coffee."

Jean Hubbell laughed. "You ain't no Dominican, then."

Jean spoke of pulping the cactuslike aloe vera plant, liquefying it, and then using the Citrus Cooperative's extractor to concentrate it, ten to one. "And you know what it brings, Winston? Eleven hundred dollars per fifty gallons, F.O.B. New Orleans. The Texas crop has frozen two years past and they got to have aloe vera in the States. Man, it's good to see you back. How long you on the island? We have to have a fête. Soylo says you're a pilot. That's splendid, Winston. You be here for the march?"

Winston's face asked his question.

"The march on Roseau. Everybody in Soufriere talking about it. It was another Portsmouth minister the Dreads took this time; motored a boat around the roadblocks and plucked him out of his house. What's the matter, Winston, you lost your Dominican ways?" Jean's glass was empty and Winston poured more rum and jelly water.

"Tomorrow, we all gonna march to Roseau and face that government. Cannot continue like this."

"I didn't know. My plans fully uncertain." Carly smiled at Winston sweet as pie.

A scratch at the door. Mrs. Polly preceded her master.

"Hello, schoolmaster. It is I, Jean."

"Yes." He sniffed. "And you two downing my rum, I see. And Winston, how are you this morning?"

"You know how I am."

Pause. "Quite so. Miss Carly, if you'd fix me something to drink, please, before these rogues drink it all."

Carly fixed his drink and placed the glass in his hand.

Jean said, "I was telling Winston about our march."

"And has he agreed to help?"

Angrily Winston set down his drink. "I think I take a little walk. I suppose all Soufriere knows I'm here."

The blind man smiled his all-inclusive smile. "Just all your friends, Winston."

Jean Hubbell said, "If you have time, Winston, Morne Patates's crusher isn't working properly. Aloe vera leaves are very stringy, you see, and they wrap around the rotor, and . . ."

Winston said, "Uh," and left, descended the timber steps in great strides and Carly called, "Winston, wait up, please."

"You know about this?"

"He said he was going to do it, yes."

"You foolish woman. You seek blows on blows. Ah!"

He lifted both fists in the air. He trembled and jammed them into his pockets, still fists. "Ahh!" he said.

"Winston, Winston." Her feet so light on the road. Her intruding *presence*. The failure, as usual, was all his, but why should she witness it? His shoulders were shuddering with the strain of keeping hands in his pockets. "I cannot!" he said. "Each time I make an attempt, I fall short!"

It took courage to touch his furious body, but she did. She hugged him, feathery light as a granddaughter's kiss.

He stopped shaking and gulped air. "I be okay," he said. "Thank you, miss."

"One wee disappointment and my name goes out the window?" And she had laughter in her eyes and after all he'd suffered, she was laughing at him and he couldn't hurt her so he had to laugh too.

The laughter fluffed the roots of his hair and loosened the skin on his cheekbones. It made his flesh dance. "Carly," he squeaked and she was laughing too, until the tears came to her eyes and she sat down, right in the dusty road and his knees were shaking so bad he sat too. They faced each other, trying to catch their breath. Carly painted sternness on her rubber features: "Poor little black plane," she said, "gone astray. Baa, baa . . ." And they started again until they couldn't look at each other and Winston's belly hurt and he wiped his wet cheeks and stuck out his hand and she took it and they helped each other to their feet.

Their legs were weak, but their spirits very light. School-children under the banyan tree waved and their teacher too. Could that be Sudy Sutpin? "Good-morning! Good-morning, Sudy!"

"Hello, Winston. Children, please!"

And, of course, they had to stop at the Disco where loafers waylaid them into backslaps and cries: "Hello, hello, *common ouye,* good-morning, Winston. Winston, how you been, man? Winston, where you been livin'? You married, Winston? This your wife?"

And Winston had to laugh. "Wait, now. Wait a minute. Dexter, how is your father, your sister? You must have children of your own: three? Somebody been workin' nights around this place. Give me a moment, now. Yes, I am a pilot in St. Thomas. Twin engine, I don't have the license for commercial jet. Yes, the helicopters too. I learn to fly, helicopters. No, Harry, do not say so. She was too young for the heart attack, say it is not so. A moment, a moment. Carly is her name. No, she not my outside wife. She nobody's. Now don't you go combing your hair, Randolph. Look, he so pretty now!"

Hand in hand, Carly and Winston walked into Soufriere and the loafers tagged along. One had a penny whistle, so their progress was attended by a musical air.

They went for penny bread and Winston embraced the baker, and the shy baker's wife came from behind her curtain. "Here, here, let me bring you glass of goat's milk to go with that."

"Carlos," Winston said, "man, you doin' pretty good for yourself. You own bake shop and pretty wife." (The girl blushed.) "And I see you keepin' the oven hot!" He laughed when the pregnant woman punched his shoulder. "Man, you in paradise for sure. Life, just a dream in the tropics, eh?"

Somebody brought a steel drum and there was an accordion too, and the penny whistle and an old man with a rum bottle danced with a child in a schoolgirl's uniform.

Winston, his hands full of penny bread, grinning. The baker's wife peeking around Carly, who is smiling in the bright yeasty sunlight.

Villagers coming down the street—there's Maxwell the grocer, still wearing his produce apron; his fat wife, Sophronia, wobbling behind; fishermen in shorts, shirtless, hurrying from the beach; and one-legged Paul Valerie on his crutches.

The penny whistle and accordion were joined by a deep-toned drum, so only a trumpet was lacking for a real steel band. Schoolchildren running down the road, released, released to freedom! And the trumpet announced its presence with a blat before settling into the rhythm, and the sun beat down long and hot on the galvanized roofs, the cobblestone streets of Soufriere, Dominica, W.I.

An old, old woman, completely black-clad, left her house, which was quite convenient, if you please, to St. Anthony's Church, and not a block from the Qwik Shop. The loaf-shaped wooden case she carried was so heavy she could make only five or six paces before pausing to put it down. Past the Qwik Shop, past the bright green house of the fisherman, Valerie. Twice she refused help with her burden. Five steps, put it down. Catch her breath and lift it up again. The dancers who packed the narrow street made way for her without losing a step, swirled, recaptured their partners and the music was hot!

Finally, she stood facing the white girl (who she did not know) and Winston Riviere, who she knew when he was too small to change himself.

"Tante Marie, Tante Marie."

She endured his hug. She flipped catches and the bun-shaped cover came away in her hand. Voilà! She smiled the same smile that used to get her anything she'd wanted sixty years ago when she'd been a heartbreaker. "My Singer machine, Winston," she said. "It is completely broken. You can fix?"

Late that night, Winston and Carly sat in Mr. Soylo's kitchen drinking tea. The schoolmaster was abed an hour since and no telling if the snores from the next room were his or his dog's.

Winston's chuckle was daylong laughter gone hoarse and run down. "At first, I think someone's joking me," he said. "Old Tante Marie. And what good's the Singer going to do her without electricity?"

Carly had her chin in her hands, watching him. His face was so much softer than it had been.

"And then Paul Valerie wants me to look at the motor on his boat and there's Jack Montgomery's generator and Hubbell's aloe vera machine. No wonder these fellas glad to see me. They want to get their lives running again."

"What are you going to do?"

Winston shrugged. "Can't have no bomber plane bombing the march."

"Winston, those Dreads . . ."

"Oh, they bad johns, is true, but who else to stop that plane? Might as well go brave."

She stood up, and calmly unbuttoned her blouse. It slicked to the floor beside her sleeping mat.

"Woman, what you do?" Even to himself, Winston's voice sounded funny.

"I'm going to bed," she said. She unsnapped her tired blue jeans. "There's two empty beds in this house, Winston, and you can sleep in either one of them."

13

Road March

"Couldn't you wear something less conspicuous?" Carly asked.

"Purple shirt, maybe? Big green flowers on it?" Winston drew his neat, white pilot's shirt out of the duffle and gave it a shake. Been underwater in a hurricane, but looked good enough for captain of a 747. Shirt was practically brand-new. Same with the light khaki slacks slung over the chair. He stepped into his underpants and Carly clasped his bare leg, pressing her so soft breasts against his leg.

"I brought these clothes for flyin' into Puerto Rico. Them Spanish funny about clothes. Fly in, dressed neat, they don't even open your bag. Manifests? 'No trouble, senor.' But one of them T-shirt pilots, oh he land they climb over him, like he is doper or gunrunner maybe. Friend of mine, Haitian pilot (he dead now) he flyin' into San Juan from the Caymans. It a hot day so he take off his shirt to get cool and open his window. 'Tum, te, tum, tum,' and the plane hit a squall and he bank and big wind suck his shirt out the window. When he come into San Juan, they not believe it. 'You a *pilot*, senor?' Oh, Charlie in the shit, then."

"But you're not going to Puerto Rico."

"I am a pilot."

When Carly sat up, the lantern glossed the tops of her sweet breasts. Her hair was mussed and tangled and the odor that rose from the disturbed bedclothes tickled Winston's nose and he felt himself getting hard again but, my, he was tender against the fabric of his underpants.

"God, you're pigheaded."

"Oink, oink, oink, oink," he bent and nuzzled her neck, "oink."

She took his face and kissed him with her love-bruised lips. "Come back to bed."

"You put some clothes on. Schoolmaster rise up soon for the road march. I want you stay in the rear of that march. That tear gas rough."

"Yes, Boss."

"You a most impudent woman. You lookin' for blows?"

"No, Boss."

Her smile lit up her face. It brought moisture to his eyes, it was so fresh and full of hope. White girl been all over the world— Winston thought—and she never able to live. I got to be careful with this one. The name *Rosemary* came to his mind and though it was just a name, nothing *personal* about it, he buried it, and scuffed sand on it, quick as a cat. Winston buttoned his shirt and she ran a hand up his leg, *way* up his leg. *Most* impudent. "Woman, I can't put on my pants with you bein' free and easy."

"What a shame."

And Winston had to laugh. Even for a white woman she was bold. He adjusted his shirt creases before zipping up his trousers and was uncomfortable, his manhood enclosed in two layers of cloth. He gave himself a hitch but that didn't help much. Winston had to think of the last time he'd been so sore after making love. Or been so stretched.

Standing, her head came just under his chin and he could feel her heat through his clothing. How perfumed she was.

She said, "I will see you after this."

He said, "Oh my, yes." He felt another twinge in his pants. "Not to worry. I be away before they know I there."

The faint hiss from Mrs. Polly sounded like a leaky bicycle tire. "All right, I be going." Winston was out before the invisible gaseous cloud could reach him.

He was down on the road, beside the lime trees when she called, "Winston?" She was a pale ghost on the veranda above. "Do not let them turn you around."

He walked off, quickstep, like regular British infantry.

Grow up barefoot and it don't hurt when you barefoot again. It felt natural and right to Winston to walk the coast road with deck shoes tied around his neck. Winston didn't care about land crabs.

The sky blued and drowned its stars one by one. Waves lapped the shore, cool wind poured down the mountains and tickled his neck hairs.

All night the shortwave radios had chattered: Petit Coulibre to Anse Du Me, Marigot to Bells, Bells to the fishing boats anchored at Castle Bruce, Castle Bruce to Melville Hall, Melville Hall to the Carib Reserve, which, recalling its warlike heritage, launched four boats to round Scotts Head, by dawn.

Marigot: We need petrol, man. Our young men can walk but old folks comin' in buses.

Bells: We got petrol—fifty gallons.

Marigot: That get us to Roseau, how we gonna get home?

Bells: When the government topple, you get all the gas you need.

Bells (to the fishing boat *Krabie*): You got petrol hoarded, is time to give it up.

Krabie: How we gonna get our (static) people to Roseau?

Bells: Ain't you got sails no more?

Static

All over the island, cached jerry cans came out of hiding, dregs were siphoned out of electric generators. St. Joseph found twenty gallons in a government road scraper. In Portsmouth, youths rowed out to the Italian yacht *Belgrave* and a not entirely happy skipper drained all the boat's diesel onto buses lined up head to tail on the municipal pier.

Winston walked by fishing boats pulled up on the beach. No fishing today. He passed driftwood trees that someone had been cutting for firewood but nobody cutting today.

The sky was very high, and the moon was a faintly printed insignia on an empress's blue silk gown. Mountains were black with shadows. The birds were starting to call.

He smelled smoke before he came into Pointe Michel, charcoal breakfast fires and some other smoke too, not so nice.

This early the women were at the standpipes, arranging which would stay with the children and which would go. They fell silent when Winston appeared.

"Good-morning, ladies. Nice morning for marching on the government, yes?"

They looked away, suspiciously. So neatly dressed, Winston might be *with* the government.

Two lorrys allotted petrol were receiving a touch-up dusting by their owners, less fortunate owners sat disconsolate on the curb, and several were drinking rum. One spat and didn't quite hit Winston's feet.

Short-haired, prick-eared pariah dogs slunk around, chickens pecked in the streets. The smoke smell was strong enough to make Winston's eyes water.

Bright houses overlooked the beach, a jumble of houses climbed the hill. The gap where the burned building had stood was as bitter as a missing tooth. Young kids picked through the smoldering wreckage. Salvaged objects were stacked beside the lintel stone: The partially melted top of a cake plate, the seats of two plastic stools mended with electrician's tape. Underneath the smoke, Winston smelled kerosene.

"Hey, man, what you want with us, here?"

He was younger than Winston and his gang was younger than him. He wore a blue bandanna wrapped around his head. His shirt was open from his navel and his genuine U.S. blue jeans were faded.

Three more young men hurried across the street.

"Lookin' for Mrs. Oregard? She friend to you?"

"Looks pretty bad in this place," Winston said. "I hope nobody burn."

The boy with the blue bandanna sauntered nearer. "Oh, it burned like a furnace, this place."

"Because of the fat grease she keep," another volunteered. He had pockmarks below his cheekbones. "Boy, what your name?"

Winston checked his temper. "Winston Riviere. Soufriere."

"Oh, that a nice place. Nice place. Soufriere. Every day a carnival in Soufriere."

"I did not anticipate running into such poor manners in Pointe Michel," Winston said. Deliberately he made the noise with his mouth, tchup!

The young man brought his hand from behind his back and he held a short, thick stick, some kind of tool handle.

Two of the others had cutlasses.

Winston said, "I got no time be playin' the ass with you boys. I got business in Roseau, for the march."

"I don't know you," the blue-bandannaed leader said.

"That's the only true thing you said," Winston said, and turned his back.

His ears cocked for the rush of running feet, the whoosh of a blow, Winston stepped through Pointe Michel at a pretty good clip. Down one slope of a storm drain, up the other. A stone cracked into a lintel beside him, but Winston didn't turn.

The young men were a presence at the center of his spine and the sweat gathered there. Fifty yards past the last houses where the road drops close to the beach, he turned. They'd stopped at the edge of town, like that's where their jurisdiction ended.

The leader lifted his fist in the air in the black power salute: "You tell 'em, we comin', man. And when we done with Roseau, no stone be standing on stone."

Broken bark marked the narrow spots where the roadblocks had been. Great broken trees, pushed aside, bobbled in the surf, floating out to sea.

No Defense Forces in Newtown, none at the intersection where Bath Road comes in from the south. People inside their houses, rare stragglers on the streets. House shutters down like when a hurricane is coming.

Roseau: There was Falconer's house and the Whitechurch Market, all closed up and nobody on the streets, shutters down, cars parked at the curb. Wind ruffling dead produce leaves in the open air market. Winston had never seen Roseau so lifeless, so still.

At the banana sheds, he abandoned the road for the beach. Twice, Defense Force Land-Rovers raced by and twice Winston crouched until they were out of sight.

Just south of Canefield Airport is a hillock where the owners of Canefield Plantation buried their dead in the days when this was the lushest and levelest estate on the island. The hillock was grown up in bush now, an annoyance to pilots who usually land into the north and can't see Canefield's short strip until they are on top of it.

Winston sat on a granite tomb. From here he could see everything.

In the haze tin roofs shimmered. The heat shimmered under
the parked planes, glittered like a shallow sheet of water at the
end of the runway. When the airport was working properly, somebody mowed the sea oats but these days they came right to the
edge of the apron.

Two planes had cockpit tarps—smooth white canvas covers that
protected the interiors from the sun. The black plane, no.

Winston plucked the wire cutters from his pocket and set them
on the warm stone. In the old days, they built tombs better than
houses. Few houses still standing, hurricanes took them, but the
tombs still here. Their builders not foolish; they'd be inhabiting
these small houses much longer than the bigger ones with windows.

Ten o'clock. Marchers would have left Soufriere. All over this
island buses laboring toward Roseau. Small boats too.

Winston started down the graveyard hill, crouched behind
clumps of skinny acacia. At the bottom, he rolled his pant legs to
ford a shallow creek. Low rushes grew in the white muck and
small fishes dashed through transparent water.

"Go brave," Winston muttered. He patted his feet dry before
slipping on his shoes. Stooped, Winston slunk through the sea
oats. It was hot and many mosquitoes made their home here. The
sea oats thrived in fine sand, which got into his low shoes.

Winston saw the V-tail of the Beechcraft first. The old Beechcraft Bonanzas are fine aircraft but unforgiving in a stall.

Hot. Whine of mosquitoes. Thump of a steel drum in the terminal building.

The Beech Bonanza and the Piper Cherokee were tied down,
the black plane not.

Two hundred meters down the strip was the terminal building.
They couldn't see Winston unless they stepped outside to take a
pee or watch a sea bird or check the weather or stretch their legs
or . . .

Winston scooted out of the sea oats, onto the Bonanza's wing,
and unsnapped the cockpit cover. Twist and tug, twist and tug,
and he jerked the handle and scriggled inside like a snake into a
tent. The plane smelled of hot plastic and oil and cigarette butts.

Winston sat in the copilot's seat and groped under the instrument panel where he snipped himself a path long as his arm. He cut wiring and vacuum lines and created spark showers when he hit a power source. He jerked the wiring until a mass of varicolored spaghetti dangled below the controls. Winston crawled into the sunlight and fastened the canopy before scuttling across the oil-streaked concrete, under the belly of the Cherokee onto the wingstep, where his fingers worked snaps, pop, pop, pop up the canvas, jerked the door, and slid into a second tent no roomier than the first. Winston breathed. This was a pretty nice Cherokee —a sixty-four or sixty-five. The radios looked brand-new. This plane'd belong to a Dominican, some Portsmouth doctor or lawyer who could afford its upkeep.

He unscrewed the coverplate of the mixture controls. His heavy cutters gnawed through the cables and aluminum control rods, ping! he heard an engine whine; tires on asphalt. His nippers clamping a solenoid lead, Winston froze. The engine stopped outside, beneath his wingtip, and backfired.

"I don't know why I got to do this, man."

"Because you told to do it."

"But I a free man. Not slave like my grandfather."

"Hand the jerry can to me, ass." A grunt. A thunk.

Winston took a quiet breath. He withdrew his nippers from the solenoid without a scrape, leaned back very, very carefully because this Cherokee aircraft rested on a tripod of tires and any weight shift can make the wingtips wobble like a tightwire walker's pole. Winston settled like a man relaxing into the electric chair.

"Gimme them flasks, man." Plastic containers clattered on the runway.

"Why ain't Rupert out here playing with petrol in the hot sun?"

"Because Rupert going to fly this black plane. Where the funnel?"

"I thought you bring the funnel."

"You continue in this manner, Roger, gonna be one more nigger in hell tonight."

"Maboya, don't be vex, I go fetch it."

The engine fired up. The groan of reverse gears, squeal of tires.

Beside Winston's right shoulder, he could see light leak through the unfastened cover. He might hook the snap with his fingernail and bring it flush. No. He might turn the stiff safety handle and pull the door to. No.

It was so hot. His shirt collar was soaked through. Winston laid the nippers in his lap.

Scritch. Winston smelled tobacco smoke. Someone sang: "I shot the sheriff, but I didn't shoot no deputy."

Winston breathed short and shallow. He could feel his heartbeat in his elbow points. Surely his heartbeat couldn't make this aircraft tremble. Winston blinked sweat.

"I shot the sheriff, but I didn't shoot no deputy. Ooh, ooh, ooh . . ."

The vehicle returned. Feet slapped on the runway. Winston's neck hurt but he didn't dare rub it.

"Hold the funnel and the flask, man."

"Maboya, why we going to drop petrol on those people?"

"Ain't gonna be us. We be right here, guardin' the government planes. Is Rupert going to do the dropping of petrol."

"When these flasks burst they throw petrol every direction, man. No telling who they douse."

"Government tell them, go to work, do your own business. No, they don't listen. They march on the government. What government to do?"

Winston listened helplessly as the two men filled their petrol bombs, wondering what on earth he could *do?*

The citizens of Dominica marched on their government festively. Most were well dressed, best shirts and dresses, going-to-church shoes. Young girls danced along the roadsides and boys, seated on the bus roofs, banged rhythms until passengers stuck their heads out the windows crying, "Stop the noise! What a terrible racket, oh my!"

Mr. Soylo took the front bus seat, right behind the driver, and Mrs. Polly lay beside him. Carly—whose heels were still tender —thought it looked different from here. No land crabs as the laden bus labored up the hills. Uphill, they went slower than the marchers and a bit faster down. The bus clunked along in its lowest gear. Strollers rapped on the side of the bus and families shouted back and forth through the windows.

"How you feeling, schoolmaster?"

"You comfortable, Mr. Soylo?"

Mr. Soylo nodded his head. "When eyes meet, lying stops. They must give us back our government."

Periodically the bus overheated and, muttering apologies, the driver pulled over and while he was finding water for his radiator, everybody got out to stretch their legs and the walkers they'd passed caught up to them again.

The Soufriere Methodist men wore short-sleeve white shirts and the women, white also. They sang: "Onward Christian Soldiers," and other ferocious hymns. Between hymns, they sang: "Rule Britannia, Britannia Rule the Waves. Britons ne-eh-eh-ver will be slaves!" They would have sung Dominica's national anthem too, had Dominica had one.

Mrs. Polly lay, head on her paws, and if she passed gas, all the windows were wide open and nobody noticed.

Three times they stopped for water before Pointe Michel and twice between Pointe Michel and Loubiere. The driver'd uncap the radiator and, face averted, he'd pour right into the heart of the steam. "Back on the bus, please. All peoples back on the bus."

Each time they stopped, the vehicles behind stopped too and their passengers got out. And stretched and chatted with the walkers, some of whom they hadn't seen since the last march on Roseau.

In Loubiere a flatbed lorry joined them. It carried a steel band seated on wooden benches and the lorry rocked to their beat.

After the Methodists, before the steel band, the Soufriere bus edged along the sea cliffs; beside it, walkers formed a single file.

"Good-morning, Henry."

"Maria, ain't seen you since your mamma died."

"You forget me too soon, Henry."

Laughter, "How I forget you?" Rapid patois. More laughter. The bus stopped at the Newtown standpipe. When Carly got out she could hear the crowd: like Roseau, ahead, was clustered by a swarm of bees. Above the hum, the wail of a police siren went on and on forever.

The engine died, and though the driver ground away, he couldn't restart it. Carly helped Mr. Soylo down the steps and Mrs. Polly hopped behind.

Umbrellas dotted the crowd. A few pure black, most brightly colored. Yellow ones bore advertising slogans for Cinzano and Pirelli tires.

The siren hooted nonstop, like a worried mother calling her children home, but nobody could pass through this crowd now. Buses and vans parked beside the road head to tail, and a flood of marchers between. Members of the Dominican Freedom Party unrolled a banner: END WRONGDOING. Many marchers wore badges, some from the Civil Service Union; the green-and-black ones, Dominican Labor Party. A few Rastafarians marched too, proud silent men, distinctly a minority, grouped close together for safety.

Winston's knees were dry, his pant knees—khaki colored. His ankles were dry—khaki colored. The epaulets on his shirt were white. Otherwise, his body was a map of human sweat glands and his pants were grungy brown, his shirt soaked through and transparent.

The men outside Winston's canvas prison worried: "Thank Jah they not marching on us, man. I never seen so many peoples."

"Watch the work you doin', man. You spillin' it!"

The pungent stink of petrol slipped into Winston's prison and tickled his nose. He jammed his forefinger against the base of his nose to halt a sneeze. It must be a hundred twenty degrees in this cockpit.

"Hand me them flasks, man."

"This the lever here?"

"Oh yes, that's it, man. Pull that and petrol falls from the sky."

Some of the marchers wore black armbands to honor the missing ministers. Several grief-stricken widows were helped by strong arms.

The government had drawn up vehicles to block off the road before Police Headquarters. Behind this barricade, Defense Force and Dreads had their rifles and machine pistols unslung. The siren cried.

"I can see fine from here," Carly said. "I'll tell you what happens, okay?"

But the blind man and his dog pressed on. "No. We must confront these scalawags. Walk on."

As they neared the barricade, the composition of the crowd changed. In the rear were elderly citizens, women with children. Forward, younger married men, some with their wives. The leading third of the great crowd was young men and boys, except for the front line of Dominican Labor leaders, priests, former officials, two exministers.

"Ah, Soylo! Soylo! I did not expect you today."

"And why not? Am I so useless I cannot raise my voice to protest injustice?"

The other wore a brown, too-tight suit and a green knit tie. On his breast, he sported a Dominican Labour Party badge.

Carly felt the press of the great crowd at her back. It was not a comfortable feeling.

The Labour Party official said, "Today a big day for us, Soylo. So many have marched I cannot count them all. Twenty, thirty thousand, easily. And many having their umbrellas. We not get painted today, eh Soylo?" He laughed.

"I don't believe that black bomber plane come for us today," Soylo said. "Has the president come out of his offices?"

"Oh that silly man. He so senile, it is said, he forget his wife is five years in her grave. Talks to her every day, tries to ring her up. A shell of a man, piteous to see."

"Then . . ."

"Rollo-Long Pre is not the government. That white man . . . There, is him coming out of the building now."

The crowd's roar greeted Mr. Bones like the squall of an angry animal. If he noticed, he gave no sign, neither slackened nor quickened his pace. He made a petulant gesture, which brought Dreads and Defence Force men running to him. They fell in behind.

At the barricade, he turned delicately to scoot through the vehicles. He stopped, clasped his hands behind his back, and rocked on his heels. Behind, his soldiers hurried into file. With a great rattling, those who had bayonets fixed them. The soldiers wore gas masks dangling from their necks.

Carly's heart dropped to her shoes. "Oh, shit," she breathed.

Clouds chased across the sun and it began to drizzle. Warm rain washed Carly's cheeks as two lines of armed men extended their weapons and took a big sliding step forward. Another.

Acting the drum major, Mr. Bones raised both arms over his head and swept them down and the armed men bellowed:

"BLACK MAN TIME HAS COME,"

and took another sliding step. Again Mr. Bones raised his arm and dropped it:

"WHITE MAN HAD HIS FUN."

it was a growl:

"BLACK MAN STRONGER THAN WHITE MAN.
BLACK MAN SWEETER THAN WHITE MAN,"

and Mr. Bones, one of the few white men on Bath Road that day shouted: "You are white man's slaves. You do his work for him."

And his soldiers sang again, louder, stabbing with their weapons: "Black man time has come, White man had his fun. Black man stronger than white man. Black man sweeter than white man."

It was a war chant and it bludgeoned Carly's ears and Mrs. Polly leaned into her harness, bared her teeth, and drooled.

In a clear, quiet voice, Mr. Soylo said, "This is intolerable behavior. This is petty and rude." He turned then to face the crowd. In the same high tenor voice he had as a boy, Mr. Soylo sang another anthem, one which he long ago learned to regard as the anthem of reason and justice. In his high, pure voice, he sang:

> "God save our gracious Queen,
> Long live our noble Queen,
> God save the Queen."

A frail voice picked up the hymn, another. First the young boys sang, and then their fathers sang. The hymn was too light to serve as counterpoint to the Dreads' rougher anthem but everyone knew "God Save the Queen"—they'd been singing it all their lives and there were thousands, thousands and thousands, and their hymn rose as a sweet chorale to the Caribbean sky and the sun peeped out and the rain quit and you couldn't hear a word the Dreads were singing. Not one word.

The armed men stopped singing and advancing and some set their gun butts on the pavement. Nobody was pointing his weapon as the final chords trembled into silence. A Dread coughed. He said, "Pardon me."

The blind schoolmaster faced forward. He spoke quietly, "Steady on, Mrs. Polly."

Carly said, "Don't . . ."

"Please to remain where you are. No need to accompany me. Mrs. Polly, walk on, please."

And, led by his dog, the blind schoolmaster marched on Mr. Bones.

Trapped in a hot cockpit, sweat streaming into his eyes, Winston was motionless.

"Time you go fetch Rupert. Time he fly this bomber plane. I stay here to clean up your petrol mess, man."

When the vehicle left for the pilot, Winston figured it was now or never and he'd lived long enough to know how to die. Like a fer-de-lance, head first, he squirmed out the hatch and slithered onto the wing.

He had luck. The enormous Dread was on the far side of the black plane, on hands and knees, scraping sand onto a torn cardboard flap. Winston came down from the Cherokee's wing onto his tiptoes, his weight was fluid, and he didn't make a whisper or a sound.

Maboya wore shorts, an olive drab T-shirt, and a canvas military holster dangling over his hard buttocks. He was digging sand with his cutlass, rattling it onto the cardboard. Winston ducked under the belly of the black plane, took a deep breath, and rushed; one step, two steps, three, and leaped into the air and dropped with his knees. The big man twisted his head but the full weight of Winston Riviere, some 180 pounds, crashed into his back with kneepoints like knifepoints in his kidneys and he went flat as a rug, open mouth jammed full of sand.

Winston grabbed the man's ears and slammed his head again and again; Maboya was so big and Winston so scared.

Half-stunned, Maboya hunched his back and bucked Winston into the air but Winston had the bigger man's pistol when he landed and backpedaled fast.

Maboya spun, dropped into a wrestler's crouch. His face was golden with sand. Winston slid the slide on the army .45 just like the army had taught him: Legs slightly apart, arms locked, butt resting in both hands, he took aim. "Halt," he said.

Maboya spat sand. "You playin' the ass, man." He rubbed his mouth.

"You not try and stop me."

"Shit!"

Winston backed onto the wing, onto the wingstep, into the black plane's cockpit. Maboya's eyes were yellow and red like a hot sunrise. Winston's right hand kept the pistol aimed as his left hand hit switches:

WHEEL BRAKES: OFF
FUEL PUMPS: ON

The Land-Rover was still parked outside the terminal, nobody in sight. Winston had a funny thought—Maybe Rupert still dressing—then he grinned. He took a deep breath, looped his arm out the window to skitter the army .45 down the runway, slammed the hatch, and hit:

IGNITION: ON

And cha-whuff, cha-whuff, as the prop whipped, whipped again and two men ran out of the terminal, stopped, stood agape. Left engine fired, settled into an irregular roar and the right engine cha-whuffing, cha-whuffing even as Winston taxied onto the runway. A thump, and the wing dipped as Maboya crawled onto it and men diving into the Land-Rover as the right engine fired too, Winston running them both up to full throttle, those great Navaho engines sucking air and Maboya struck at the door with his cutlass, a great slash in the Plexiglas. The Land-Rover rolling toward him, pilot standing, waving a pistol, his long white scarf streaming behind and Winston's engines nowhere near full power, but this was every bit of all the time he had, so Winston released the brakes and the black plane lurched down the runway, engines screaming. Wham—Maboya struck at the canopy, wham and they sped right at the Land-Rover—collision course—and there was a hard *cluk* and a magic hole appeared in Winston's windscreen, but he didn't think of that, didn't fear the onrushing Land-Rover because there was just room for one big moving thing on this airstrip now, and that him. "Lift off, lift off!" How she wanted to fly!

Wham. Maboya had turned his attention to the thin aluminum fuselage.

Winston paused, paused, *now,* pulled the gear-up lever and the plane climbed as White Scarf dove for safety and the Land-Rover spun out of control. Ten feet altitude, fifteen, the runway flashed by, the light green sea, turning dark green-blue immediately, and there was a rattling of the door latch but Winston didn't turn to see, he dipped his wing and shook it and a hundred feet below, in nice deep water, Maboya created a white plume.

"I hope that fella swim," Winston said.

Winston completed the preflight check and the inflight check, oil and fuel pressure nice, set his mixtures. Left engine too rough. His hands flicked over the controls, tuning the plane like a fiddle player tunes, musical again, in full flight again, plenty of fuel and the reserve tanks topped off, heading north by west, Dominica's sheer foggy mountains beneath his wings and all the green Antilles, the happy world ahead of him. Winston *free*.

During the singing, government workers came out of headquarters. One clerk held his mug of tea. A woman hurriedly applied lipstick.

Propped up in his progress by Mal Esprit, the old president, Sir John Rollo-Long Pre, appeared. As they hobbled on, like a four-legged beast, Mal whispered in the old man's ear and gave his arm emphatic squeezes.

The old man wiped spittle from the corner of his mouth. His shirt collar was three days old and he had patchily shaved. "Yes," he said. "Of course. Yes."

His cream-colored tropical suit hung on him like swaddling clothes. He was blind to the crowd though several old friends shouted his name.

"You see what injustices are done in your name, Mister President?"

"Mister President, we protesting today."

"Quite close enough," Mr. Bones said.

Mrs. Polly halted. Mr. Soylo licked his lips and said, "I am Mr. Maurice Soylo, Schoolmaster, Soufriere, retired. I voted for the West Indian Federation in '61, worked for Associated Statehood in '67, served on the Dominican Constitution Committee, struggled for full political independence from all nations, Great Britain too, and now, sir, I wish to know by what authority you sell our nation to the highest bidder, by what authority you assassinate our ministers?"

Mrs. Polly didn't growl but bared her teeth.

Mr. Bones lifted his face to the sky and rolled his eyes. "This is a filthy little island," he said. "Chickens in the streets, cattle tethered on the shoulders of the roads, unemployment, illiteracy, superstitions."

Mr. Soylo waited for his answer.

"Filthy and boring. In the capital city of this Negro nation they pull in the streets by nine o'clock. Do we have art? No, crafts. Music? No, steel bands. Subtle intellectual discussion? 'No, mahn. We talkin' good shit.' And you claim to be a schoolmaster."

When Mal Esprit turned the president loose, the old man wobbled in an eccentric circle, seeking his aide. Eyes on the drama ahead, his clerks sidestepped.

"All around," Mr. Bones jerked a contemptuous thumb, "we see the evidence of educational achievement."

"You have not answer my question, sir," Mr. Soylo pressed. "Where is your authority come?"

The white man stalked around the schoolmaster, like Mr. Soylo was statuary. Mrs. Polly's glare and bared teeth attended his circuit.

"My authority, you ignorant wog, is my willingness to put you to death."

The crowd's hush was absolute. Nobody sniffled or rattled an umbrella.

Mr. Soylo said, "No. That don't give you no right to—"

Mr. Bones backhanded him across the face and he reeled, and, furious, Mrs. Polly seized Mr. Bones's pant leg, and he hopped, trying to kick her, and she took another, firmer, grip and had his ankle this time and bit hard.

He yelled, "Damn! Damn!" And from his suit jacket, he plucked a nickel-plated automatic, a lady's gun, and it barked at the dog once, twice. Mrs. Polly yelped and let go to lick the place where bullets had taken her and, pointblank, Mr. Bones emptied his automatic into the blind man's dog.

That great crowd roared and rolled forward and Mr. Bones went down. Perhaps the soldiers might have saved him but one soldier broke for safety behind the barricade, and others ran after him, like soap suds going down a drain.

The black plane came down Bath Road, skimming the electric wires and seemed to fill the air space between the buildings, wingtip to wingtip.

The disheveled Dreads and Defense Force men greeted it with a cry and even Rollo-Long Pre turned to follow its passage. It soared steeply and those who could cluster under umbrellas did so. Others pressed onto the sidewalks. In the middle of the street, before the barricade, nothing remained except a man-sized bloody pile of rags, and a dead black dog, lying on her side.

Mal Esprit rallied the government. "To me! To me!"

Soldiers were pulling the tear gas masks over their chins and tightening goggle buckles, and the black plane was a speck in the sky, turning lazily, sun glinting off its wings.

Mal Esprit formed his force into files, tear gas guns forward, and the panicked clerks bolted for the safety of police headquarters and a bewildered president circled the square like a parrot gone mad.

Down it came, down, like a dropped stone, and all the crowd cried out. The street filled with a roar and the doors in the gut of the plane opened and a streamer of white plastic jugs toppled and burst at the Defense Force barricade, while others whumped the pavement, one exploding inches from the president; another knocked a Defense Force soldier to the ground and he screamed and huddled around his broken arm.

Then the plane was a speck again, in the eye of the sky. The president was screaming, hands pressed to his eyes. The air was saturated with petrol vapor. Everybody felt fear.

"No matches. No fire," a Dominican Labor Party leader cried, and, on tiptoes, the great mass of people began to withdraw with gentle, shuffling feet.

A drenched Defense Force man unfastened his gas mask and sniffed the fuel cooling his hands. Gently, he laid his weapon on the pavement and laid his shirt, boots, and pants beside it. Wearing only undershorts, he walked into the crowd and though nobody welcomed him, nobody molested him either.

Other soldiers and Dreads followed this example and disappeared into the crowd, ordinary Dominicans again. They had looked so very fearsome minutes before.

14

Chak pe jwen fromage-li
(Every bread finds its cheese)

It rained and washed the streets. Clerks and government workers slipped out of Government House. Dr. John Allen, who had treated Rollo-Long Pre for as long as anyone could remember, came and took the president away. Firefighting units from the Department of Public Safety pumped great quantities of water down Bath Road and into Police Headquarters courtyard. They washed the barricade too, because those vehicles belonged to the Dominican people again.

The Soufriere marchers brought Mrs. Polly home in state. The priest said it would be blasphemous to bury a dog in consecrated ground so the villagers buried Mr. Soylo's companion under the banyan tree at the schoolyard. On Carly's arm, Mr. Soylo attended the burial. He was in shock, dry-eyed.

By nightfall, the rightful police reoccupied their offices, removing the Dreads' goats and ganja plants. The assistant commissioner of police took the office Mal Esprit had used and the commissioner planned to occupy Mr. Bones's office as soon as it was scrubbed with carbolic from floor to ceiling to remove the stench.

By nightfall, the electric plant at Lolot was operating and the police began searching government files for evidence of wrongdoing. Judicial Magistrate Wiley issued warrants for arrest. Road-blocks were set up. Constables dispatched to every village.

Soufrierians hoped Mrs. Polly would be an object lesson to school-children—loyalty, patriotism, fighting for Dominican rights. Mr. Bones was unceremoniously bundled into a pauper's grave in Government Cemetery. He was an object lesson too.

A constable was stationed outside Rollo-Long Pre's hospital room and police officers were ordered to Canefield Airport and Melville Hall. As soon as power was restored, Radio Dominica began broadcasting, "Ministers working round the clock to restore essential services, election promised soon." And they'd play the Mighty Sparrow's calypso, "Capitalism Gone Mad" again and again.

Engineers worked all night on the boards at the telephone and cable headquarters. The first phone calls were from the government to the State Department of the United States.

Then the government made assurances to Martinique, Guade-loupe, and London.

At dawn, the Liat plane landed at Canefield. Three weeks be-fore, when the strike closed down their airport, the Layou Young Men's Cricket Club had been playing a match on Martinique; thus the first passengers to land in Dominica were twelve-year-old boys in shorts and blue blazers. The plane kept its engines run-ning and stayed on the ground only minutes. The Dominica gov-ernment had phoned the School for the Deaf and Blind in Philadelphia, Pennsylvania, United States, and Mr. Soylo was one of the outgoing passengers.

Winston said, "You be gone three weeks only. Bring a new dog. Everything be fine."

"Won't be Mrs. Polly," Mr. Soylo said as the flight attendant helped him aboard. When the attendant tried to take Mrs. Polly's harness from his hand he wouldn't let her. Winston told him they'd have a new harness in Philadelphia, but it was as if Mr. Soylo was deaf as well as blind.

The Liat flight was full going out: Canadian Aid officials, two Englishmen, several German and Scandinavian tourists who'd been trapped by the strike. As the plane lifted off, another circled overhead, ready to land. A short white man approached Winston.

"You are Riviere?" he demanded.

Winston stared; apparently rudeness was epidemic here on this once polite island. The white man's face was puffy, red with anger.

"Well?" he demanded.

"I am Winston Riviere, yes. And who might you be?"

The man went into his jacket for a morocco wallet. As he presented his card, his fingers shook.

> Mr. L.D.B. Reeves
> Solicitor
> Portsmouth #9
> Dominica, W.I.

"There," he said. "Sir, there you are."

"There is what?"

"There he is, the person who is going to bring you before the bar of justice, sir. There"—he tapped the card—"is the man who is going to sue you for the damage you have done. And the personal anguish, yes sir."

"Damage?"

The man looked at Winston like he'd gone mad. He angrily pulled at his forelock. "My airplane!" he squeaked. He pointed at the Piper Cherokee at the end of the strip. "You have destroyed her." The white man shook a finger. "Believe me, sir. You will pay."

"But Winston was fighting for Dominica," Carly said.

"That what he say? My plane is destroyed from patriotism?"

Winston put an arm on Carly's. "You cannot argue with such a man as this."

"Such a man as this? I am a property owner, yes. I am a solicitor, educated in Sheffield. Such a man as what? Do you ever hear of slander, sir?"

As Winston walked to Jean Hubbell's borrowed Land-Rover, the white man pursued them, still shouting.

Enterprising merchants had used the ham radios all night and by first light, several freighters were tied up at the deep-water jetty in Woodbridge. The Land-Rover's radio interrupted its bouncy calypso beat to say: "Good news for all you shoppers, now. Darlin', listen to this news. First shipment of chicken parts, frozen, have arrived at Whitechurch Market in Roseau, and it will be first come, first served until they gone, so hurry down to Whitechurch and replenish your pantry now. Chicken parts, canned goods, household necessities, now in the store."

Winston got in line at the BP Superservice. Lorries and cars were sucking petrol as quickly as the tankers could fill underground storage. Five gallons was all they would sell at two dollars a gallon, which was not the price posted on the pumps. The attendant, wrapping a ten around his inflated roll of bills said, "Take it or drive on, man." Winston took it.

The radio said, "The government nearly finished with official telephone calls, so if you want to be phoning off island, you can make appointments at the Postal Bureaus."

Carly asked, "What are you going to do?"

Winston shrugged.

The sun shone on the nation. Laborers in the back of flatbed lorries waved as they returned to work on the estates. Jitneys cruised the roads, picking up and letting off passengers. The radio talked about a Festival of Gratitude. A solemn announcer read the proclamation. "The Dominican People have cast out their unjust government and replaced it with one more representative." The proclamation made no mention of Winston or Mr. Soylo or Mrs. Polly. The radio announcer's voice became intimate. "Oh this going to be one bon fête," he said. "All you darlin' women, I been missin' so long, I see you at this fête. Look out for Marko, that be me. I the one winkin' at you."

Carly said, "What are you going to do?"

"About what?" Unnecessarily Winston tapped the horn. They zipped across the Roseau River and downtown. A throng of people waited outside the Barclays Bank and those supermarkets that had been resupplied. Winston drove by what had been the Fort Young Hotel. "Hurricane David ruined this one," Winston said. "Ruined everything else on this island, too. Oh, many people died that day."

"Rosemary," Carly said.

"Ah, Rosemary. We been seein' each other, now, five years. You know what they say here, in Dominica. . . ."

"In California, we say, 'Don't shit a shitter,'" Carly said.

Winston had meant to stop at La Robe Creole, but he drove by.

In Pointe Michel, he pointed to the burned building where a sturdy young man was picking rubble. Winston said, "Gang of bad johns waylay me here yesterday morning. I fear for my life, oh yes."

Carly didn't see fit to comment.

In Soufriere, at Mr. Soylo's steps, Winston said, "I take his Land-Rover back to Jean, take a peek at his broken machine, eh?"

He waited for her questions, if any. "We fly out of here day after tomorrow. After the fête. Black plane full of fuel. I fly us to Puerto Rico."

She didn't look back. Winston missed his shift and bashed the gears, which made him angrier than he was already.

He fixed Jean Hubbell's crusher. Jean tried to press money on him—five dollars, which was what he paid one of his agricultural workers for a day.

Winston said, "No, man, keep your money. We pilots all rich men."

All the way down the mountain, Jean Hubbell's driver raved about the fête, what a grand time, how his cousins were coming for the celebration. "Man, all Dominica be dancin'," he said.

"Watch out for that cow," Winston said.

Tante Marie greeted Winston like it had never crossed her mind he might not come. He fixed her sewing machine. Tante Marie tested it thoroughly on thick, stiff cloth and scraps of ladies' lingerie. Satisfied, she went to her coin purse, counted out three twenty-five-cent pieces, reconsidered, and withdrew one. Then she smiled, toothlessly, sweetly, "Thank-you, Mr. Riviere."

"No trouble, Tante. This was not troublesome at all."

Winston went to the rum shop, hoping somebody would have something for him to repair. The same loafers greeted him and several had rum, which they were willing to share with yesterday's hero. Winston told them about hiding under the airplane's canopy, he told about taking off with men shooting. He didn't tell about dropping Maboya in the sea. In an hour or so, he'd retold his story several times and the rum was gone, and since Winston was the only one with money, he bought the next round. Since the rum shop owner hadn't heard the complete story, Winston repeated it and the shop owner bought the next rum for Winston only. Other men had to return home to beg money from their wives.

"And, man, I lift the wheels, because I need airspeed and the plane bump and I think, oh, shit, but she fly right over that Land-Rover and them gunmen so surprise."

Other men had stories to tell. Most had made the march to Roseau and several saw Mr. Bones shoot the schoolmaster's dog. Most had been in the rear and all they saw of the action was Winston's plane diving on them, like, one said, "A crazy Jack Spainard hornet. I tumble to my knees when it pass over me, give thanks to God."

And as other men told their stories, they homogenized Winston's deed so it didn't seem so much. He flew a plane low over a crowd and pulled a lever—big deal. Winston bought another rum for himself but nobody else and when he came out into the roadway, he blinked; it was dark. He went behind the rum shop to take a piss. From the smell, many others had preceded him.

The stars were out. To hell with them! Winston walked past the darkened schoolhouse feeling unloved.

At the banyan tree he said, "Good-night, Mrs. Polly," and felt very sad for himself and all life which must come to an end. Why can't we live forever, he asked, which, he was sober enough to realize, wasn't the first time *that* particular question had troubled the chilly stars.

The stairs were awfully steep and he wondered how an old man like Mr. Soylo negotiated them. She sat at the kitchen table, reading that book on cricket.

"You'll never understand it," he said.

She closed the book on her finger and looked at him coolly.

"Cricket," he said. "Got to be born in the islands to understand what it *means!*" He flung his arms apart, wide.

She said, "Go to bed."

He sat down on the couch to remove his shoes.

"Not here," she pointed, "there."

He said, "I didn't get my dinner."

She said, "Maybe Rosemary'll cook it."

One shoe on, one off, Winston hobbled into the next room and collapsed on the bed.

In the old bad days, when Winston fell asleep drunk, he never dreamed. But not tonight. Over and over he dreamed of Maboya, the man he'd dropped in the sea. He hadn't seen his face, had heard the scrabble of the man's hand on the cockpit handle. In his dreams Winston couldn't keep from turning to face his victim, and when he did, he saw a child on that wing, politely asking: "Please let me in" as the wing tilted, tilted, and the child dropped away. Winston woke early Saturday morning drenched in sweat. His sweat smelled very bad and the clothes he'd slept in smelled bad too. When he sat up his eyes felt hot.

Though he didn't hear a sound from the other room, Winston knew from the air tension she was awake. One sock on his foot, the other on the floor. Winston peeled it off. A Dominican can go barefoot anywhere.

He padded out to the wooden veranda. Overcast. He hoped it was clear tomorrow morning for the flight north. He thought about Mr. Soylo, in Philadelphia, probably still clutching Mrs. Polly's harness. Maybe Mr. Soylo would pick a new dog who smelled worse than the old.

She came and sat on the railing. She wore a man's shirt, nothing else. "Do you want me to make coffee?" she asked.

"Yes."

So she was busy for a few moments, grinding and boiling water. He said, "This morning I telephone Rosemary. We enjoy the fête, fly north tomorrow."

She looked at him.

"I tell Rosemary about us," Winston said. "That me and Rosemary not getting married."

She made a sound in her throat and took him in her arms—so strong those arms, might make a sailor out of her yet—and she was crying on Winston's chest, hot tears.

He said, "Don't you be foolish now, woman, or I give you blows. Just because I say I not marrying Rosemary, don't mean nothing."

But she couldn't be made unhappy now and hummed all the while she made Winston's coffee, and while he drank it, she sat in his lap.

As he changed into the shirt she'd washed for him yesterday, she said she'd phone too. Her mother.

As they walked to the Catholic rectory, they held hands, which was *Winston's* idea.

The rectory was wide open. "You want to go first?" he asked.

She shook her head. She gave his hand a squeeze.

"This not take so long." He got the operator on the phone and told her who he was and where he was calling from and gave her Rosemary's number and said to please make it a collect call but the operator said they couldn't because of the crisis and Winston said to charge it to the Rectory and she said fine. He heard the faint hum of undersea cables and relays clicking into place, like pinballs into slots, and the ringing, very faint, at Rosemary's home. "Hello? Hello? Is that Montgomery? Montgomery, is me, Winston!" In Montgomery's silence, Winston could hear the underwater pinging of the sea.

"Get away from me, Jumbie," Montgomery hissed and hung up.

Winston went through a second explanation with the operator before she dialed again. This time it rang just once, before Rosemary answered.

"Hello," she said cautiously.

"Rosemary, it is I, Winston. Do not hang up the phone, please."

"Winston, oh, we thought you were dead. We hear how the great hurricane sink all ships in Anegada Passage. So many ships go down."

"This time the ocean let me live until another day, ha, ha."

"That's why Montgomery hung up, Winston. He thought you dead." Rosemary put her hand over the mouthpiece and Winston could hear her saying something, but not what.

Montgomery came back on. "Winston, you give me the shock of my life. Oh we were grievin' for you, brother. We were grieving so hard. Hundred-eighty-mile-an-hour winds. How can small boat live through storm like that? And somebody say you have a white girl aboard. Tourist girl. Is true?"

Winston said, "That fine weather report you give me, brother."

Montgomery rolled on: "Oh we mourning you, man. David and Megan so upset they cancel DMS flying for a 24-hour day and Richie take the Twin Beech out to the Anegada Passage and drops a wreath for you. Forty dollars of flowers."

Winston began to get suspicious, "Montgomery..."

"You been havin' bad luck in St. Thomas, man. That crazy Indian woman..."

"Mrs. Indarsingh?"

"Yes. Her. She get a court order about some appliance you fixin' and police break down your door to retrieve her machine. I fix the lock, brother, but not so good as it was. And, brother, that Haitian

Obeah man standing outside your door? I never like that ugly thing but I don't think anybody thief it."

"Thief the Obeah man?"

"Well, he gone. When I fix your lock I notice. Maybe he up and walk himself away. Maybe he gone down island, ha, ha."

Winston interrupted impatiently, "Montgomery, what you doin' in Rosemary's house before breakfast in the morning?"

Silence. Again, a hand muffled the phone. When it lifted, Rosemary was back, more serious now. "Winston, when you return, we have many things we must talk about."

"Oh, I'm sure of that! I am sure of that!"

"Winston . . . We thought you were dead."

"Well, I am not one bit dead. I am in Dominica in the Rectory at Soufriere, telephoning, and I am quite alive, thank-you, and won't be needing no forty-dollar flowers from Richie or David either, if you please."

"When you come home, Winston, we talk then."

"Fine!" He shouted. The second time he shouted, "Fine!" it was into a dead phone. He clattered the phone into the cradle. "Them two, what they doin' up there? Oh, that St. Thomas is an island full of temptations."

Carly's eyes were too merry for Winston's taste.

"We see about that!" he said. "That Montgomery, he my brother, damn him."

She looked at him very solemnly. "I thought Montgomery only liked white girls," she said and clapped her hand over her mouth.

"We see about that," Winston said, knowing he was a fool, the echoes of his speech dying in the empty room. The Rectory furniture was unchanged from when his mother had cleaned it but everything had new slipcovers. "Oh," Winston said, "them betrayers." And he didn't want to laugh but a snort escaped him and a snuffle. "Montgomery think I am a Jumbie," he wailed. "Oh, I took some growth off that boy. He so afraid he drop the phone."

Carly's mother had left Sandpiper Cay. No, they didn't know where she'd gone.

Carly dialed her home number.

"Hello."

"Mother, this is Carly! I . . ."

Uncaring, the answering machine rolled on. "You have reached

Magdellana Hollander. I am in mourning over the loss of my daughter, missing, believed drowned in the Caribbean. All my friends who wish to send memorials may send them to DayTop Village, the center for substance abuse. If you wish to leave a message, wait for the beep. And have a *nice* day."

When Carly hung up, she had tears in her eyes.

"Darlin' . . . ?"

"Nothing will ever change her."

"She not going to be what you want her to be?"

"Did I want so much?"

There wasn't any answer to that except what Winston offered, the consolation of his strong arms.

At noon sharp, Radio Dominica kicked off the big fête with speeches by the government and tributes to the slain ministers. The acting president promised early elections and a return to normal and legal ways of life. The commissioner of police vowed to bring members of the renegade government before the bar of justice. Soufriere's steel drummers waited, heads bent, arms folded during the minute of silence. Deep in the bush a Sissourou parrot chattered.

"We give thanks for those who gave us our freedom," the announcer said. "Let bon fête get commenced today!" And with a shout, the steel bands struck up.

Winston switched off Mr. Soylo's radio. The steel bands clattered in the village below. A great shout lofted, like someone had just scored a cricket goal.

"You go down there, darlin'. Listen to them fellows now."

"Aren't you coming?"

"Oh, I be coming. I got to make myself pretty. All the fine women waitin' for Winston today."

Her look promised trouble, but at least it was a new trouble. Carly'd been brooding about her mother ever since her unsuccessful phone call.

Hot water boiled for Winston's shave and as he skidded white suds from his dark cheeks he wondered just what he'd got himself in for now. Oh dear. He didn't miss Rosemary, no. He hoped her and Montgomery be happy together. Whenever Rosemary and Montgomery together they very witty. It would be a good joke to watch Montgomery saving for a house.

Lather sticking to his face, he answered the soft rap at the door and the breath gasped right out of him. He took an involuntary step backward. "Leon."

"Winston, my old friend. Good-afternoon, yes."

His shirt sleeves had been ripped off and his breast pocket dangled like a loose patch. One cheek was bluish purple like steak left in the sun too long. His red eye was squeezed shut. His khaki pants were filthy. Around his left arm he'd swaddled bloodstained rags over the place blows first land. "Oh, Winston. This country gone mad."

Winston gaped.

Leon chattered, "They tryin' to kill me, true. Outside Newtown, crazy woman fly at me brandishin' a cutlass, try to slice my hand off. She gonna do to me what I do to the ministers. Wasn't me, man. I didn't do none of that business." He heeled the door shut and limped to Mr. Soylo's chair. "Man, I in the shit now."

His cheeks were swollen, lined with dirt, and his hairline was much higher but it was Leon Balla's face and Winston said stiffly, "You want rum?"

Painfully, he turned his neck. "Too long since I been in this house," he said. "Garvey, Falconer, DuBois, King. I asked the schoolmaster why Huey Newton not there. Where is Cicero, Jupiter, the Maroons. 'They violent,' he say."

When Winston set a glass before him, Leon pushed it around like a chess piece. "Was that you pilotin' my airplane?"

Winston swallowed. "Yes."

"You always skilled at that thing. A wonder with machinery. Chieftain of the pistons, General of the sparking plugs: Winston Riviere, man of the hour." Though the words were bitter, the tone was pure sadness for what might have been. "Boy gang assault me. Oh they pull at me, kick me like I soccer ball in their game. I leave the road then, follow bush tracks like runaway slave. President appoint me you know. Dominican president has power to appoint what ministers he like. . . . Oh, Winston. New ideas worthless if you don't try them out."

"What you want with me?"

Leon winced. "I come to say good-bye."

"Good-bye."

"Why so vex, Winston? We good friends once."

"Murderers your friends!"

From the village, a shout soared free over the persistent thump of drums. Leon eyed his untouched glass of rum. "I never want none of that," he said. "Mr. Bones..." Leon shuddered.

"Man, you workin' with that white man. Doin' he bidding."

"What you think happen I stand up to him?" Leon flared. "What you think happen to the government? Winston, we was bringing in the petroleum industry to Dominica! We was doin' mighty things."

"You thief my examination," Winston sputtered. Things weren't going as smooth as they should.

"What you talk?"

"My sixth form examination for the scholarship to University of West Indies. I done bettern' you and you switch my examination for yours so I don't get no scholarship and you get to go."

Leon Balla looked at Winston for the longest time. Winston poured himself a rum and downed it, so.

"Winston, Winston. You grow up easy like...like...Your mamma, she loves you. You know your daddy's name. Nobody laughin' behind Winston Riviere's back, no. Nobody sneerin' at he hopes and dreams. Important men bend over backward help Winston Riviere. 'Winston, he a clever boy.' Schoolmaster gives him books and priest help pay for he education. What you been doin' for the black man, Winston? How you payin' you debt?"

"I got no time for politics."

"Shame, Winston. Politics got plenty time for you." Leon put the glass to his ruined lip but it dribbled. "When I fly into Kingston, Jamaica, I was short-pants boy. Thought I knew everything what was, me and my cardboard suitcase. Bob Marley alive then, makin' music all over the island. The Rastafarians gonna set the black man free, go home to Ethiopia, talk to Haile Selassie, ask he give Rastas African land. There were ongoin' negotiations too." His clear eye was dead serious. "Ongoin' negotiations with the Lion of Judah, you see. Oh those were some times, Winston. Been so happy if you'd been there."

Below, the steel bands swelled and faded, like the surf.

He pointed at Mr. Soylo's gallery of pictures. "One day my face be there, Winston, with all the black saviors. Dominicans never gave me a chance. Me and them other ministers appointed less than six months and can't get anything done on this island in six months. Want to build a road, got to talk to the man owns the land

and the man who covets it. Mus' learn whose nephew out of work. 'He a first-class surveyor.' And then they start calling for election and then they go on strike. Winston, to me, this is extremely disappointing."

"Why you thief my examination?"

Leon's pained headshake. "Winston, I did no such thing. I study day and night. I cram my poor head with fact and opinion. I neglect my girlfriend, all else. Winston, I want the scholarship more'n you do."

"Lie!"

"Winston, you happy fixin' things. Fly the airplane, sail the boat. Why you want more'n you want?" Although it must have hurt him, he created Leon Balla's grin, that prankster grin that once charmed Winston's heart. "You want to trade places with me?"

Winston's head swirled. He was very excited, everything turning topsy-turvy like hurricane.

"Your friend Rupert, he dead now. Rupert runnin' to Scotts Head where his cousin has a bateau. 'Come along,' Rupert say to me. 'We sail to Martinique, easy.' At Tres Pitons Estate, they catch him and cut him to pieces. Rupert is unrecognizable." For an instant, Leon's grin turned strange. "More ganja in the world for others now that Rupert gone." He paused to savor the thought. "Oh yes, clock pendulum swings to the other side now." He emptied his rum like it was a decision. "I save your white lady's life, you know. Rupert is all for turning her over to Mr. Bones. I say no. I save her. You know she is CIA?"

Winston felt a flash of deep repugnance. Leon had so many ideas whirling through his head, like metal seahawks, slicing through tissue with sharp beaks and wings. Ideas were real to Leon in a way they'd never be for Winston, who knew, in that moment, how it would be for the rest of his life; how strong and how limited. Even as a hero, he was so limited.

"Old friend," Leon said. "I ask you to fly me off this island."

Winston felt a great calm, like a circle completed. Perhaps it was time for him to start making children. "Old friend," he said, "it's far too late for that."

15

Home Island

It was one of those rare Caribbean mornings when you can be forgiven for thinking you might—just might—live forever. The dawn sky lightened from rust to pink to tangerine and the new moon on the dark blue was sharp as a fingernail cutting.

"Carly, you must lift," Winston said as she dragged the copilot seat off the wing to the ground. "Watch you step, man," he spoke sharply to Jean Hubbell's overseer, who'd come to help with the aloe vera drums.

Carly's earthly belongings were in the duffle bag at her feet. They'd load it after the drums were in.

Behind Canefield Airport, the sun peeped through a gap in the mountains lighting the olive-drab bush, spinning rainbows.

They'd delivered Mal Esprit to Police Headquarters an hour ago.

From the moment Winston refused him, Mal fell silent, sitting quietly in Mr. Soylo's kitchen while arrangements were made. The fête wound down. Carly cooked up chicken and pigeon peas but Mal didn't touch any.

Yes, Jason would loan his Rover but, "Since you're flying to Puerto Rico, man, why not take a small cargo for me? We've had no product for sale since the strike started. You know," he added thoughtfully, "there's plenty of work for a man like you on the island."

Winston said sure, sure, and Mal Esprit made his predawn trip to Police Headquarters squeezed beside two concentrate drums and Jean Hubbell's overseer who nervously fingered the cutlass in his lap.

Winston worried they might be stopped and searched but Dominica was exhausted from its celebration and only drunks and stragglers walked the road.

The constable at headquarters didn't want to let them in. "Wait until regular hours, man, you got business with the police."

While they debated, Mal Esprit sat up and looked so solemn. "Winston," he said, "you certain you wish to do this thing?"

"No," Winston said, "I am not sure."

The constable opened the gate. "But leave your lorry outside. I don't know that you is a car bomb or something."

The duty officer wore a name tag: LT. BERGUAY. He was a white man and he was buttoning his shirt. "My," he said. "What do we have here?" He called for others.

They weren't rough with Mal Esprit. Nor were they unkind. But the police were such big men and Mal Esprit was a child in their hands. Winston hurried out without saying good-bye.

Jean's aloe vera concentrate was packed in 25-gallon drums and even with the copilot seat out, it was a sweaty couple hours getting them loaded.

Winston was so particular. Carly wondered if she'd ever known any man so particular with his life as Winston.

Before Winston had everything just so, others started arriving at the airport and the Liat plane came in, wings outstretched, like a gull landing.

The pilot brought his manifests into the customs. Relatives greeted each other with hugs and cries.

Winston took another half-turn on each of the seat bolts. "Okay, man. You tell Jean his concentrate on its way."

It rained while Winston was in customs and Carly let the warm rain wash her face. At the end of the runway, a crew was cutting sea oats. They seemed to be in great good humor. Scattering sea birds, the Liat flight took off for Martinique.

She thought: What extraordinary lengths he will go to defend the ordinary.

He stepped into the sun and waved. "Darlin', come in here. Immigration fellow want to talk to you."

It should have been a simple formality, but the immigration officer was young in his job, trying to overcome inexperience with punctiliousness. No, Carly could not fly without a passport, without a valid entry stamp *plus* the exit stamp he'd be so happy to give her *after* the passport was properly stamped for entering.

Winston explained again, "We come in by boat and nobody on that beach to stamp passport. My passport ain't got no entry stamp either."

Silently, the officer put out his hand, flipped all the pages in Winston's passport, dropped the passport in his drawer, and closed it. "You better be talkin' to the official," he said.

"Man! You *is* the official!" Winston cried.

To no avail. A Mr. Bosserman at Government House, he would issue a chit and when this was done they could fly, not before.

So.

So they took a taxi back to Government House where the policeman on the gate let them pass without protest, but all ministers were in urgent conference and could not be disturbed.

So they went outside and bought some rotis and fruit juice off a push cart. When they returned to Government House, yes, the conference was concluded, but all ministers had gone to lunch.

They strolled around Roseau. "Hello, hello . . ." Winston must have shaken a hundred hands. Carly bought a Carib basket at the open market.

Mr. Bosserman was apologetic. He'd gone to school with Montgomery and had many questions to ask and once Winston had satisfied his curiosity, he happily signed their exit chits.

"The Government should give you a medal, Winston," he said. "I am so sorry for all this." He asked Carly if it was true that she was CIA.

The Portsmouth solicitor, L. D. B. Reeves, was waiting for them at the airport. He had two constables with him to arrest Winston right now. "Otherwise," he argued, "this man who wreck my aircraft fly off island, scott free."

Winston looked up at the sky but found no relief there.

The solicitor produced his trump, a summons to appear before the Portsmouth magistrate who "will give you as fair a hearing as any man, sir, on the date written here, Tuesday next, in Portsmouth. Magistrate Thompson is a fair man, most eminent jurist. Everybody knows him well."

Winston sighed. "I don't have any tools," he said.

The solicitor beamed. Not a problem, no sir. Plenty mechanics in Roseau happy to lend their tools. His own cousin a diesel mechanic in Roseau. Let no man say L.D.B. Reeves lacked understanding.

While Winston went into Roseau for tools, Carly waited in the terminal. The immigration officer shuffled papers. A poster in the waiting room bore a photograph of a waterfall and the legend: DOMINICA. NATURE ISLAND OF THE CARIBBEAN. Carly wondered where the waterfall was.

After he ran out of papers, the officer came over and said he was sorry to have detained them but he was new on the job and wished to do it properly. He hoped to have a government career. He asked about California.

He was disinterested in California citrus but was delighted to hear about freeway rush-hour traffic. When Carly said men in helicopters monitored traffic conditions he got angry. He thought she was pulling his leg.

It rained again. The men returned with tools. The sun came out. Winston lay across the wing, his torso in the cockpit, splicing the electrics he'd cut. The airport snack bar opened and the solicitor chatted up the snack-bar girl. Carly drank an orange juice and brought one to Winston, who said, "Thank you. Hand me the box end wrench. There, by my foot."

Carly sat on the wingstep, handing him tools, thinking she should buy a new pair of socks.

The afternoon Liat plane landed. Emptied. Took off again.

The solicitor brought them bottles of beer. Winston said, "No. When I finish this, I be flyin'." Carly drank hers. It rained. The sun came out.

Winston climbed down and tossed his borrowed wire pliers into the borrowed toolbox. Carly said, "Stand still," and dusted him off.

Monkey quick, the solicitor hopped into his plane, switching switches, checking gauges. He fired both engines and shut them down. "Mr. Riviere," he said. "Altimeter light not working."

"It was not working before," Winston said. "Put a new bulb in it."

And then the little white man shook Winston's hand and Carly's hand too and, gaily, he ripped up the summons and the scraps blew down the runway. He tapped his watch. "Four-thirty-three," he noted. "Plenty of time for flying."

Winston stretched and shook out his arms and cricked his neck and told Carly they'd go as soon as he made the preflight check. He pulled the wheel chocks and stowed them in back, under the duffle bag. He wriggled the rudder and ailerons. He ducked under the wing to inspect the engine cowlings. He hunkered under the left engine for a long time. He said something.

"What?"

"Goddamn that Rupert to hell!" he cried. He waved his oil-stained finger like a flag. He held it up before Carly's eyes like an accusation. He jammed his eyes shut and rocked back on his heels. After a moment he breathed deep. "Life is a dream in the tropics," he said.

One of Rupert's bullets had struck the left engine behind the cowling and no telling how much damage it had done. Not too much oil leaking out of the neat hole, just a little. "Two and a half hours over open ocean to Puerto Rico," Winston said. He rolled his stiff shoulders inside his shirt. The sun was too hot to look at directly. A pair of frigate birds flew past, heading north. Absently, Winston wiped his hand on a rag. His eyes followed the birds until they were dots. He said, "Castaways Hotel pretty nice. To-morrow, we will see..." He set the wheel chocks again, exactly, fastened the canopy and shouldered the duffle bag.

The snack bar was closing but the girl sold Winston a green bottle of beer. Wordlessly, he drank it.

The mountains lifted steep and green. Patches of mist hung over narrow valleys. There were several rainbows.

In the taxi, they rode in silence. Carly put her hand in Winston's. She traced his callused palm. "Let's stay," she said.

VIOLON EN SAC, BAL FINI